Saskia Noort is a novelist and journalist. Born in 1967, she studied theatre and journalism in Utrecht, is married and the mother of two children, and writes columns for such publications as *Marie Claire* and *Playboy*. Her novels are highly acclaimed literary thrillers and are sold in 13 countries. They are bestsellers in the Netherlands, where *The Dinner Club* has sold over 300,000 copies since its publication in 2004.

THE DINNER CLUB

Saskia Noort

Translated from the Dutch
by Paul Vincent

BITTER LEMON PRESS
LONDON

BITTER LEMON PRESS

First published in the United Kingdom in 2006 by
Bitter Lemon Press, 37 Arundel Gardens, London W11 2LW

www.bitterlemonpress.com

First published in Dutch as *De eetclub* by
Anthos, Amsterdam, 2004

This edition has been published with the financial support of the
Foundation for the Production and Translation of Dutch Literature

Bitter Lemon Press gratefully acknowledges the financial assistance
of the Arts Council of England

A CIP record for this book is available from the British Library

ISBN 978–1–904738–20–6

Typeset by RefineCatch Limited, Broad Street, Bungay, Suffolk
Printed and bound by Cox & Wyman Ltd., Reading, Berkshire

For my dearest Marcel

He poured himself another glass of red wine, spilling some, swore and wiped the wine off with the sleeve of his jacket, which wasn't like him at all. He was usually very tidy, but it didn't matter now whether there were stains on his grey jacket, or on the oak table. His life, their life, was ruined anyway. He might just as well ram a concrete wall at full speed and relieve everyone of his superfluous presence in this world. Somehow he had always known that it would end like this, that one day he would lose everything. But he had taken the risk.

He tried to remember who he was before she had come charging into his life. He couldn't remember. Some sort of lonely, hard-working zombie, living thriftily and frugally and at the same time searching for something. Until the girl with the blond ponytail had floated into his shop, swept him off his feet with her charm, dazzled him with her passion and within a month had moved in with him. The girl who had once crawled onto his lap, frightened and in tears, whom he wanted to protect, to give everything to and who finally consented to be his, to be the mother of his children, now wanted to take away all he owned.

His eyelids were heavy, so heavy that he needed all his strength to keep them open, but he had no wish to go to bed, even though he was terribly tired. He didn't want to sleep alone yet again, in the dusty attic, lying awake, longing for her warm body. His limbs glowed with weariness, but he would stay sitting here, at the kitchen table, smoking and drinking, until he had worked out what to do next. He couldn't live without the boys. The idea of waking and getting up without their cheerful hubbub, seeing their sleepy, happy faces at breakfast, without feeling their young bodies on his lap now and then, scared him so much he could scarcely breathe. There would be no point to anything, he would go gradually to pieces and eventually lose his mind, he was sure of it.

1

He nodded off, started awake, and again it dawned on him what lay ahead. It was a nightmare, and he simply couldn't believe it was happening to him after all he'd had to swallow. He got up unsteadily, but his legs were limp as spaghetti, and he slipped and fell, striking his head against the sharp corner of the table. He was obviously drunk. He felt warm blood trickling down his cheek. Death had him in its sights, but he wasn't afraid, at least not as afraid as he was of the life that awaited him. The throbbing pain in his head was pleasant, comforting even, compared with the pain in his heart. His eyelids closed, and he wanted to lie down, sleep and never wake up. But surely he couldn't make it that easy for her? Didn't she deserve to pay for all she had done to him, to suffer until she longed for the end just as he did now? Wincing with the pain in his heavy heart, he felt a failure and lonelier than ever. Why couldn't they just go away together, disappear? In his head the image loomed up of an azure sea, fine, snow-white sand and a shabby wooden boat onto which the boys were clambering nimbly with their gleaming, dark brown bodies, before jumping off again in delight. He heard them calling his name. That's how it had been, not long ago, on the beach in Thailand. And that's how it should be: his family, together to the bitter end. He smelled the fire. The boys roared with laughter. He poked the blocks of wood again with a stick. The flames flared up, he breathed in and savoured the smell of burning wood. This was happiness, true happiness and that's how it should be forever.

1

It was the middle of the night when Michel shook me awake gently and mumbled drowsily that the phone was ringing. I groaned, burrowed further into the pillow, hoping the ringing would stop, until it slowly dawned on me that a ringing telephone in the middle of the night generally means something terrible has happened. I turned on my bedside light and looked at the alarm. It was three o'clock. The ringing stopped, and Michel said we might as well go back to sleep. It was probably some idiot, wrong number or something.

At that very moment the telephone rang again. The sound seemed louder and more piercing: like a siren. My mother-in-law's heart had given out. My sister had lost her baby. I got hurriedly out of bed, slipped into my dressing gown and ran downstairs, followed by a naked Michel. I found the angrily ringing phone on the sofa. My heart was pounding. I picked up the receiver, looking at Michel, who folded his arms protectively around his naked body.

At the other end of the line I heard shouting and lots of noise. A man called out "Patricia!" in a panicky voice. I heard footsteps and panting: the high-pitched, subdued wheeze of someone gasping for breath and then a low whimpering voice.

"Karen! Sorry to wake you up . . ."

"Patricia? What's going on?"

". . . It's awful. You've got to come. Evert and

Babette's house is on fire . . . We've got to save what we can . . . Everyone's coming over here. I've called them all . . ."

"Oh God . . ." Michel took my hand and looked questioningly at me.

"Evert and Babette . . . the boys . . . how are they?"

"Luuk and Beau are unhurt. Babette's injured . . . They're still looking for Evert . . ."

It felt as though everything had frozen: time, my blood, my heart. Michel began asking in a panic what was happening, and where, where on earth, we had to go to.

"There's a fire at Evert and Babette's . . ."

He swore. I saw our youngest daughter Sophie sitting on the stairs with her thumb in her mouth, observing us wide-eyed.

"We've got to go, everyone's there. To see if we can do anything . . ."

In the distance I heard sirens wailing. I realized I had already heard them in my dream.

I ran upstairs to dress, and then back down again because I realized we couldn't leave the children behind by themselves but couldn't really take them with us either. I rang Ineke, our neighbour, who said she had also been woken up by the sirens and yes, she would happily come and watch over the children. With the receiver in my hand I ran through the living room and opened the curtains. I could smell the fire and could see an orange glow in the distance beyond the trees.

We threw on our clothes, watched by Sophie and Annabelle, who bombarded us with questions: why were we going to the fire, why couldn't they come too,

4

were all Luuk and Beau's toys burnt, where would they would live now and were they dead? My thoughts were so absorbed by what we were probably going to encounter that I could only react curtly to their questions. Sophie began to cry.

"I'm frightened!" she sobbed. "You two are going to be killed in the fire too! You've got to stay here!"

I kissed her head, wiped the tears from her eyes and said that I wanted to help my friends, and that if all of us did our best, we might be able to save some of Luuk and Beau's toys.

Ineke was standing at the foot of the stairs in her pink slippers. She had thrown a trench-coat over her pyjamas. I hurried over to her, with two still weeping girls trailing behind me, gave her a kiss and grabbed my coat from the coat hook. Her grey hair stood on end and her watery blue eyes looked worried. "Everyone's out in the street," she said. "It's really a huge blaze."

She put her arms round the girls.

"Off you go, I'll sort things out here," she said, before asking with feigned cheerfulness why these two little girls weren't in their beds. Michel and I put our coats on, slammed the door behind us and leaped onto our bikes. Outside there was a thin dusting of snow. A crescent moon shone from a clear sky, and if we hadn't been on our way to the scene of something dreadful, we would probably have told each other what a wonderful night it was.

Head-high flames were leaping out of the thatched roof, and the outside walls, once plastered in white, were now scorched pitch black. Thick, dark grey clouds of smoke were billowing from the windows and

5

the roof. Neighbours were running about, carrying their crying children, yelling to each other, while others, holding their breath and red-eyed, were watching the fire that was eagerly devouring the detached house. The street had been cordoned off, and firemen were running to and fro, unrolling hoses and entering the smoking house with breathing apparatus. Water roared through the hoses, but the flames seemed stronger, as if being constantly refuelled.

A week ago we had celebrated the seventh birthday of their son Beau in this house. We sat round the open fire drinking red wine with a wonderful bouquet, while the children rampaged through the house. Now the fire was consuming everything that Evert and Babette had built up together.

We squeezed our way through the spectators, looking for familiar faces. We wanted to help, though we realized at once that there was nothing we could do. A policeman came over and asked us to make way for the wailing ambulance that was following him at a crawl. Everyone fell back. Michel took hold of my numb hand, and we watched the flashing light disappear round the corner. The fire had spread so fast it was a miracle there were any survivors, certainly at this unearthly hour, we heard people whispering around us. No one could tell exactly what had happened. Only Evert was still in the house.

Again we were pushed aside by yelling policemen, and a second ambulance roared past. Patricia came running after it, her dark red curls straggling down her slightly sooty face. When she saw us, she stopped. The corners of her mouth trembled with stress, and her eyes darted in all directions, like those of an animal at bay. She kissed me quickly, and I caught a whiff of sulphur. She gestured with her head in the direction of her black Range Rover, which was parked carelessly among the trees.

"I'm going to the hospital with them, Babette and the boys are in those ambulances . . . The rest are over there." Panting, she pointed at a police van, where a group of shattered-looking people stood together.

"There's nothing more to be done, my loves . . . We can only hope and pray they can rescue Evert . . ."

At the mention of his name she faltered. She knew it was highly unlikely he would get out of the burning house alive: it was taking far too long.

We pushed our way through the throng towards our friends, who were staring at the fire in disbelief. When Angela saw me, she spread her arms and began crying. We hugged, and I felt her hot tears on my cheeks. "Oh God, Karen, this is so awful! So appalling . . ."

Simon broke down in Michel's arms and started swearing, his voice breaking with emotion.

"It's so fucking unfair! What a god-awful mess! Fuck! He came round to see me only yesterday . . ."

He clung to Michel's shoulder's, digging his fingers into his jacket.

"And now . . . he's dead! He must be! He can't possibly survive that. He's dead! My friend is dead!"

I looked over Angela's shoulder and saw Hanneke sitting against a tree in a daze, taking short drags on her cigarette. She seemed to be in shock. I freed myself from Angela and went over to her. At that moment we heard yelling. I turned and saw everyone racing back, ducking down and screaming. The burning roof collapsed. I looked back at Hanneke, who had put her arm round her head and was rocking gently to and fro. Firemen raced past, shouting to each other that none of their team was in the house, followed by four policemen carrying a long, grey bag. Angela squeezed my arm. I felt my stomach turning and became so giddy I thought I was going to faint. The bag was carried carefully into the ambulance. It drove slowly off, this time without screaming sirens.

2

Day was slowly dawning by the time the fire brigade finally brought the fire under control while we, chilled and drenched with the water from the hoses, sought refuge in the kitchen of Simon and Patricia, who lived round the corner from Evert and Babette. Their neighbour, a plump, elderly lady, made coffee. Thom, Thies and Thieu, Simon and Patricia's three sons, sat huddled together on the sofa in their pyjamas.

"They didn't want to go to bed," whispered the neighbour. "They wanted to wait here for their Mummy and Daddy. So I let them."

We listened in silence to the cheery bubbling of the coffeemaker and the clatter of cups, spoons and saucers. The tense silence in which no one dared look at anyone else made me nervous, and I got up to help. Simon looked most distraught of all. He didn't seem to be aware of his three sons, who were staring at him anxiously and with their eyes full of questions. Michel took a cigarette from a packet lying on the table and lit up. He inhaled deeply and then exhaled the smoke angrily, as if trying to blow away the image etched on our retinas. My hands were trembling as I served the cups of coffee. We were all trying in our own way to get a grip on the situation.

The sound of sighing, sniffing and slurping became almost intolerable. Fortunately Simon broke the silence.

"Why haven't we heard from Patricia? Why doesn't she give us a call? Would someone ring her? We have to know how Babette is . . . and the boys . . ."

We fell silent again, turned to our cups of coffee and lit up cigarettes, though most of us hadn't smoked for years. Simon got up, went to the fridge and took out a bottle of vodka and six chilled glasses, which he deposited on the table with a dull thud. He poured the vodka into the glasses. Michel rested his elbows on the table and hid his face in his hands. I asked Simon gently if Evert's mother had been told yet. He nodded and said that she was probably at the hospital too.

We heard the front door open. Angela sprang to her feet and went into the hall. We all held our breath and avoided eye contact.

The wailing of Evert's mother went right through me. Her anguished cries came from deep inside and sounded exactly as I had always thought utter despair would. I emptied my glass in one, in the hope that the fiery liquid would protect me against the grief welling up. Simon refilled my glass without looking at me.

Patricia came into the kitchen and opened her mouth to say something, raised her hands in the air and could only shake her head, while the tears ran down her cheeks. Evert had not survived the fire. Babette was still unconscious but stable. Luuk and Beau were doing fine, but they were being kept in overnight for observation. She gestured towards the hall, where the animal howling of Evert's mother still rang out.

"I couldn't leave her there all by herself . . . He's her only son . . ."

Simon put his arms round his wife and pushed her gently onto a chair. The neighbour said she didn't feel well and ran out of the kitchen. I took over her job and made sure the coffeemaker kept bubbling, that my hands were busy, that I didn't succumb to helplessness and break down. I was afraid that otherwise I would flee this grief-filled house. I was a powerless onlooker, an intruder in the tragedy that had struck this family, an outsider. But flight wasn't an option: we were friends. One of us had become homeless and a widow in a single night. Our place was here and nowhere else.

'One minute you have everything and the next nothing at all,' someone murmured. All we could come out with were clichés like these. But we did not want to go to our own homes yet. We were putting off the confrontation with the outside world for as long as possible. There seemed to be no way of talking to other people about this. Outside we heard children going to school, everyday sounds that suddenly seemed terribly far away. We were still drinking vodka, and when the cigarettes ran out we smoked Simon's cigars.

3

When we got home Ineke made us tea and fried eggs. She had taken the children to school and given them rolls for lunch. We had until three-fifteen to get some sleep. We let the eggs go cold; we couldn't eat a thing. We kept getting flashes of the grey bag and hearing the ghastly screams of Evert's mother.

I went for a shower to wash off the smell of burning, the odour of sulphur and charred wood that made me sick, because it reminded me of Evert's burnt body. I stood under the hot jet of water, washed my hair three times and scrubbed my nails with soap, but still my hands and hair smelled of last night, of smoke and soot.

Then I got into bed to try to catch up on some sleep, next to Michel, who was tossing and sighing. I cuddled up to his naked body and put my cold hand on his burning-hot belly. He shivered.

He turned towards me and looked at me sadly with his blue-grey eyes.

"I'm still wondering . . . We knew that Evert wasn't in good shape. Shouldn't we have done more for him?"

"Do you think his crisis has something to do with the fire?"

"I don't know. I just feel like shit . . . as if we had let friends down. Did we ever really listen to him?"

"I don't think we need to feel guilty. In the end Evert turned his back on everyone . . . even on Simon, his best friend. No one could help him, not even his own wife."

I laid my head on his chest and thought of Evert. Actually I knew him mainly from other people's stories. For the past few months my girlfriends' conversations had focused almost exclusively on his mental problems, although we had said nothing about it last night, as if this dreadful accident had come like a bolt from the blue, suddenly disrupting our carefree lives. But we had all felt the threat before, the putrid smell of approaching doom, and we knew that things were not right between Evert and Babette. Perhaps we should have intervened, should have been less cowardly.

When I went to collect my daughters I was accosted by mothers who normally never spoke to me. They wanted to know all about the fire and Evert's death, and they had heard from the children that we had been there. Beau and Luuk's teachers had talked about it in class. All the children had done a drawing for their grieving classmates, and the parents of both classes had decided to buy two big cuddly bears for them. Would I take charge of buying them and handing them over? After all, I was a friend of the family. Some women, who scarcely knew Evert and Babette, started crying when they saw me and even hugged me. I wanted to push them away, grab my children and get the hell out of there, but I managed to control myself and answer all the questions in a friendly way. Children streamed out of the school entrance, yelling and running, followed by Marijke, Annabelle and Beau's teacher, holding Patricia's sons by the hand, with my daughters bringing up the rear. Sophie leaped into my arms. I hadn't seen them since I had left home the night before, and they had had to hear at school that Beau and Luuk's father had died and that their friends were in hospital.

They looked at me with serious faces and told me

13

Beau and Luuk were in hospital and their mother too. They asked if we had been able to save any things and whispered that Beau and Luuk's father was dead. Could they come to the funeral too?

Marijke offered her condolences and asked if I would take Patricia's boys with me: she couldn't collect them herself, as the police were at her place. The children ran over to the climbing frame.

"The police were here at school too," she said, looking at me earnestly.

"I'm really shaken up."

"So are we all," I said.

I searched in my thick head for words that could really describe how empty and distraught I felt.

"I just can't imagine that he . . . He was a real family man. A nice father, really involved. I knew there had been problems recently . . . I had regular chats about it with their mother."

"That he what?" A shiver went down my spine.

"Well, the police think the fire was started deliberately. They kept asking me about the family situation: how Beau and Luuk were doing at school, whether they ever let slip anything about home. . . . The very idea! Suppose it had gone differently . . . that all four of them . . ."

I walked with the children down the path through the woods to Simon and Patricia's house, which was behind the school. In a strange way I longed to be with people who had been through the same thing, and who felt as bereft and desperate as I did. The children ran on ahead of me, climbed trees and screamed excitedly, as they always did, or perhaps a little more frantically than usual: it was their way of expressing themselves. A watery sun shone momentarily through

14

the trees, and it was as if nothing had happened, as if this were a normal Tuesday and in a few moments I would go into Patricia's house and find Evert there.

Just as I reached their drive, Simon drove up in a silver BMW. A slight tingle of excitement shot through my lower belly and for a few seconds drove away my sadness. He got out of his car, and his eyes were bloodshot. He strolled over to me like a footballer after losing a match, put an arm round me and pressed a gentle kiss on my temple.

"It's getting more awful by the minute,' he said softly. Furtively I took in his smell, cigar smoke mixed with a coconut-like aftershave, and patted him consolingly on the back. We went into the house arm-in-arm. It seemed perfectly natural that we should touch each other like this. We wanted uninterrupted contact, both physical and mental, as if that would help us drive the horror of what had happened out of our systems.

Inside it was a hive of activity. People were sitting in the kitchen, in the living room, there were flowers in cellophane everywhere, and a girl was serving coffee.

"It's unbelievable . . ." murmured Simon, scratching his head and running his hand slightly nervously through his black locks.

"Our house has been transformed into a kind of funeral parlour . . . Typical Patricia . . ."

He pulled himself together, conjured up his well-known grin and began commiserating with everyone. Neighbours, a number of members of Evert's staff, some business associates, relatives, mothers of friends of Beau and Luuk, everyone had dropped in to give their condolences. Patricia had opened their house to receive them.

I followed Simon awkwardly and did not know what

to do with myself when confronted with these sobbing strangers. We reached his office, where Angela and Hanneke were sitting smoking.

"Listen . . ." Simon's fingers were trembling.

"I've just come from the police . . . Patricia has gone to see Babette and the boys . . . and yes . . . it looks as if it's true."

He slumped into his desk chair. Hanneke's eyes filled with tears, Angela got up and started cursing. I was the only one who had no idea what they were talking about.

"Have you seen the note?" asked Angela.

He nodded.

"They asked if I recognized his handwriting . . ."

"What did it say?"

"They found the farewell note in his car, in the glove compartment. It's his handwriting, I was able to confirm that. There's no heading, but it's obviously addressed to Babette. Evert says that he will do everything to keep his family together, whatever it takes, that he loves her . . . He asks for forgiveness . . . It's very jumbled up, and a piece of the paper has been torn off. They also found traces of tranquillizers in the blood of Babette and the boys; and in the kitchen, where Evert was found, there was a jerry can."

I went weak at the knees, as if I had had an attack of vertigo, except that I was not standing on the edge of a precipice but in Simon's study, listening to a weird story, which was set among my circle of friends, around the corner from where I lived. One of us had set fire to his own house, with his family inside it. This happened in deprived areas, in problem families, among social outcasts or people living in isolation, but surely not here in our village, among our exclusive homes, in a generally liked and respected family?

16

Angela cried and wailed. Hanneke mumbled that she had to go to the toilet. I sat staring ahead in a daze. Simon rubbed my thigh and asked if I was OK. I nodded.

"Things can take a funny turn,' he said hoarsely. He rolled a cigar back and forth between his fingers. Then he began yelling.

"Christ almighty! Why? Why?"

He kicked his desk a couple of times and then pulled himself together, sat down again and pressed his fists against his temples.

In the evening we gathered again around Simon and Patricia's kitchen table. How were we supposed to tell our children? What would it do to them? We couldn't shield them from it. A news team from regional television had already shown up at the gutted house, as had a journalist from the local newspaper. The police spokesman mentioned "relationship problems". Tomorrow there would be articles in the papers. One way or another, our children would hear that Beau and Luuk's Daddy had tried to kill his own wife and children. The trust our children had in their parents would be damaged, and none of us knew how to alleviate the pain.

We kept wondering what our own part had been in this drama, and whether we could have prevented it. After all, every one of us knew that Evert had problems, and we heard daily from Babette how difficult her life with him had been for the past six months. We had seen it for ourselves, from his gloomy face and aggressive reactions.

The week before the funeral we lived together at Patricia's as if it were a commune. We wanted to be together to share our bewilderment and despair and to find answers to our questions. We smoked, drank gallons of coffee, beer, gin and wine, ate the meals that were provided every evening and talked about mourning, those we had lost, grief. We told each other our deepest doubts and fears, and an intimacy was created that felt almost like love. The children roamed around the house and every few moments were stroked and hugged, given sweets whenever they asked and ate pizza or chips every night. Luuk and Beau also flitted around among their friends, avoiding any conversation or contact. Their only comment was that every day seemed like their birthday.

If we could turn the tide
We would take you in our arms
Rock you gently like a baby
Whisper your name
And tell you we love you
Evert, you left us with so many questions

Perplexed and dismayed we say farewell to

Evert Hubertus Struyk

12 June 1957 – 15 January 2002

whose act of despair we shall never understand.

Dear Babette, Beau and Luuk, we will always be there for you.

Your friends from the dinner club:

Angela & Kees Bijlsma	Hanneke Lemstra & Ivo Smit
Lotte, Daan, Joep	Mees, Anna
Patricia & Simon Vogel Thon, Thies, Thieu	Karen van de Made & Michel Brouwers Annabelle, Sophie

4

The day we moved to this village I was ill, sick with fear. In the intervals between lugging boxes around and making coffee for our friends who were helping out, I threw up all over our new toilet and shivered as I nibbled a dry biscuit in an attempt to settle my stomach and quell the feeling of panic in my body. The decision to leave Amsterdam, the city we loved so much, for more countryside, more peace and quiet, more parking space and more safety was a thousand times harder for me than any decision I had ever made. It was as if, by leaving everything I loved behind in the city, I was finally tying myself to Michel for life. My girlfriends, my work, my favourite baker, the Thai restaurant round the corner, the option of going out on the town some Tuesday night, ending up at some wild dance party and staying anonymous. In Amsterdam you could have secrets. Not that I partied these days: I hadn't done that for years, and I no longer had secrets. But for me the thought of walking through town as someone else occasionally, for once not a mother or "the wife of" but just Karen, a designer – always up for adventure – made life a lot less dreary.

So why were we coming to live in this village? Michel had to keep reminding me: because we were being driven crazy by having our car regularly broken into, by the stressful daily bike ride to school and nursery, because we wanted our daughters to be able to play safely in the street and have their own garden, because the city was becoming more and more of a threat now that we had children. The last straw was being mugged by an aggressive junkie while taking the children to the dentist. That finally convinced us that this was not the place where we wanted to raise our kids. We started looking for a house with a garden, where I could work from home, in a nice village not too far from Amsterdam.

Moving from the city to a village meant that we lost friends. For the first year they kept coming, especially when the weather was fine and provided they could stay the night. That first summer we barbecued for Holland: every weekend we had guests with dogs, children and new lovers, and while they went off on their bikes or dozed in the sun, I was hauling a trolley bulging with rosé, spare ribs and baguettes out of the local supermarket, before making up the guest beds at home. It was fun, especially once the children were in bed and we all sat outside round the fire raking up memories of our old life in town, but by the second summer the conversations were a little more forced and the reproaches started. We never got up to town anymore, we showed no interest in their lives or their concerns, and we were turning into boring yokels. They were right, although we didn't agree at the time. Even though the distance wasn't that great, we grew apart: we forgot their birthdays and they forgot ours. Increasingly we dreaded night driving, and they dreaded sleepless nights in our spare bed. Our girls made new friends in the street, my girlfriends visited each other and had less and less need of me. Sometimes I went along, to prove I hadn't turned into an uptight provincial cow, but actually I always dreaded those evenings. Their conversations were always about

21

people I didn't know, cafés I had never been to, films I hadn't seen and problems I didn't have. It felt as if the rhythm of their lives had speeded up while mine was becoming slower and slower.

A second summer passed, rain and thunderstorms set in, and there were scarcely any visitors. Old friends had dropped out of the picture, and we had not made any new ones – that was no easy task in a village like this. The locals hate you because you are helping ruin their birthplace, and the newcomers are each on their own little island maintaining the anonymity of city life. Here the women's favourite mode of transport was SUVs, and they hid behind thick, heavy sunglasses. It was as if they wanted to avoid any kind of human contact with us. Shopping and children were loaded and offloaded, after which the mothers disappeared behind high gates into their golden cages to tidy up the house for their ever-absent husbands. And I was well on my way to becoming just as isolated as they were.

By now our house was finished, and it had turned out wonderfully. A big window had been fitted in my study, giving me a view of green fields and grazing cows. Annabelle and Sophie each had the room of their own they had so longed for, and I had my big dream kitchen, with a hearth and a big armchair for reading in, and Michel had his garage where he could tinker with cars and bikes. Our dream of a garden with fruit trees, a pond and a terrace with a barbecue pit and a pergola covered in roses had been turned into reality by the local landscape gardener. When, to cap it all, Michel bought a new Volvo to celebrate the success of his business, we laughed and said to each other: "Our city friends mustn't see how bourgeois we've become."

Michel left for his office in Amstelveen at seven-fifteen every morning. At eight-thirty I took the girls to their school in the wood on the bike. Then I got to work in my study and sat there alone all day until three-fifteen, which heralded the loneliest moment of the day: collecting the children. I had the choice of either standing and waiting alone next to the other mothers, who chatted to each other and looked right through me, or waiting in the car hidden behind black sunglasses. Only when the doors opened, and the excited little darlings ran out did everyone seem to thaw; some of them were suddenly capable of communicating with me about who could play at whose house and until what time.

In the village you're always bumping into each other: at gym classes, at the hockey club, in the supermarket, at swimming lessons, on Saint Nicholas day, at the baker's, on the tennis court and at the sports club. It was all wonderfully familiar and safe for our daughters, who consequently had hordes of girlfriends in no time. I was less enthusiastic: some mothers, whom I met at least three times a day, still didn't say hello.

"Dear, you'll have new friends before you know it through the children, that's how it was for me," my mother assured me, but those days were obviously over. I played tennis, drove the girls to windy hockey pitches at the crack of dawn, wore myself out doing odd jobs at school and, with Michel, paid regular visits to the most popular local café. Apart from a few superficial acquaintances, it produced no new friends. And I gradually became depressed from being alone all day. I had to do something about this oppressive feeling of being a social outcast, about the fear that I was incapable of making new friends, that there was something seriously wrong with me. I longed desperately for a girlfriend, someone I could have a coffee with on the spur of the moment, bump into at the supermarket, to whom I could unburden myself about my children, my husband, my house, my mother, about all the things you can't discuss with your children, your husband or your mother. There was nothing for it but to go out and look for one.

The first target of my girlfriend offensive was Hanneke, a woman of about my age, dressed in trendy clothes, whom I saw running hurriedly in and out of the school every morning and afternoon, dragging her little son behind her by one arm. The way she acted made her seem more like me than the rest of the mothers, who arrived in plenty of time, with their perfect hairdos, make-up and clothes. Hanneke obviously had another life besides that of a mother and wife, and I was curious about it. Since my daughter Sophie got on well with her son Mees, it wasn't difficult to arrange for him to come and play and when Hanneke came to collect Mees at the end of the afternoon, sighing with stress, I already had the Chablis uncorked in the wine cooler and offered her, supposedly spontaneously, a glass of white wine to help her relax. She flopped down immediately in my kitchen, threw her bag on the table, asked if she could smoke and before I had a chance to say yes had already lit up. Only then did she look around in mild surprise, as if suddenly realizing where she was, and said she thought our house was divine, especially the open hearth in the kitchen. What a good idea. She wanted to do the same thing. She thought it would be marvellous to snuggle up in that chair in front of the fire with a good book, and I told her that had been my fantasy too, but that I hadn't done it once in the eighteen months we had lived there.

"Tell me about it," cried Hanneke with a loud laugh. "Last year I was given one of those deckchairs for my birthday, you know, for the garden, and I still haven't stretched out on it, while my husband Ivo thinks nothing of snoozing in it, in *my* birthday present!"

Complaining about our husbands, we finished the Chablis, after which she told me about her work as an interior designer, which gave her the chance to see the nicest houses in the village from the inside and to do them up.

"They may be loaded, but they've got no taste. They buy it from me. It's really funny how it works; if their neighbour has a new white sofa, they want one too, only bigger and covered in more expensive material. That's fine by me."

It turned out that Hanneke had also only been here for two years, after living for ages in Amsterdam, and they too were seeing their city friends dropping off one by one. She told me she felt like an alien outside the school. We discovered we had both landed in the kind of life we used to be scared of. During our first pregnancy we had declared optimistically that we would go on working fulltime and that child care would be shared equally, since our husbands had promised to work one day a week less. Nothing would change because we would simply continue going out, taking long trips and living in town. And here we were, in this village, in our lovely house with an open-plan kitchen, with our half-hearted one-woman businesses, our absent husbands and our children, whom we were doing all this for. "Before you know it," said Hanneke excitedly, "he'll be taking off with some young bimbo, and the cliché will be complete. Then something else will happen, or I'll take a lover. Ha, ha. Another pretext for a good fight."

We got drunk and gave the children microwave pancakes. I uncorked another bottle, put a ciabatta in the oven and served up the French cheeses I had bought for the weekend. Occasionally we stumbled over our words, we were so eager to tell each other everything we had thought of over the last few years and were so glad to have found we were in the same boat. Partly because of her work, Hanneke knew more about the village than I did. She told me all the gossip that was doing the rounds about the fathers and mothers from the school, and I hung on her every word. I made tomato soup and put the children in front of the video, and by the time Michel came home at eight-thirty we were completely wrecked, slumped over the table laughing our heads off and had decided to set up a dinner club. Hanneke knew some "fun women", customers of hers, who were also dying to meet more people. She would organize the first gathering, at her place. She had the room and liked cooking. Glowing from the drink, I slipped under the covers as happy as a sand boy that evening. Perhaps I had made my first friend in the village. I thought a dinner club was a terrific idea.

5

Holding a glass of wine and swathed in a red woollen dress, Hanneke opened the wooden door of her converted farmhouse on the Bloemendijk. She greeted me with an excited cry, hugged me and exclaimed that I looked great and that she was so glad I'd come.

I hadn't known what to wear for this first meeting and had gone for a plain black dress with a little cardigan and simple black high heels, an outfit that wasn't too showy and in which Michel always found me irresistible. With my hair up and a string of fake pearls round my neck, my look could be taken as a knowing wink at the 1950s, which would hopefully show I had a sense of humour and wasn't a grey mouse. Now, face-to-face with the fashionably and sexily dressed Hanneke in her imposingly large hall, I suddenly felt insignificant and drab.

We walked together towards the glass door flanked by two outsized earthenware pots with strange stalks sprouting from them. The click of our heels on the concrete floor of the hall was rather disconcerting and seemed to emphasize our awkward silence. I was so overawed by the minimalist design of the space that I could not get a word out.

Three women were seated at the long wooden table, and their conversation immediately ceased as we entered the kitchen. For a moment I didn't know where to look first: at the gigantic stainless steel kitchen

island, the women looking me up and down as unob-
trusively as possible, or the ballroom-sized living room,
which seemed uninhabited. Big, bigger, biggest: that
was obviously Hanneke's style. Even the wineglasses
were buckets on stems. Thick candles in all kinds of
colours provided atmospheric illumination for the
kitchen and the living room.

I introduced myself to Babette, a tall, slim woman,
strikingly brown for the time of year; Angela, dark-
haired and plump; and Patricia, small and worryingly
thin, with aubergine-coloured curls bobbing around
her head. Hanneke put her apron back on and took up
her position behind her kitchen island.

"Have a seat," she shouted. Cautiously I sat next to
Angela, who was talking about some deep book she was
reading. Babette was the first to turn to me, asking me
how I liked living in this hole.

I replied that it was OK and that I was getting used to
it. She asked me how long I had been here.

"Almost two years," I replied, noticing that I was
blushing slightly.

"As long as that? I've never seen you before! What
school do your kids go to, then?" Coming from Angela
these questions sounded like the third-degree.

"Plover School."

"God, fancy my not having seen you there . . ."

An uncomfortable silence ensued, and I had the
feeling I'd put my foot in it. From behind her pots and
pans Hanneke called out that Patricia had only been
here a week, in that wonderful white-rendered house
on the edge of the woods behind the school.

"And I love it already," enthused Patricia. "It's so
quiet . . . The woods right outside the door, room to
park everywhere. I've got such a terrific house, partly
thanks to Hanneke! Really, girls, if you are ever

converting or moving, call her in. She's the best. Cheers, Han!"

A large glass of wine was thrust into my hand, after which we toasted the hostess. For the first time in years I was longing for a cigarette to hide behind, as they were all doing.

We ate crusty warm bread, a salad of mozzarella, Parma ham and figs, grilled prawns *en coquille*, fresh pasta and creamy, pungent cheese. The wine did its work, and after a few glasses we were talking to each other about school, the children, the tennis court and other safe topics. It turned out that Angela and Babette played at the same club, and that triggered a long-winded discussion of tennis tournaments and tennis coaches. They made it clear to me that for the last eighteen months I had been a member of the dreariest tennis club for miles around and that I should quickly join the Dune Hollow club and have lessons with Dennis because he was terrific.

"Tennis with Dennis!" screamed Angela. "You couldn't make it up!"

"Say, girls, haven't you anything better to do than play tennis and rattle on about tennis," called Hanneke from behind her kitchen island, cigarette in mouth, shaking a *tarte tatin* out of an oven dish.

"Is there something wrong with that?" asked Angela.

"I hate sport and all that yapping about it. Let's change the subject."

She set the fragrant, steaming apple tart down on the table with a bang.

Angela took a tense drag on her cigarette. "I mean, is there something wrong about our 'having nothing better' to do? You seem to have a problem with that."

Again there was an awkward silence, which I tried to break with silly chatter.

"Of course not, come on now, it's OK, everyone has to decide for themselves, don't they? My, what a fabulous tart, did you make it all yourself?" I cackled in a cowardly attempt to steer away from this subject, knowing from experience where it could lead.

Hanneke shrugged her shoulders and began slicing the tart.

"Anyway, I'm very glad I've got something else to do."

Angela assumed a pious expression. "And I think staying at home for the children is the most worthwhile job there is."

"I can't stand the thought of working again," added Babette sourly. "After my last job, I resolved never to work another day in my life."

"It must have been an awful job in that case . . ." I said, rather taken aback by the adamant tone.

"I worked in Evert's sports shop. He's my husband: that's how we met. I loathed it. Not him, but the work, being a shop girl."

Hanneke exchanged looks with me and rolled her eyes.

"There's such a thing as pleasant work," I said, "and I can't bear being financially dependent on my husband – that really goes against the grain with me. If you want to be equals, you've both got to contribute, I think," I blurted out.

"So a woman who doesn't work, let's say that's us," said Angela, pointing to Babette and Patricia, "is inferior to someone who works? However many useful things we do, like looking after children, the housework, helping out at school . . ."

"Not inferior as a human being, but in your relationship . . . The one who earns the money often has the power, doesn't he?"

Babette hooted with laughter.

"Not with us! We may not earn a penny, but we still wear the trousers."

After a bittersweet espresso by the fire Angela was the first to leave.

"I've got to drive the children to hockey at eight o'clock tomorrow, so I want to stay in shape. It was a great evening, Hanneke, wonderful food and a good discussion too. We really must do it again."

She kissed us all and squeezed my cheek for a moment.

"Bye, sweetie. Nice to have met you. I hope we'll have lots more arguments."

After all that rosé it was as if we'd known each other for years, not just one evening.

"Wait," cried Patricia. "Before you go: next week Simon and I are throwing a party, a housewarming you could call it, and I'd love you all to come too. With your husbands, of course: I'm very curious about them now."

I left too, rather high on all the caffeine, alcohol and excitement. I longed to be able to snuggle up to Michel and tell him everything I'd experienced that evening. For the first time since we had left Amsterdam, I felt a degree of happiness: it would all work out. I had finally made some girlfriends, and although they were completely different from me, it didn't matter. We were all women, mothers, wives, dying for a vibrant social life.

I sang as I jumped on the bike and realized that country life had its own delights: croaking frogs, the smell of new-mown grass and open fires, skies full of stars and enormous moons. I no longer felt small and insignificant in the landscape but was a part of it. I lived here. I cycled down the gravel path with a smile on my face. My life was not half over: it had only half begun.

A black Golf was parked on the verge and a thread of smoke curled from the window. As I rode past I saw Angela sitting at the wheel with a cigarette in her mouth, staring blankly ahead of her. I stopped and asked if anything was wrong. She took a drag and laughed.

"I'm just sitting mulling over the evening and having a last cigarette. I can't do it at home, Kees gets furious."

"Oh. OK . . ." I was suddenly lost for words.

"You're surely not going to cycle home all alone in the middle of the night? Come on, I'll drop you off."

I had been cycling at night for years and had never had a problem. But I had only just got to know Angela, and I suspected she would take a refusal of her offer very personally.

"Leave your bike here and pick it up tomorrow."

"OK," I said, going back to the fence, and chaining the bike to it.

The car smelled of new upholstery and tobacco smoke. She put it into first and shot off down the Bloemendijk.

"What did you think of it?"

She changed up impatiently from second into third, and then fourth. We were doing at least sixty on the narrow road through the polder with ditches on either side.

"I thought it was great. It's really nice to have met you all. And a party next week! I've suddenly got a social life again! I was really missing that. And how about you?"

Angela pointed to the packet of Marlboro in the glove compartment and I handed her a cigarette, which she lit with the car lighter.

"It was fun, though I felt rather sniped at by you, about work and all that."

"It wasn't personal, it's more my own fear of being dependent. Independence was drummed into me from an early age by my mother, who'd been left in the lurch by my father with two children and without a penny."

"It doesn't matter. Probably it's just as well that we're all so different."

She put her foot down even harder. We were now doing nearly eighty. If I had known her better, I would have made a joke of asking her to slow down.

"That Babette . . . Have you known her long?"

"A year or so. Not that well, though. Our husbands know each other. This was actually the first time I've met her without having the men along. Why?"

"I don't really know what to make of her."

I immediately regretted the twist I had given to this conversation. I didn't want to come across as a gossip.

"She can be a bit loud sometimes. It's insecurity, I think. She was married to a terrible creep, who went on stalking her for years after the break-up, so she told me. If I'm honest, I have more of a problem with Hanneke. She can really let fly . . ."

"Hanneke tells you things straight to your face. I like that . . ."

"Yes, great. Until you get it in the neck. But you won't, because you're interesting, you work! And your husband's a television producer – also interesting."

This wasn't the kind of conversation I'd been expecting, and it gave me a sinking feeling.

"But OK, don't let me be too quick to judge. At any rate I think the idea of a dinner club is a brilliant initiative. What do you think about our clubbing together for a present for Simon and Patricia?"

We entered the built-up area – there were 20 mph signs along the road, but she scarcely eased off the accelerator.

"I think it's a great idea."

"Have you seen the house they've had built?"

"I've driven past it. It's huge."

"That Simon's a multimillionaire. He was in *Quote* magazine."

"Should be a fun party . . ."

"I think so too. Terrific, isn't it?" Angela grinned. "I think Hanneke should organize the present. I'm sure she'll think of something, being an *interior designer.*" There was a hint of sarcasm in that last remark.

"It's ages since Michel and I have been to a party. I'm really looking forward to it. I hope there'll be dancing."

Angela slowed down and turned right into our street.

"Right, home safe and sound," she said with a smile.

She leaned over to me and we kissed each other on the cheek. Then she looked out of the window.

"What a lovely house," she cried enthusiastically. "I'll give you a call about tennis! OK, see you next week. Good night!"

I got out, closed the door gently and waved as she drove off.

6

The hospital room was dark. Babette was sitting on the bed staring at the closed curtains, with her weekend bag beside her. Her long straight blond hair hung greasy and dull over her shoulders. I was about to go over to her, put an arm round her and console her, but Angela held me back.

"Leave her a moment. Come on."

She pulled me out into the corridor, in the direction of the coffee machine, and began pressing the buttons impatiently. A white cup was dispensed, the machine began to hum, and the cup filled with milk and then with coffee.

"Do you want one?"

I nodded.

"Cappuccino?"

"No, straight black please."

I got sugar and plastic stirring sticks and sat down on one of the faded orange bucket chairs. Angela gave me my coffee and remained standing up. We tore open the sugar sachets in silence, tipped the contents into our cups and stirred with the flexible white sticks.

"If ever there's a place you need a cigarette, it's here," muttered Angela, walking about restlessly and waving her free hand.

"You know, I've been giving it some thought . . . I don't really think it's a good idea for Babette to go home with me . . ."

I looked at her in surprise. We had discussed it at

length just the night before, and Angela had been the first to offer to look after Babette. The boys were to stay with Patricia for the time being, until Babette was back on her feet. Angela had said that she had the space and the time, that Kees would have no objection and that she was happy to do it for her friend.

"But it's all arranged, isn't it? Babette will be counting on you, won't she?"

She avoided my gaze.

"I talked to Kees about it. He doesn't want us to."

"And you accept it just like that?"

"He thinks that having her in the house will be bad for our relationship, that we'll start fighting about her. It's true we've been talking about nothing but Babette and Evert for months now. They were already virtually living with us. Let someone else take over for a bit."

"Your friend has lost her husband and her home, has to live with the thought that he wanted to kill her and the children too, and you let her down?"

"She's your friend too, and Hanneke's and Patricia's. You've all got enough room too. Kees is sick of coming home and finding her at our kitchen table. He thinks we have to get on with our own lives."

"You're closer to Babette than Hanneke and I are. She's counting on you! Angela, her husband's dead! It's his funeral tomorrow! And now you come up with this?"

There was a dull thudding pain behind my eyes. I was too tired to get really angry. Babette was in her room waiting for us. She wanted to leave the hospital as soon as possible. We had enough room too. There was nothing else for it.

"OK, she can stay with us."

"Don't you need to discuss it with Michel?"

"If I feel I have to do it, he'll go along."

It sounded very definite, although I wasn't at all sure of myself.

In the car on the way home, when we told her that she could stay at my place for the time being, Babette burst into tears. She stroked my arm and kept repeating that it was so sweet of me, that she was so afraid she would have to go into a hotel, or into some summer cottage, and I told her that of course she wouldn't have to do that. We would never let her down, she could stay as long as she liked; it was no trouble. She looked fragile. Her thin brown arms were covered in goose pimples and her big brown eyes were red and swollen. Her movements were jerky, and she was trembling the whole time.

"I thought the children would be coming too," she said, and Angela replied that the boys were with Patricia and it seemed less upsetting for everyone just to let them go on playing at her place. Babette nodded, and her lower lip started trembling.

"It's a miracle, do you know? That they're still here, that they're back playing with their friends again."

She closed her eyes and rested her head against the cool car window. Tears were running down her cheeks, leaving a trail of black mascara behind them.

"I thought Luuk was dead. He wasn't in his cot, he'd come into bed with us . . . I couldn't find him. In the smoke . . ."

She groaned. There was an awkward silence. I patted her thigh rather awkwardly as I tried to imagine what it must have been like for her.

"Little Luuk. He was lying there so still . . . I couldn't wake him up. I actually hit him . . . Then I tried to lift him out of bed, but he was so heavy I couldn't manage it. A nightmare, that's what it was. I just couldn't get my legs to work. Everything was going greyer and greyer, and I thought: we won't be able to get downstairs! We'll have to jump out of the window! I'd already taken Beau outside. He did wake up: he was in his own bed and was able to get downstairs. I jumped out of the window with Luuk. You just jump: anything rather than fire, dying in the fire, I thought."

"You did the right thing," said Angela hoarsely from the back seat. "Really, we're all very proud of you. You saved your children. You fought for their lives. And now you've just got to keep going for a little longer, my love, with the help of all of us. We won't leave you on your own, all of us will make sure that you get your life together again as soon as possible, that you get another nice house of your own, and new things . . ."

Suddenly Babette let out a shriek, and I was so startled that I almost drove into the verge. She slumped forward and howled with grief, as if she only now realized what she had lost.

"It's all gone! It's all gone!" she screamed, covering her face with her hands. I parked the car at the side of the road, and Babette threw open the door, got out and looked around in bewilderment. Angela went after her and took her firmly by her upper arms.

"Go ahead and yell, my love, scream, let it all out." They clung together, and Babette moaned that it hurt so much, so terribly, unbearably. Angela looked at me, motioned in the direction of Babette's bag and then pointed to her mouth. I opened the zip, rummaged until I found a bottle of pills and dashed over to them with the pills and a bottle of water.

"There you are, darling, take these, it will calm you down a bit."

Babette gulped the pill down, and Angela wiped her

face with the corner of her white blouse. I stood there, searching for words, something to say that would be consoling. Again I was surprised that Angela did not want to have her in her house. She cared for Babette like a mother. Suddenly the feeling came over me that Angela was trying to show me that only one person could help Babette, and that was her. Babette may be coming to stay with me, but I mustn't think that I could usurp her role.

Michel wasn't angry at my agreeing that Babette could come and stay with us without discussing it with him. Of course she was welcome. He was actually happy that we could really do something, and he assured her that she could stay as long as necessary. Our home was her home. They hugged, and her back heaved. Michel hugged her tightly, took her face in his hands and gave her a kiss.

"All of you, all of you are so sweet, so sweet , , ,"
Angela intervened.
"Come on, you need to lie down for a bit."
She took Babette by the hand and led her out of the room.

Michel looked at me and made a helpless gesture. He suddenly looked old. His dark curls were sprouting in all directions, and his face looked dull grey from all the sleepless nights. I realized with a jolt how much I loved him, as if I'd forgotten for years. He was a sensitive man with a big heart. I should count myself lucky. I must hold on to this feeling, for always and have no more doubts. I put my arm round him and kissed him on his sad mouth.

"Sorry I arranged this without discussing it, but I had no alternative. Angela suddenly pulled out."

"It's OK. I understand. And it won't be for that long, will it? Once she's back on her feet she'll start looking for something for herself and the children. Kees and Angela have put themselves out for Babette and Evert for long enough, and I can understand that they want a bit of peace and quiet."

"I still find it strange. They're such good friends."

"Leave it, Ka. This is not the moment. We're all doing what we can. We're all shattered."

We let go of each other. Michel dug a packet of cigarettes out of his trouser pocket and lit one.

"Why are you starting again? And you know I prefer you not to smoke in the house . . ."

He looked at me in irritation and went outside. The feeling I'd had for him just now vanished instantly.

7

It had been a beautiful day, too beautiful for the funeral, as if it were mocking our grief by having the sun shine through the bare trees. The children played outside in the snow, while the men sat round the fire in the kitchen. Babette spoke. Again she told us about rescuing the children from the burning house, about Luuk's silent face, the despair that had seized her when she realized that Evert had started the fire. We nodded in sympathy, hugged her and stroked her hands. Our cheeks were glowing from exhaustion and from the full-bodied red wine Simon had opened. We were special, friends forever; there was no denying it. The love that had grown between us during this week lessened the pain, at least for us friends. We had assured each other that we were not to blame, that Evert was ill and that no one could have foreseen this. All the tragic moments were shared, and we had voiced thoughts and feelings we would never have uttered if this tragedy had not united us.

Hesitant laughter came from the kitchen. Babette smiled and said she liked hearing the men laugh again. She got up, taking her empty wine glass with her, and went to the kitchen. All of us watched her go. When she was out of sight, we took a deep breath.

"I have such admiration for her: she's so strong," I began. "Sometimes she doesn't seem to have a clue what's happened to her yet."

Angela gave me one of those strange, cold looks that were always the prelude to some spiteful remark. But instead she swallowed her words with a superior laugh, and the nape of her neck went red, as if something had startled her. At the same moment Hanneke squeezed my leg.

"That cow is driving me nuts," she whispered in my ear, nodding towards Angela. "Are you coming for a smoke outside?"

The icy cold cut into my cheeks as we left the house, still holding our glasses of wine. I was glad that Hanneke had swept me off, away from Angela, with whom I never really felt at ease. Hanneke brushed the snow off a cast-iron bench, laid her coarse-knit woollen scarf over it and sat down. Her hands were trembling as she pulled a cigarette out of her packet.

"Damn," she muttered, taking a hefty gulp from her glass and with her thumb wiping away a tear that was rolling down her pale cheek. "You know, I just can't hack it anymore."

"Then why don't you go home and have a good sleep? We're all shattered. It was a draining day . . ."

"I don't mean that . . . I mean, of course I'm tired, but . . ." She rested her head on my shoulder. My eyes were now full of tears too, I cried in sympathy because I'd been crying in sympathy all week, since crying was now OK. No one gave you a funny look, you could just cry about all kinds of things, and in fact it was wonderful to give free rein to your grief. Best of all, there was always someone there to console you, and you were constantly being touched and caressed. I put my arms round her and felt her shudder, our cheeks were wet and sticky against each other, and slowly the pain ebbed away, at which point we withdrew from each other's arms, sighing fitfully. She looked at me.

"We're all stuck, you know."

"How do you mean?"

"Well, the way Evert was stuck. We're all like him. Stuck."

"Stuck where?"

Hanneke turned her face away and took a long drag on her cigarette. The she threw the end on the ground and stamped it out. I took hold of her wrist.

"Hanneke, what are you talking about?" What she had said frightened me. She took my hand and looked back at me.

"I'm just rattling on. That's what it feels like some-times, though, doesn't it? Stuck in your marriage, in your career, in your village. The sense that noth-ing more will ever change in your life can be very frightening."

"I don't think that was Evert's problem. Evert was ill. If anything, he was stuck in his psychosis."

"That's what we tell each other, that he was crazy. Nice and convenient: it wasn't our fault, because he was nuts. No one wonders aloud how things could have reached that point."

"But he had treatment, didn't he? Babette says he'd had problems with mood swings for years . . ."

"Evert just couldn't take the pressure anymore! He wanted to get away from us, away from this village, he felt stuck in our group. And it *is* stifling for me too. Karen, you're so naïve, you really have no idea . . ."

I stared at her open-mouthed.

"We're a bunch of hypocrites. We're addicted to but-tering each other up, but there's a high price to pay. Evert refused to pay the price any longer, and we wrote him off. That's the truth."

"And what is the source of all this wisdom?" I asked in annoyance.

"I knew Evert, and unlike the rest of you, I didn't give him a wide berth when he was in bad shape."

"Are you saying what happened was our fault?"

"In a certain sense, yes. You all abandoned him. And so did I, ultimately. I could have prevented this catastrophe, and I didn't. I don't know how I can go on living with that . . ."

"I think you're drunk. I just can't follow you. Sorry, but I'm going back inside."

Her words were spinning round in my head and making me feel sick. I turned away and went inside. She called out my name, but I didn't look round.

Patricia was rinsing glasses in the kitchen. Two girls from the catering company were calmly drying glasses and putting them on the kitchen table.

"Hi, Karen. I bet it's cold outside." Patricia turned around and dried her hands on a tea towel. Her eyes were darting in all directions, as if she had to keep a constant eye on everything, her body was taut with tension in her clinging black dress, which made her look even thinner than she was.

"What a day, what a week. I'm completely drained, completely finished, it's all so . . ." She blinked back her tears, turned away and walked impatiently to and fro, transferring the glasses from the table to the cupboard.

"Yes, it's still impossible to take it in. I think it will really come home to everyone tomorrow, and certainly to Babette."

"Keep a careful eye on her. How is she doing at your place?"

"She sleeps a lot or she sits in her room gazing out of

44

the window. But she's taking care of herself, she gets dressed, does her face, eats well. Meanwhile there's been a lot going on the whole time, what with all the arrangements."

Patricia shook her head.

"Isn't Hanneke in here?" Ivo poked his head round the kitchen door.

"No, she's outside."

"Why? It's freezing!"

"I think you should take her home . . ."

Ivo's expression darkened. He knew how violently his wife could react when she'd had a drink or two.

"Why's that?"

"She was pretty angry and down . . . Well, you know her. She's at the end of her tether and very tired, I think."

"Stinking drunk, you mean," said Ivo angrily, walking outside past us. Patricia grabbed a cloth and began wiping the draining board like a woman possessed.

"Drama queen," she muttered. "Why does she always have to attract all the attention, even on a day like this?"

There was an uncomfortable silence, because I did not know how to reply. Patricia vented her irritation on the draining board while waiting to see if I would tell her exactly what had happened. I felt nervous, harassed and a little guilty.

Out of the kitchen window I saw Ivo look around frantically and finally throw his hands in the air. He ran off and a little later came back into the kitchen.

"I can't see her, and I'm not going to comb the whole garden: that will take forever. At any rate the car's still there, so she hasn't driven off."

"Don't get into a state, she'll turn up."

Ivo grabbed his coat off the hook and said he was

going to look for her. He asked me if I would drive his children home. He kissed Patricia, thanked her for all her kindness and then kissed me. There was a frown between his tired eyes when he looked at me and tried to smile. Ivo always reminded me of a walrus, probably because of his short, bristly grey hair and his heavy eyebrows, combined with his excess weight.

"You know what she's like," he said.

"It'll be all right. See you soon."

8

We couldn't find Hanneke. No one had seen her after she had gone outside with me. I took their children Mees and Anna home, where I found Ivo, by this time furious and worried. He shot straight off again in his Range Rover, leaving me behind with his son and daughter. I heated up some milk, gave them both a cheese roll and comforted them by saying that Mummy was still at Simon and Patricia's.

"And you've come to look after us?" asked Mees, his lip trembling. I gave them as sweet and relaxed a smile as I could.

"Just for a bit. Till Daddy and Mummy get back."

I put them to bed and promised them that their mother would come and give them a kiss as soon as she was home – and I believed it too. Ivo would find Hanneke in a bar or at someone's house, or she'd reappear of her own accord. It was often like that with Hanneke. When she'd had too much to drink, she became confrontational, with Angela or Ivo, for example, which usually ended with her furious departure, leaving everyone feeling desperate. We all thought she drank too much and maybe worked too hard as well and wondered how we could say that to her without becoming the target of her wrath.

I suspected that Hanneke was unhappy. Perhaps she no longer loved Ivo. In the two years I had known him he had put on at least forty pounds, something that he seemed to find no problem at all. I couldn't imagine that Hanneke still found him sexually attractive, however sweet he was. We didn't talk about that; we complained about our husbands, but it was always because they were away so often, threw their socks in the laundry basket and missed and left childcare entirely to us. We didn't dare go much deeper in our conversations for fear that our marriages would be put down as unhappy. And perhaps also because voicing discontent, admitting that our marriages had become dull and predictable, would lead to the bankruptcy of our relationships and so to failure. We might sometimes be saddened by the prospect of never again being ambushed by love or passionately desired, of compulsory sex till the age of eighty with someone to whom we had plighted our troth and who was now also dreaming of someone else's body – but the thought of ending up alone, living on meagre alimony payments in a small rented apartment, was even more depressing. So we suppressed our doubts and desires and instead raved about anti-wrinkle creams, nice holiday destinations, the divorces of other, less successful couples and the conviction that nothing like that would ever happen to us.

I woke with a start at the barking of Droef, their brown Labrador. For a moment I didn't know where I was, and then I realized that I had fallen asleep on Hanneke and Ivo's red sofa. Hanneke had disappeared, and Ivo was looking for her. The large car that was coming up the drive probably contained Ivo with a drunk and furious Hanneke beside him. I became nervous and was dreading her anger, which would undoubtedly be partly directed at me. After all, I had turned my back on her and said she was drunk. I got up, stretched my stiff back, slipped my feet back into my tight black high heels and went into the kitchen to put on a kettle of water.

The bell rang, and the dog went on barking. I hurried down the endless hall to the door, looked through the small glass window and saw Babette standing there in the cool light of the porch lamp.

"Hi, Michel said you were here . . ."

She rubbed her hands to get warm, and then blew on her fingers. I opened the door and she came in.

"Oughtn't you to be in bed? Come on, I've made tea. That'll warm you up . . ."

Babette folded her hands round the teacup and cautiously blew into it. She sat on the extreme edge of the sofa and stared straight ahead, sniffing. I scarcely dared look at her and was ashamed of my cowardice and helplessness in the face of this mourning woman. I was afraid of saying the wrong thing to her, intruding on her, and at the same time felt guilty for saying so little and keeping my distance. To compensate for my helplessness I tried to take as much work as possible off her hands: I did her washing, ironed her clothes, cooked a lot, put her sons to bed, ran baths for her, made her bed and helped with the funeral arrangements. I had farmed out my own work for a month.

"Are you OK?" I handed her a handkerchief, and she blew her nose.

"Yes, I'm OK. I just think it's a rotten trick of Hanneke's . . . After all that's happened. That's why I came here, to tell her what I think of her when she gets back."

"I can't understand either. Everything got on top of her, I think. She'd been drinking, hadn't had enough sleep . . . We're all confused, wondering whether we could have helped Evert, whether we're not indirectly responsible."

Babette sat up and gave me a disconcertingly fierce look: below her brown eyes her mascara had run.

"Oh come on, Karen. You must know why Hanneke is acting like this!"

I was alarmed by the irritation in her voice and by her assumption that I knew what was going on in Hanneke's mind, making her doubt my honesty.

"No, really, I haven't the faintest idea! She was angry, I don't know what about. She thought we were all hypocrites, she said. I assume she didn't mean you by that. I think she meant that we left Evert in the lurch a bit when he got depressed, that we are only interested in each other when things are going well. Something like that."

"If anyone's responsible for anything, it's *her*."

Babette's voice faltered, as if she were being throttled.

"How do you mean?"

She took my hand and played with my fingers. Black tears trickled from her eyes. "Hanneke had an affair with Evert," she whispered.

"What?"

"For at least six months."

"How did you find out?"

"Angela told me. She saw them together. In the dunes, arm-in-arm." Droef laid his heavy head in her lap and looked at her. Babette stroked his chocolate-brown coat.

"Walking arm-in-arm doesn't necessarily mean you're having an affair."

"He admitted it straightaway when I confronted him with it."

"Christ."

"I don't know what she did to him, but I do know that the whole mess started with her. That affair just made him more ill, and when it ended he went completely to pieces."

"Do the police know?"

"No. What's the point? I don't want anyone to know. You know now, because you're my best friend. I told Angela that it was all a storm in a teacup and that they were just walking through the dunes as friends. Ivo knows too, and we decided between us to keep it a secret. The humiliation is bad enough as it is, and the children have to be protected."

"I think you're ready for a drink," I said, leaping to my feet, while my heart beat wildly. I hadn't a clue what to make of this story. I was hurt that Hanneke hadn't taken me into her confidence, and I was shocked that the woman I regarded as my best friend turned out to have had an affair with the husband of another friend, who was now dead. I didn't dare ask either Babette or myself whether Hanneke might have anything to do with it, but it kept gnawing at me.

Ivo looked dejected when he entered the kitchen. His cheeks were red from the cold, and a drop hung from the tip of his nose that he wiped away with his sleeve like a child.

"No sign of her," he panted.

"Should we call the police?"

I poured three glasses of Chardonnay and gave him one. He looked into the living room and saw Babette sitting there.

"No, I don't think that's necessary. She's sure to come waddling in rat-arsed any minute. Hey, Babette, shouldn't you be tucked up in bed?"

"I couldn't sleep anyway," she replied.

At that moment the telephone rang. Ivo raced over to it. I looked at the kitchen clock. It was one-thirty.

"Hanneke?

"Bloody hell, where are you?

"How on earth did you get there?

"Shall I come and fetch you?

"No, I want you to come home . . .

"Christ woman, don't make such a fuss.

"No, no, I can't. The children are asleep.

"Have you got money?

"Yes, if you have to . . .

"Go to bed then, OK? Please. Take a room.

"You too. Wait . . .

"Amsterdam. The cow's in Amsterdam," muttered Ivo. "She'll call again tomorrow. She says she wants to be alone . . ."

Babette went over to him, took his hot head in her hands and kissed him on the forehead. "It'll be all right," she whispered.

9

It was the first thought that came into my head when the alarm went off at seven: "Party time. What shall I wear?"

Michel had already left, the children were still asleep, and my stomach was gurgling with excitement. On the one hand, I was looking forward to it like an impatient child, and on the other, I felt the kind of terrified paralysis that seizes you before an exam. I thought of how lonely I'd become, how I longed to be rescued from this dreary round of getting up, taking the children to school, working at home, collecting the children from school, racing to the tennis club and hockey training, shopping, cooking, putting the children to bed, Michel coming home shattered, watching TV and off to bed again.

All day long there was the tingle of nervousness in my belly, a pleasantly itchy, excited sensation that propelled me from the hairdresser to the beauty parlour and then into town, with Hanneke, who talked me into buying a red, gypsy-style dress, a water-filled push-up bra and absurdly high black heels.

"These are for your entrance, my love. If there's dancing you can just kick them off, and then in bed you can put them back on!"

I had never bought such expensive clothes: my head was spinning as I paid the bill, and I was a little afraid too. In two hours I had gone right through my monthly income. If Michel were to see these amounts, he would be furious. Hanneke laughed when I told her.

"It's your own money, isn't it? What do you think one of his work suits costs? Come on now. Anyway, he doesn't have to know."

She pulled the price tags off my dress and bra and threw them in the fire with the bill.

"Right. In a bit you can put the whole lot into a chain-store bag, and no one will be any the wiser."

We drank prosecco in her garden, which looked out over a meadow full of buttercups and cow parsley, through which our children were skipping noisily. My daughters were to stay over here and eat pizza with the babysitter. Hanneke modelled the dress she had bought for this evening: an asymmetrical white halter dress with frayed seams, and she asked me what I thought of it. 'Lovely,' I said, although I didn't really like asymmetrical clothes, especially if they looked as though they were being worn inside out, but she was my friend, my first real friend in this village, and I had never once been so cheerful in the last two years as I was with her today.

"We're going to drive those guys completely wild tonight," she said, swaying her hips alluringly and pushing up her breasts.

"Absolutely." I raised my glass and downed it in one, after which Hanneke ran inside in her bare feet, holding her dress off the ground. A little later "It's Raining Men" blared out across the terrace, and she tripped back out, dancing and singing. She dragged me out of my wicker chair and, waving her arms furiously, ordered me to dance with her.

The evening was unusually balmy. Even at the top of the leafy street we could hear the dreamy mood music and smell the paraffin of the torches. When we saw the huge Bedouin tent rising up among the pine trees, Michel and I broke into nervous laughter. We navigated our bikes between the off-road vehicles parked all over the place, staring open-mouthed at the garden lit with Moroccan lanterns and the marvellous house built completely of wood and glass that loomed up among the pines. When Michel took my hand, I could feel his was clammy.

"You look amazing, darling," he said, to reassure me, and he planted a kiss on my forehead.

"This is unbelievable, isn't it?" I squeezed his hand. I felt privileged to be here. I had always thought I cared nothing for wealth and status and had always decried these kinds of people, although I didn't know them, but now I was standing here, on the threshold of Patricia's palace, I was secretly grateful for the invitation.

Patricia was waiting at the door. When she saw me a radiant smile lit up her face.

"Karen! You're the first of the club!" She hugged me warmly and gave me three kisses. A sweet heavy fragrance surrounded her, and her small breasts swelled modestly above a black satin top.

"And this is your, let me think . . . Michel! Isn't that right?" She put out her arms to Michel and gave him three kisses too. He submitted awkwardly to her embrace.

"I'll show you round later, if you'd like that," she said, after which she let go of Michel and descended on the next new arrivals.

"Show you round: people like this always want to do that. And then they tell you how difficult every tile, every door handle was to obtain."

I gave him a nudge.

"Don't be so cynical. Be open to other people for a change, without prejudging them!"

Feeling somewhat lost, we wandered through the large empty room to the garden, where everyone was standing together looking rather embarrassed. The champagne, which stood waiting on a table covered in gold brocade, tasted wonderful.

"For the time being I'm in the right place," muttered Michel and he took a second glass, which he knocked back in three gulps. There was a strange, expectant atmosphere, and I searched desperately for a familiar face, someone who could give me the feeling that I belonged here. Thank God, at that moment Hanneke came into the garden, with a man who must be her Ivo.

The drink did its work. An hour later we were all beaming as if we had known each other for years. Michel was holding forth to Evert, Kees and Ivo; and we women were commenting on the other guests. We knew some of them vaguely, but most of them we had never seen before.

"All business colleagues of Simon's," said Angela, and Babette asked what kind of business was Simon in, for goodness sake, to be making such a pile.

"Something to do with property. I don't know exactly, very complicated. What it comes down to is that he's loaded, which helps him to get even more loaded," replied Hanneke, sucking frenetically on her cigarette and blowing out the smoke with a hiss.

"Talk of the devil . . ." whispered Angela, nodding almost imperceptibly in the direction of someone who was obviously standing behind me. I turned around and found myself face-to-face with Simon. The man who was shamelessly surveying me from head to toe with his fierce blue eyes was exceptionally attractive. Not that he was all that handsome: the lines around his mouth were a little too sharp, his black hair was a little too artificially tousled, and he was only slightly taller than I was, which gave him a rather boyish air, but he exuded blatant sex. He was aware of his masculinity as only boys of eighteen can be, the kind of consciousness that men lose when they pass thirty and it no longer concerns them that their jaw line is sagging and their belly expanding.

"Hanneke, I get nothing but compliments about the fantastic job you've done here."

He put both hands on Hanneke's hips and kissed her on the cheek. I began blushing vicariously. Hanneke introduced us to him as the girls from the dinner club, and he said he'd already heard a lot about us from his wife.

"And the gentlemen here must belong with you?" Simon introduced himself jovially to everyone. I couldn't take my eyes off him. Completely at ease in his white suit, running his tanned fingers nonchalantly through his tousled hair, he had a hypnotic, eager look. I had rarely met anyone so self-absorbed without it being irritating. His grin seemed to be making fun of his own persona, as if he really enjoyed playing the part of a millionaire and were laughing at everyone who took him seriously.

Euphoric from the alcohol, we danced like idiots to the music of our wild youth. Michel and Ivo found each other playing air guitar, Hanneke tipped barefoot around a man enveloped in a red pullover who every so often grabbed her and lifted her in the air, and I moved in and out from one person to another, in a kind of blissful trance. It was years since I had last danced, although it had once been my great passion. Michel and I had met on the dance floor, which was where I met all my boyfriends, since it was where I spent every free evening. Nowhere did I feel lighter, freer or more beautiful than on the dance floor, where I could let myself go, spurred on by the music, entranced by the other moving bodies. I had always found it difficult to strike up a conversation with someone at the bar, but I hadn't the slightest inhibition about dancing up against someone, sliding my buttocks against his hips.

Floating on the music, I again became a seductress and it was wonderful to feel so alive, young and sexy. Michel danced after me possessively, but I kept wriggling subtly out of his grasp. Hanneke handed me a fresh glass rather unsteadily and put her arm round me. She hung heavily and drunkenly round my neck and yelled in my ear that everyone was as horny as could be, after which she wandered over to the Bedouin tent. As I bent to get rid of my glass, I suddenly felt two burning hands on my hips.

"Want to dance with me now?" asked Simon in my ear, as he came up behind me, and I felt his sex hard against me. My first impulse was to slap his face for grabbing me in such an impertinent way, but I did nothing, said nothing. I turned around, pushing myself against his groin, and finally thrusting my breasts into his chest. The champagne made me bold and, putting my hands on his hard hips, I led him to the centre of the dance floor. Silently our bodies met, we were unaware of the people around us, and Simon's hands did not let go of my body for an instant. He was obviously unconcerned about the presence of my husband and his wife just a few feet from us.

Sometimes his voluptuous mouth came so close to mine that he seemed about to kiss me and I knew that if he did I would be unable to resist, regardless of the consequences.

"You smell wonderful."

His nose brushed against my ear, and I could hear him breathe. I looked down and stared at the dark curly chest hair revealed by his unbuttoned white shirt. He smelled of cigars, soap and a whiff of sweat. His grip on my buttocks became firmer, and he stroked my lower back with his thumbs, giving me goose pimples and making my heart beat even faster. The rhythm of the music accelerated, giving me the opportunity to push him gently away. Our movements became more violent, we shook our hair about wildly, I jumped, threw my arms in the air and laughed at myself, at him, at the fact I could still seduce and out of pure happiness at his interest in me. Meanwhile the sweat was dripping from his forehead.

"I've got to stop for a moment . . . Are you coming to chill out?" He laid his hands on my shoulders and nodded towards the tent with his flushed face. I was about to follow him when Michel grabbed me by the elbow.

"Come on. We're going," he said gruffly.

Michel described my flirting with the host as embarrassing, and although I knew he was right, I denied it with all my might and professed to be insulted. Nothing had happened between Simon and me, we had just had a wonderful dance, Christ, why did he have to make such a fuss about it? Why can't I have a nice evening for once, I screamed while he cycled off angrily and I started crying. I cycled after Michel, sobbing. The cold, damp air of the woods brought me back to my senses somewhat, although a burning, frustrated desire continued to glow in my belly. Deep inside I was certain that it would happen sooner or later, that there was no escape, that one day Simon's mouth would find mine. I should feel bad and guilty about these emotions, but I just wanted Simon all the more.

"Please let me experience this one more time!" I whispered to myself in my befuddled state. Through my head flitted images of Simon closing his lips round my nipple, gently opening my legs, kissing my inner thighs, holding my buttocks with his strong hands and thrusting into me. With a jolt I realized that for the first time since the birth of our youngest I felt like a sexual being again, was aware of my body and my breasts and felt my vagina throbbing hard against the saddle. Simon had kissed me awake from a long, deep sleep and with one dance had given me back my libido. I had already forgotten all about the zombie I had been for years until tonight.

10

The following summer seemed to be an endless succession of dinners, parties, birthdays and beach barbecues with our new circle of friends. Since Simon and Patricia's housewarming it had been perfectly natural to celebrate the children's birthdays together, drop in for coffee on the spur of the moment, and for our husbands to play tennis on Friday evenings, after which we would meet at Verdi's, the local café on the square. In the space of a few months we became close friends. We had in common the fact that we came from outside the village and were absorbed in our unstoppable business success. Evert's sports shop grew into a chain, Kees opened one wine bar after another, Ivo progressed from an accountant to an asset manager and built a golfing holiday complex on the south coast of Portugal, and Hanneke was so busy remodelling houses she had taken on an au pair. Thanks to the sale of a number of programmes, Michel outgrew his premises in Amstelveen, and through my new circle of friends I acquired so many lucrative business clients that I stopped designing layouts for magazines. We revelled in the inspiring optimism that all this success brought with it, in the positive chemistry that surrounded us like a collective love affair. Recognition was perhaps the greatest driving force. we were in our mid-thirties, settled in our family lives and careers, but despite that we felt far from old. We still wanted to have wild parties, before the inevitable decline set in, to dance on the edge of the volcano, as if we knew that this beautiful life could not last for long and that one day we would have to pay for our hedonistic lifestyle.

There was still a certain tension in the air between Simon and me, but the morning after the party, when I woke with a feeling of guilt as oppressive and real as the hangover, I swore to myself I would never let things go that far again. Not another word was said about it, not by Michel, not by Patricia and not by Simon, and I followed suit. Words would make this innocent flirtation seem more serious than it actually was, I convinced myself. My sometimes shocking fantasies about him made it painfully clear that my feelings for him were deeper than I dared admit to myself. But this was strictly off limits: if I sought to get closer to him, I would be risking not only my marriage but also my friendships and the good life that went with them.

One autumn night with dense fog outside, Michel came home late and very excited from tennis. I was sitting downstairs in my dressing gown waiting for him, frightened that he might have had one too many and crashed into a tree or driven into a ditch. I had tried a number of times to reach him on his mobile but kept getting his voicemail, and out of pure anxiety I had polished off half a bottle of red wine. He came in at nearly two-thirty, reeking of pub, beer and cigars and slapped a full, greedy kiss on my mouth, something he had not done with such passion for years.

"I've been having this amazing conversation with Simon. Sorry I'm so late, but it was just so special," he apologized and got a beer out of the fridge. Then he sat down opposite me at the table and looked at me with slightly bloodshot but shining eyes.

"We're going to do great things, Simon and me. Ka, he's got so much dough that he'll never be able to spend it in one lifetime. He's got to invest it, so he's always on the lookout for interesting projects to put money into. For example, property: I'm hunting for new premises, and you know I've looked everywhere and nothing fits the bill. Now Simon has suggested that we build something together, near Amstelveen. He'll buy the land, build to my specifications, and I'll rent the place from him."

He smiled, put the bottle to his lips and took a good swig.

"For an exorbitant amount, I expect . . ."

"If I can expand, I can earn more. And with Simon as my backer, Christ, Ka, I can do really great things! He knows all the big players . . . What kind of sponsorship do you think that could mean?"

"Of course it's wonderful, to be able to work with a friend like that . . . But it can just as easily go wrong, can't it? I mean, you'll be more or less dependent on him financially. Do you want that?"

"What difference does it make if I'm dependent on him or on someone else? I can talk to him. He's so smart and so positive that when you've talked to him you have the feeling anything is possible. I find that inspiring, and our conversation really gave me a terrific rush."

He ran his finger along my cheek and neck and took my warm breast in his cold hand. I shivered. He bent over and kissed my ear.

"I just have a good feeling about this. I feel I'm on the edge of a breakthrough . . . With Simon's help our dreams can come true. Then in a while I'll be one of the big players too."

I thought cynically that he had obviously in the

meantime redubbed *his* dreams – a lovely house, the Volvo, a sizeable company, a villa in Tuscany and membership of the local golf club – as *our* dreams, although I didn't give a damn for any of that, but it didn't seem sensible to discuss this at three in the morning with a husband who'd had too much to drink.

"Shall we have this conversation tomorrow, when you've sobered up?"

His tongue played over my cheek, searching for mine. I turned my head away as a reaction to the smell of cigars on his breath.

"Come on, Ka, it's been so long. I want you . . ."

I knew that if I refused, there would be days of sulky silence, until I broke it and convinced him of my love for him. And I didn't fancy that, so I let his hands wander over my body. My thoughts strayed to Simon. I got up and unbuttoned my dressing gown. Michel took hold of my hips and looked appreciatively at my breasts, then bent his head and kissed them. Gently kneading, his hand slid across my belly to my thighs. I opened my legs obligingly and let his fingers in, whereupon he groaned and said I was a wonderful woman, his own wonderful woman. As I grabbed him violently by the hair and kissed him roughly on the mouth, I realized that I was no longer his wonderful woman, that I was drifting a little further away from him every day, that I was playing at happy families and that it hadn't felt real for a long time. Michel wasn't turned on by me, he was excited by money, the vistas Simon had opened up for him, and I was turned on by the thought of Simon himself.

11

Michel was asleep when we got back from Ivo and Hanneke's in the middle of the night. Babette did not want to go straight to bed, and nor did I; although my body was shivering with cold and exhaustion, my brain was still working overtime, and I knew that if I went to bed now, I wouldn't be able to sleep. So I made us two large mugs of hot milk, stirred in two generous spoonfuls of honey, lit the candles on the living-room table and nestled next to her on the sofa. The warmth and sweetness of the milk were not comforting: for some strange reason I felt deeply hurt by the story Babette had told me an hour ago. Hanneke was my best friend, and we sometimes joked about the others, whose main concerns seemed to us to be tennis, dieting, shopping and never-ending chatter about the kids. For real understanding, trust and intimacy, Hanneke and I sought each other out, or at least I thought so. It now turned out that she hadn't trusted me enough.

"How do you think I felt when I found out?"

Babette dipped her finger in the liquid candle wax and watched the hot liquid setting on her finger.

"Terrible. What a betrayal. I think it's really . . . I would never have expected it of her, never, and not of Evert either. How can you bring yourself to go on seeing her?"

"I forgave her and Evert. What choice did I have? I wanted to keep my family together, and our circle of friends. So we agreed to keep it secret and to go on behaving normally with each other in public. But I shan't be calling her a friend again in a hurry. To be honest, I thought Hanneke would have told you. You two are so close. Promise me you won't talk to anyone about this, not even to Michel."

She bent her head as if she were about to cry. I took her by the shoulders, pulled her to me and stroked her thick blond hair, which smelled of perfume.

"You can trust me. My lips are sealed."

She lifted up her head and gave me a broken-hearted look.

"Evert fell into a huge hole after their relationship broke up. I'm afraid it was the last straw. Hanneke unleashed something in him, something destructive. She's a bit destructive herself, don't you think? She's violent woman, she smokes a lot, she drinks a lot, and she always wants to tell everyone the truth. I sometimes think she's depressive, just like Evert, and that they recognized that in each other. But I don't blame her; the only person I can blame is myself. I should have seen it coming: I knew he was having problems again, but I refused to see it. So stupid . . . I was too bound up with my own misery, my own rage, and I just left him to get on with it."

Her lips were trembling, and my stomach contracted. I fought back my own tears and the cowardly feeling that I couldn't take all this. I wanted to be there for Babette, so there was no going back. Obviously she had singled me out to share her secret, and I couldn't shame her trust by being afraid. But I was.

Babette leaned heavily against me.

"It feels good to be with you, Karen," she sniffed, rubbing my arm as a gesture of gratitude.

66

"You're such a warm woman . . . Without you, I think I'd go crazy now. If ever you have a problem, you know I'll be there for you."

I stroked her back and rested my head against hers, surprised at how easy it was to be intimate with her, although we never had been before. Even with Hanneke I had never been this tactile, and in fact I disliked women being physical as a gesture of friendship. Yet here I was in a close embrace with a friend, without feeling at all uncomfortable.

"That's great, but for now it's you that matters. We'll all help you get back on your feet. You're not alone."

"You're sweet, really sweet." She sat up, pursed her lips and gave me a kiss. The she got up, stretched and put out her hand to pull me up from the sofa too.

"Now we've got to go to bed. Go and snuggle up to that lovely husband of yours."

"Sleep? What's that?"

A sad smile appeared on her face. "It'll all come right one day, I keep telling myself. However hard it is, life goes on, and I'm determined not to wallow."

My sleep was restless, and I woke in a kind of panic. Hanneke. Something was all wrong, and I hadn't handled it properly yesterday. It was obvious she had a problem, had taken me aside to talk about it, and I had rejected her honesty by walking away, leaving her in the lurch, condemning her harsh words instead of trying to understand as a best friend should do. If I hadn't turned my back on her, she wouldn't have gone away. She might have confessed her affair with Evert, told me the source of her unhappiness. How could I be so quick to judge her without first hearing her side of the story? She had always been good to me, the only person I could really talk to. I realized how difficult it must have been to keep her love for Evert secret from me and that she hadn't done so out of distrust but rather out of respect. She didn't want to burden me with a secret and had opted to sort things out all by herself.

I looked at the alarm. It was six-fifteen. Another fifteen minutes and it would go off for Michel, who left at seven every morning. Perfectly timed, to avoid the rush hour at its height. When I complained, he invariably replied that he would much rather be at the breakfast table with his family than sit in a tailback but that he couldn't help it if he had a business where as managing director he had to be in before nine. He just laughed at my suggestion that he try swapping with me for a day and then seeing if he preferred being at home at the table instead of in the snarl-up. It was no wonder that we women at home abandoned ourselves to fantasies about other men, seeing that our husbands abandoned us daily. And of course these things could get out of hand, hungry for attention as we were.

I jumped out of bed, slid my feet into grubby pink slippers and went into the hall. I wanted to shower before the girls woke up and warmed up the cold house with their boisterous din. From the bathroom came the sound of the shower. Babette had obviously woken as early as I had.

I turned up the thermostat, put a kettle of water on the gas, fetched the paper from the letterbox and turned on the radio before making sandwiches for the children's school lunch. Upstairs I heard Michel and Babette saying good morning. As I picked up the paper, I saw my mobile lying there.

You have 1 new message, it said on the screen.

Dear K, sorry about yesterday. Can I see you today? Back in B. late afternoon. XHan.

12

It smelled of an open fire and spiced biscuits in the De Beiaard café, and it was noisy and busy. I found a table by the window and ordered a beer, hoping it would perk me up. I had the kind of headache that felt as if my brains were slowly pushing my eyes out of their sockets, the result of prolonged lack of sleep and over-indulgence in alcohol. In my experience, only more alcohol could temporarily relieve these symptoms.

I ran my hand nervously across the coarse surface of the tablecloth, picked at the thick white candle and then scrunched up a beer mat, meanwhile looking outside for Hanneke to arrive. I sensed she had decided to tell me everything this afternoon and had resolved to listen to her without prejudice. It would be difficult playing piggy-in-the-middle between her and Babette, but I was determined to be as objective and under-standing as possible towards both of them. At any rate I wanted to do what I could to ensure Evert's death did not lead to the disintegration of our circle of friends.

Outside dusk was falling. I drank the last of my cold beer and glanced at my mobile: Hanneke was over fif-teen minutes late. I tried to call her but got her voice-mail. There was no answer on her home phone either. Hanneke was notorious for her lateness, and usually I didn't mind, but now it irritated me beyond measure. She couldn't keep me waiting with this feeling: I had had to move heaven and earth to find somewhere for the children to stay, as Babette had gone to town with

Angela to choose a stone for Evert's grave. I ordered another beer and decided to wait till I'd finished it. Then I would go and leave it up to her.

I stared out of the window at the bare, gnarled beeches around the church. How dare she keep me waiting here like a fool after what had happened? I tried to ring her again, or at least to leave a message on her voicemail telling her exactly what I thought of this behaviour. This time there was an answer.

"Good afternoon . . ."

"Uh, it's Karen, is Hanneke around?"

"This is Dorien Jager, Amsterdam South Police. Do you know Mrs Lemstra?"

"Yes, Hanneke Lemstra is my friend . . ."

This was not the news I wanted. This was completely wrong. My hands started trembling so badly that I could scarcely hold my phone.

"Perhaps you should contact Mrs Lemstra's husband."

"Why? What's happened?"

"Your friend has been admitted to Amsterdam General Hospital. Her husband is on his way. We found this telephone in the hotel room where your friend was staying."

"Oh, God . . ."

"Hello, madam? Could I take a note of your name?"

"Karen. Karen van de Made. What's happened?"

There was a moment's silence at the other end of the line.

"Your friend has had an accident. She fell off the balcony."

71

13

Ivo was sitting slumped forward in the black plastic chair, supporting his head in his hands, eyes closed, immersed in his own despair. Round his shoulders hung the camel coat that he recently been given for his birthday by Hanneke.

I put my hand on his head, and he looked up, at first alarmed, then surprised, and immediately afterwards his shoulders began heaving. He got up, put his long arms around me, his sobs punctuated with long, piercing wails.

"They don't know, they don't know, they don't know anything."

His rough cheeks were scraping my neck, which was gradually becoming wet with his tears. I took hold of his head and rubbed the salty tears off his face with my thumbs. We stood there together for a while, under the cold fluorescent lights, both wondering what kind of hell we had found our way into. First Evert, now Hanneke – it was as if our families were being punished one by one.

Ivo let go of me and took my hand, and we both sat down.

"No one's saying anything about whether she's going to make it. No one can say."

He ran his hand neurotically through his stubbly hair.

"I'm glad you're here."

"Of course I'm here," I mumbled and thought that if

I'd been there for Hanneke earlier, we might not have been here now.

"Can you tell me exactly what happened?"

"It's vague, very vague. After that row at Simon and Patricia's she obviously went to Amsterdam by taxi or train and took a room in a hotel in Jan Luijkensstraat. That night she rang me, you were there . . . This morning she rang again. She'd calmed down a bit and said she'd be coming home at the end of the day. Then, at four o'clock maybe, I was rung up to say she'd jumped off the balcony. She's in a terrible state. Everything's broken. They're operating on her now for a, what's it called, a haematoma, a haemorrhage in the brain. It's not certain she'll make it, and if she does, what sort of shape she'll be in . . ."

"But Ivo, surely Hanneke wouldn't jump off a balcony just like that?"

"No. I don't understand it either. She wasn't feeling too good, that's true: she was confused and very upset about Evert. But this . . ."

I took hold of his hand and stroked the dark hairs that lay over his swollen veins.

"We're all upset about Evert. But I don't think Hanneke would do something like this. It must be an accident."

"It is. I'm sure of it. She drinks too much. I've been telling her so for months. For Christ's sake give the wine a miss for once. But what can you do?"

His voice broke, and he made a helpless gesture.

"I didn't realize that it was bad as that, that she had a problem."

He sprang to his feet and started pacing about.

"Problem? Problem? We've got everything we could wish for, for God's sake. Why did this happen? Please explain it to me!"

I cringed, and my cheeks were burning. I wanted to disappear, dissolve into thin air, melt into the chair. Ivo clenched his fists and yelled.

"Goddammit! My wife! Why my wife?"

Then he staggered off down the chilly corridor like a drunk.

The hurried click of heels down the corridor startled me. Simon looked breathtaking in a black, tightly fitting woollen suit, under which he wore a starched white shirt with the top buttons undone. Along the lapels hung an ice-blue silk tie. I could see from the dark rings under his eyes that he was tired. I caught my breath: I didn't dare look him in the face, frightened as I was that my head would start shaking involuntarily.

"Hi, baby." He put his warm hand on the back of my neck.

"Michel is on his way. Babette is staying with the children. How is she?"

"Bad, I'm afraid. They're operating. Ivo's says everything's broken . . ."

He stood in front of me, feet apart, rocking his knees nervously.

"Christ . . . What a weird situation. Where is Ivo?"

"He's just gone for a bit of a walk. It was all getting on top of him, I think."

"OK, baby, I'll go and find Ivo. I'll be right back."

Hanneke lay small and lonely in her bed, her head wrapped in thick bandages like a mummy, and attached to a respirator. I didn't dare look at the tubes filled with blood that poked out of the bandages. Seeing her lying there like that made me nauseous and dizzy, but I forced myself to stay, to touch her blood-smudged hand and whispered in the direction of her ear that I was with her, that I was terribly sorry for everything and that she must fight to come back to us, for the sake of Ivo and her children. Michel fled the room gasping for breath, followed by Simon. Ivo sat helplessly beside his wife, who had been transmuted into an extraterrestrial.

Her life was still not out of danger, and the doctor said it was worrying that she was still unconscious.

"So she's in a coma?" Ivo had asked; and all the doctor would say was that "she was in a comatose state, from which she could awake at any moment", but this might well take weeks.

A police officer came into the room and asked if he could speak to us for a moment.

"Your wife and your friend checked into the Jan Luijken Hotel at about one this morning and made a confused impression. She had no visitors last night, or today, although the hotel owner can't be absolutely sure: the reception desk is not always manned. This morning Mrs Lemstra indicated that she would be checking out at about three. We found her things packed on the bed. The incident took place at three-thirty. No note was found, and we cannot yet establish whether this was an attempted suicide or an accident. My colleague and I would like to ask each of you some questions separately."

Ivo's face was completely drained of colour, and he nodded blankly. Simon put his arm round him and with his other hand patted the policeman on the shoulder in encouragement. "Of course, officer. It's just that I have to go right away, I've got an appointment. I'll give you my card and you can just call me, right?" He pressed his card into the policeman's hand and said goodbye to Ivo with a firm hug. As he was leaving he turned round again and pointed in our direction.

"We'll stay in touch, OK?"

I was questioned by Dorien Jager, the policewoman I had spoken to on the phone earlier. She was plump and had short, bristly brown hair. Her contemptuous air came as an unpleasant shock. I told her immediately that I didn't believe it had been an attempted suicide, that wasn't like Hanneke at all. She was a fighter, someone who always turned a negative into a positive. She could be hard and cynical, bitingly sarcastic at times, but that was typical of her resilience. With a look of displeasure Dorien made an entry in her notebook.

"Does your friend drink?"

"Sometimes, yes. But I wouldn't want to call her an alcoholic. The evening she went off, though, she had had a bit too much to drink, but so had we all. We had just buried one of our best friends."

"So she was in mourning and drunk. What was her relationship to that friend like?"

This question startled me. If I were to give an honest answer I would be breaking my promise to Babette. The consequences would probably be hard to predict. Evert's suicide would also be seen in a completely different light.

"Just normal, he was the husband of a friend of ours. We women had our own dinner club. That's how we also got to know each other's husbands, and in the meantime we've all become friends."

"And this friend, Evert Struyk, is the man who burned down his own house?"

"Yes. Because he was ill, mentally, that is, of course."

"Don't you find it odd that there should be two

suicides in your circle of friends in the space of two weeks?"

"What happened to Hanneke was an accident, I'd stake my life on that. Perhaps it happened because she was drunk, but it definitely wasn't deliberate. I think it's a coincidence that this happened just after Evert's funeral."

"But she didn't wind up in a hotel in Amsterdam for no good reason, did she? It seems to me that one thing led to another. On the day of his funeral, your friend runs away to a hotel . . ."

"We've all been thrown by Evert's death and by the fact that he tried to take his family with him . . . We've sat up with each other night after night. An event like this makes you look at your own problems, and you start wondering what your life really means. Can you imagine how guilty and inadequate you feel when one of your best friends does something like that? We're all taking sleeping pills, I can assure you of that. I think it all got too much for Hanneke. She was feeling vulnerable, and she'd been drinking, and she wanted to get away from it all for a bit. And Hanneke's the sort of person who does just that."

"So mightn't such an impulsive person equally well jump off a balcony?"

"Impossible. She'd texted me and rang me again to arrange to meet. She was planning to come back and she sounded like her old self."

"Could someone have pushed her?"

For a second I gasped for air, as if someone had punched me in the stomach.

"No. That's impossible."

"Experience has taught me that nothing is impossible, Mrs Van de Made. Could I finally ask you where you were at about four this afternoon?"

"In the shower: I was hot and sweaty after a workout. I had a date with Hanneke half an hour later."

"Can anyone confirm that?"

"I'm afraid not. My children were out playing, and there was no one else at home."

Dorien Jager wrote everything down precisely with pinched lips.

14

When I drove into our street, my head spinning from exhaustion, I found that everyone had gathered at our place. The cars were parked carelessly around our house, and through the big kitchen window I could see them sitting at my dining table. A stab of irritation went through me, and I wondered if enough weren't enough. I didn't want to talk and drink, I wanted to sink into a hot bath without a word and finally get some proper sleep, but their appetite for togetherness was obviously insatiable. I immediately suppressed such negative thoughts: they were of course all sitting in my kitchen to support us and Babette after this terrible accident, and it was wonderful that they were able to find the strength yet again.

When I entered the room, I felt at once how much I already missed Hanneke. She was my buffer, my anchor in the group. Without her I felt lost and uncertain.

Patricia gave me a big cuddle. 'You'll probably need this,' she said, pushing a glass of red wine into my hand. Babette looked at me meaningfully with her red-rimmed eyes.

"Well, my love," said Angela, putting her hand on my shoulder. "It just goes on. We're really being singled out."

I sat down, took a sip of red wine and felt the calming effect of the warm glow that spread through my body.

"I expect Ivo's still there?" asked Patricia, and I nodded.

"How is she?" Everyone looked at me tensely.

"Bad. She's broken more or less every bone in her body, and she's had an emergency operation for a haematoma, a swelling on the brain. It went well, but she hasn't regained consciousness, and that's pretty worrying."

There was a dejected silence, which grabbed me by the throat and forced me to go on talking. I searched for words, for something consoling or uplifting, but I couldn't say everything was going to be all right or better than we thought. It was never going to be all right, ever. Evert was dead, and Hanneke as good as. As friends we had failed them. There was really no point in our still sitting together in supposed solidarity.

Simon broke the silence.

"Hey, come on! For goodness sake don't let's get depressed. It's terrible, but we can't blame ourselves for this. Everyone is responsible for their own life, their own actions. Apart from which, we don't even know for certain that Hanneke jumped. Probably it was an accident, a tragic combination of circumstances."

Angela smiled sarcastically. "We know she'd been behaving very strangely over the last few days."

"Hanneke is an emotional woman," said Babette quietly. "That's one of the nice things about her: she gives it one hundred per cent when there's a celebration and one hundred per cent when she's unhappy. Please don't let's judge or get into recriminations that don't do any good. As friends we must be united now. There's enough gossip in this village already, don't let us contribute to it . . ."

"I'll drink to that," said Simon raising his glass.

We had a Chinese meal and drank cold beer. Patricia

and Angela both went home in time to relieve their babysitters. All Babette wanted to do was sleep. After they had gone the gloom gave way to an unstable, hysterical mood, with the kind of giggling that can easily turn into floods of tears. Simon was in a talkative mood, telling one anecdote after another about dodgy businessmen. Michel and I hung on his every word. It was wonderful to laugh for a change and talk about something other than death and grief, although it felt almost illicit, something that wasn't really allowed during this period of mourning, while Babette was probably feeling terribly lonely and churned up.

We stayed there talking and drinking till we finally sat puffing drunkenly on Simon's cigars and were incapable of saying anything but sentimental nonsense.

"Where would we really be without each other?" slurred Simon, opening his arms wide and putting them round Michel and me.

"That's what it's all about, isn't it? What everything's about? Love, friendship . . ." He hugged us with all his might and gave us both a smacking kiss on the top of our heads.

"Money, my loves, money doesn't mean a thing to me. Believe me, I don't give a damn about it anymore. It's the game I like, the risk, acting quickly, having balls, that's great. And surrounding myself with talent, inspiring, positive people, like you."

He patted Michel playfully on the cheek, and ran his other hand down my back, sliding it via the base of my spine into my jeans, where he tugged teasingly at my thong. My heart was pounding so hard I was frightened the others could hear it. Simon got up unsteadily and stammered that he must go home. Michel rose too and muttered that Simon couldn't drive in that state. Then he sprinted for the toilet, where he dutifully vomited up the complete contents of his stomach.

With unsteady hands I helped Simon, who was hiccupping with laughter at my vomiting husband, into his coat and pushed him gently out of the house before Michel left the toilet. At the door he took my hand and pulled me with him into the biting cold. "Just look at that," he said pointing upwards at the full moon with dark clouds scudding across it.

"Wonderful," I stammered, shivering with the cold. He put his arms around me.

"Simon, what you just did isn't on."

"What did I do, then?" He gave me a mocking look.

"Putting your hand down my jeans, with Michel there."

"So what's your problem, my touching you like that or my doing it while Michel's there?"

"Both."

"It looked so terrific. That black thong above your jeans . . . I couldn't help it. You've got a body that has to be touched."

"Surely you're not going to drive in that state?"

"I'll be home right away. It's just straight ahead. Don't worry."

His intense gaze made me lower my eyes.

"Take Michel's bike, please. We've had enough grief already . . ."

"All right. Give me the bike then. It's a wonderful night for cycling."

I hurried indoors to get the key of the shed, just in time to see Michel hoisting himself paralytically up the stairs.

"I'm going to bed, Ka, I've got to lie down . . . I'll clear up tomorrow," he groaned.

"It's all right, love. I'm just getting your bike for Simon. He really can't drive."

Michel could only moan in reply.

With my heavy ski jacket round my shoulders I tripped as nonchalantly as possible down our gravel path to the shed. I knew that Simon was following me. The moment I saw Michel hanging so limply from the banisters I knew it was going to happen.

I breathed in the smell of the freezing cold, so as not to faint with excitement and to sober up a little. I tried to feel guilty about what was about to happen but couldn't manage it. Trembling, I tried to put the key in the lock, and when I failed Simon took over. We giggled about our fumbling, and I stammered something about Michel, who was so wrecked, while Simon started to stroke my hair, put his forefinger under my chin and kissed me. He pressed his full, rough lips carefully against mine and as our tongues slowly touched he groaned. My knees went weak, as if my muscles had suddenly become liquid, and my doubts vanished. I wanted this man: this was the inevitable moment I had felt approaching for two years.

We stumbled, still kissing, into the shed, our mouths not separating for a moment and my whole body seething with desire. The jacket slid from my shoulders, but the cold did not bother me, I was capable of taking off all my clothes in order to feel his hands on my bare skin. Breathing heavily, Simon wriggled out of his coat and slid his cold hand into the back of my jeans. His drunken clumsiness had gone instantly. I could feel his erection against my belly and without hesitating I undid his belt, unzipped his trousers and wrapped my hand round his warm, hard, throbbing cock. I kicked off my boots, Simon peeled off my jeans together with my thong, knelt down and pressed his face into my pubic hair. He took my buttocks in his hands and pulled my hips greedily to him. His warm breath made my crotch tingle, and I shuddered as his tongue slid into me after slowly dwelling on my outer lips. He moved upwards again, licked my navel and grabbed my breasts, which were still imprisoned in my bra. He started fiddling impatiently with the catch while straining to bite my mouth.

"Taste how wonderful you are," he groaned. I licked his lips and tasted my own salty moisture. A bottle fell and broke, he lifted me up, pushed me against Michel's workbench, and I caught my breath as he came into me with a deep thrust. We screwed like hungry animals in the dark, panting, smacking, trembling and grunting. If Michel had come in, we would probably have simply continued, we were so obsessed.

"And now one last vodka and a cigar." He brushed my cheek with his bruised lips and grinned. "You're a wonderful woman, Karen. Your body is so soft, you're made for sex. I knew that the moment I saw you."

Simon put his hand between my thighs, pinched my flesh gently and groaned again. I kissed him and began groping around for my jeans and thong. What I most wanted to do was cry, something that hadn't happened to me after making love for years. Simon hitched up his trousers, zipped his fly and put his coat back on. I wriggled awkwardly into my jeans and boots. Only now did I feel how the cold was numbing my fingers and toes.

"I don't want to leave you, beautiful, I wish we could make love all night and then fall asleep in each other's arms. But we've got to be very careful . . ." He hugged me and kissed the tip of my cold nose.

"Off you go . . . Michel will be wondering what's happened to me . . ."

"Don't you worry, Karen. No one will ever know about this. You're my secret."

I nuzzled up to him and thought of the vows Michel and I had made. We would let each other know in good time if one of us had feelings for someone else. Playing away had no place in our relationship and, if it ever happened, should be admitted honestly. Should it ever come to it, we would do it safely and never, ever with someone from our own circle. In less than ten minutes I had broken every promise without feeling a moment's guilt. Simon let go of me, put his hands in his leather gloves and took Michel's bike out from among the others.

"I already look forward to bringing it back," he whispered with a grin.

I watched him cycle off into the dark, with his dishevelled hair waving about. He didn't look back. I couldn't go inside and lie next to Michel as though nothing had happened. My heart was pounding too hard, and my head was full of a restlessness that bordered on panic. I wanted to run, just run to empty myself of everything and not to have to think.

15

It was a present from Ivo, for the first anniversary of the dinner club: an all-in week's holiday in Portugal at a villa in his golfing complex. The men would look after the children. He had arranged everything. There would be a Saab convertible waiting for us at the airport, three days of golf lessons, one day's beauty treatment at one of Portugal's leading spas and to round it off dinner on a yacht off the coast of Carvoeiro. We were just starting on the tiramisu in Angela's country kitchen, when the men, in drag and well oiled, burst in. They waved the tickets about while Ivo, looking like some kind of Sugar Lee Hooper, came in hooting with laughter holding the model of his golf resort. We squealed with enthusiasm like a bunch of hysterical schoolgirls. A whole week basking in the Portuguese sun without husbands or children – that was something we had been fantasizing about for the past year.

An hour later we were all swinging round the kitchen table, bottles of beer in hand, the men still in our dresses, their faces blotchy with makeup. We stamped and clapped along with the Gypsy Kings, embraced each other in drunken excitement and shouted and yelled for all we were worth. Hanneke climbed onto the table and showed her stocking tops. Patricia joined her and unbuttoned her purple satin blouse. Urged on by the gentlemen, Hanneke also took off her sweater, and Patricia lifted up her miniskirt with hips swaying to reveal her thong. I didn't know whether to find this wonderful or embarrassing. They jumped off the table, Hanneke almost slipping over, and cheerfully went on dancing half-naked.

One by one the others too, faces flushed, removed their clothes, giggling as they did so. I didn't feel like it at all. What was happening gave me an uncomfortable, unsettled feeling. I did not want to be part of this vulgar crowd. The arousing guitars of the Gypsy Kings gave way to Marvin Gaye, whose sexy voice fitted the overheated mood. I saw Babette dim the light and then start tugging impatiently at Michel's top. He smiled in awkward embarrassment but to my great annoyance just let it happen. Angela's breasts were swaying attractively in a black lace top, as she bore down on me with her arms outstretched and smiling radiantly.

"Come on, Karen, let your hair down a bit! Just let yourself go!"

With her arms around my waist, she tried to get me to sway along with her, but my body was locked tight, as stiff as a board. I had to get out of here. It was crystal clear how this party was going to end and that was a step too far for me.

Michel said I was being childish, making a fuss about nothing and thought it was OK. We were walking home, and the wind was so strong we had to raise our voices to make ourselves heard. Branches were creaking and swishing menacingly over our heads, which made me feel even more agitated. Michel looked ridiculous, in my long red dress under which he had put his own loafers on again. He started sniggering. I asked him why he was laughing.

"She showed me her new breasts . . ."

"What?"

"Really, I came out of the toilet, and she was waiting. She pulled her sweater up, took hold of her tits and asked me what I thought of them."

"And?"

"I said I was very impressed. Then she told me they were a present from Evert, after the birth of Luuk. And that she'd wanted boobs like those ever since she was a young girl."

"Christ!"

"Oh, she was pretty pissed. Don't go passing this on to Hanneke, will you!"

"I think this is pretty offensive . . ."

"I think it's a turn-on . . ."

"Fake boobs?"

"They looked bloody real to me." He roared with laughter.

"And I'm supposed to go to Portugal with someone like that. With a cow who shows my husband her boobs . . ."

"Don't get all worked up. Nothing else happened. Everyone let themselves go a bit. I liked it; it was a breath of fresh air . . ."

"So next time I can show other men my tits?"

"You'd never do anything like that." He took my hand and kissed it. "That's why I love you. You've got class."

For the first time since the dinner club had come into being I wondered if we belonged in this club, if in fact we were not worlds apart from the others.

Hanneke gave nothing away the next morning, except that it had got very late. They had danced and drunk, smoked a few joints, nothing else. She had a splitting headache and yes, she was thoroughly ashamed of herself for having stood on the table in her stockings. She screamed with laughter when I told her that Babette had shown Michel her boobs.

"Should I confront her about it?" I spooned the thick creamy foam of my cappuccino and looked inquiringly at her.

"Get real! Of course not. Leave it. Those kinds of things happen when people have had a few. Don't make a mountain out of a molehill."

Hanneke coughed. A heavy rattle rose from her chest.

"Perhaps you should light another one . . ." I said. She frowned at me.

"I just think it's not on for a friend of mine to pull something like that. . .and surely being drunk is no excuse?"

"Oh Ka, don't get all serious. She didn't proposition him, did she? And even so. . .it was just a bit of fun. You do the same, don't you? Flirt a bit, see if you're still a marketable item. . ."

"Not so publicly. And I don't wave my boobs around the moment there's a man about. I think that's pretty vulgar."

"I don't know. It takes some nerve . . ." She sniggered and coughed at the same time. I patted her on the back until the coughing fit passed. Hanneke grabbed my wrist and looked at me seriously.

"Don't make a fuss, I'm telling you! It won't do any good; it'll just get you in a lot of shit. And then you'll be the one who looks foolish, not her."

"I expect you're right. But I just like people to be open . . . What does friendship mean if you can't trust someone, when someone shows her boobs to your husband behind your back?"

"In the first place she didn't do it behind your back

and in the second place you're being hypocritical. If Simon feels up your bottom at a party, you don't tell Michel and Patricia. Of course not: if we all did that, there'd be no end to it."

There was a silence. Hanneke grinned triumphantly, and I smiled back. She had a point.

"You don't want to know everything, and you don't want Michel to know everything, do you? The thing is to enjoy your husband and enjoy your friends. Keep it that way."

Cycling back home, with the biting wind piercing through my heavy woollen coat, I thought about what Hanneke had said. I didn't want to bang on, play holier-than-thou; I just wanted to have fun, like everyone else. It was great to be part of this group of crazy, successful, creative people, to belong with them. We basked in each other's reflected glory. Although we had known each other for a year, I still had the feeling that I had to tiptoe around them. It was the same gnawing, uncomfortable feeling I'd had as an adolescent at secondary school, among my radiant, popular friends: I could be rejected at any moment; any word, any gesture could mean exclusion. In exchange for a place in this group I was sacrificing myself. I shook my head to expel these thoughts, because I didn't want to doubt my friends and my own role in our group. I should be happy with my new, full life. This was the life everyone dreamed about, and I was living it. So what was I moaning about?

It was not their fault that I felt so tense and uncertain, they had long since shown they liked me. I must simply stop being afraid of being not found good enough.

Again I saw Babette snuggling up to Michel and trying to get his clothes off. His hand sliding along her bare back. It was part of it all. It didn't mean anything. That was just how we acted with each other, playful and free, experimenting in our own safe, familiar environment. I resolved to play along in future and to stop questioning the rules.

16

The villa with its faded yellow walls was on a hill and looked out over a rolling, fluorescent-green golf course, punctuated here and there by cypresses and pools full of flowering water lilies. It had a veranda, a large balcony with bougainvillea growing over it and a beautifully laid out terrace at the back. Hanneke and I had bought sea bream, courgettes, fennel, garlic and tomatoes at the market and transformed them into a glorious baked dish, which we were now serving at the edge of the swimming pool. We had been at the white wine for five hours, and our faces were glowing with the sun, the alcohol and complete relaxation. Patricia raised her glass and proposed a toast to our friendship, which thanks to this week had grown even closer. We agreed with a cheer. "And what wonderful husbands we have, to have made all this possible!" cried Angela with a broad smile.

"Though you might wonder why they've sent us packing for a week," replied Hanneke. The only one of us not yet at table was Babette. We were just starting to wonder where she had got to, when she arrived looking glum. Her make-up could not hide her swollen, red eyes. Patricia immediately bent over her with motherly concern.

"Hey, my love, come here, what's wrong?"

"Leave it. I'm over it now. Please. Let's eat."

"Come on, you can tell us what the matter is."

Hanneke started serving.

"Yes, we'll go on eating."

"No. I don't want to spoil your holiday. It's nothing."

She shivered, and despite the heat her brown arms were covered in goose pimples. I poured her a glass of white wine and handed it to her. Trembling, she took the glass and drank a big mouthful.

"Now tell us, is there something wrong with the children? With Evert?" Hanneke placed a steaming plate in front of her.

"Yes, Evert," she said hoarsely. "He's not in very good shape. Hasn't been for a while, actually. I'd rather no one knew about it. So you must all keep it to yourselves! It's so humiliating. But anyway, it'll probably all come out."

Tears flowed gently down her cheeks. It was the first time one of us had shed tears in this company, and what tears they were. Most of us became ugly when we cried, but not her. I had never seen anyone suffer as beautifully as Babette. It was the kind of unhappiness that begged for consolation and touch. There was an awkward silence in anticipation of what was to come, and Hanneke lit a cigarette, in spite of the food in front of her.

"At this moment . . . a doctor is seeing him and they'll probably admit him."

"Admit him? To hospital?" We stared at Babette open-mouthed.

"Is he ill? What's wrong?"

Babette shook her head and raised her hands protectively in the air.

"It's nothing serious or anything, or at least it won't kill him. It's psychological." She tapped her head with her varnished nail.

"That sounds pretty serious to me."

"I had Simon on the phone. He thinks Evert has completely flipped."

Babette cleared her throat.

"Simon? What's he got to do with it? Did he ring you?"

Patricia's look changed from sympathetic to irritated. She kept her hands folded in front of her mouth and stared severely at Babette.

"No, it was all very messy. First Evert rang, and he was really talking gibberish. I knew at once that there was something badly wrong. I had to come home at once, he said, as they were trying to murder him because he had the divine gift, and when I told him that I couldn't be there until tomorrow at the earliest, he started calling me names. I was the whore of Babylon . . . I was colluding with diabolical powers against him . . . I got so scared: I could only think of the children. I asked him: Where are the boys? He muttered that he would take them to safety."

"I'm going to call Ivo: he's got to go over. Or the police, perhaps we should call the police." Hanneke had her mobile at the ready.

"There's no need to call. Simon's with him. He took the phone from Evert. It turned out that Evert had been swearing at him in the restaurant of the golf club and had then driven off like a madman. Simon drove after him and found him shivering in the wardrobe in the bedroom. Thank God the boys were out playing with friends. Simon phoned our GP, and he came. Now they're waiting for the emergency team."

There was a silence. I stared blankly straight ahead at the white tablecloth and didn't dare look at anyone. The helplessness that came over us was almost tangible. This shouldn't happen; this did not belong in our club. It was too difficult, too confrontational. None of us put it into words, but that was how we felt. It was no accident that Babette had described the situation as "humiliating".

"Emergency team?"

"Yes, to take him to the psychiatric unit at Amsterdam General Hospital."

"Couldn't you have seen this coming?" Hanneke's voice sounded sharp.

"No! I don't know . . . He's been gloomy for months. Sleeping badly, worrying. He thinks we're on the brink of bankruptcy, though I don't think things are that bad. He accuses me of the oddest things: of frittering his money, of flirting with every Tom, Dick and Harry, of neglecting the children. He watches every step I take, rings up the whole time. We had a fight about it just before I came out here. I asked him not to call every hour, and he flipped completely . . ."

"Surely people don't go crazy just like that?"

"Listen, girls," said Angela, placing her hands on the table and starting to smooth the folds in the tablecloth. "Evert isn't crazy. He may be stressed out or having a burnout and that will blow over with rest and the right therapy. That can happen to any of us. You mustn't forget the enormous pressure those men work under. Babette, you've simply got to shelve everything and be there for Evert, support him, make sure he's his old self again as soon as possible."

The chirping of the crickets rose to a crescendo, no longer tropical, but alarming.

"And where are the children going to go?" Patricia tugged nervously at her dark curls and looked at us searchingly one by one.

"Simon's going to collect the boys and take them home with him."

Angela got up and went over to Babette. They embraced.

"Oh, you poor thing ... What a business. What a terrible mess. Why didn't you confide in us earlier? We could have helped you ... We're going to help you."

Babette began sobbing.

"Most of all I'm very frightened. Awful, isn't it, being afraid of your own husband. ..? He even hit me during our fight!"

"That wasn't him, that was his illness. Get that clear in your mind. He'll pull through, you'll see. More than that, it'll probably make him a better person. A burnout can also be a huge learning experience. The worst is behind him, he's getting help ..."

"And what about me? What am I supposed to do? I've been hit, he accuses me of all sorts of things! I can't just ignore that. It hurts! None of you knows what it's like when your husband suddenly turns against you, what it's like to be afraid of him and to be humiliated!"

Her voice faltered. The despair ringing through it moved us. We were all fighting back our tears.

"Of course we understand," I whispered, in the hope that it would help calm her down. "And now he's being admitted, it will give you some peace for a bit."

Babette nodded dejectedly and said she wanted to be alone. With a glass of wine in her hands she went into the villa and left us behind in confusion.

I couldn't sleep that night. From my bed I looked through the cream-coloured curtains at the almost luminous starry sky and thought of the last time I had seen Evert. We were both taking the children to school, and he had greeted me as enthusiastically and cheerfully as ever. He had ask me if I was looking forward to the week in Portugal and joked about all the things the men would get up to when the women were away. I didn't notice anything strange about him.

I felt cold, although it was a balmy night, and pulled the sheets up over my nose. Hanneke was snoring gently beside me, and I suddenly felt terribly lonely and afraid. Something wasn't right, I was suddenly sure of that. I tried desperately to suppress these imaginings. What I had suddenly got into my head made no sense at all. I had drunk too much white wine, and it was making me paranoid. What had happened to Evert had nothing to do with us. No one could have prevented this, not even his own wife. He was sick in the head, and it had probably escalated because he was alone. I also felt a kind of anger and something like disappointment. His sickness was a crack in our paintwork. A word kept buzzing round in my head, a word that didn't suit me at all. I didn't want to think in those terms. Before I lived in this village, before I knew these friends, the word had no meaning for me. But a new voice had forced its way into my brain and whispered forcefully: "Loser. Evert is a loser." It was this voice that frightened me. What kind of person had I turned into, for God's sake?

17

The only reminder of last night's drinking session was a stale smell of cigars and my nagging hangover. My lips were inflamed and swollen, and through my body surged waves of memories of Simon's hand between my legs, his mouth on my nipple, his warm breath in my pubic hair. While I made sandwiches for the children, I found myself becoming wet all over again. I shook my head in the hope that these images would disappear. It had been good, fantastic in fact, and inevitable too. But I would leave it at that: it was once but never again. He was too close, and the husband of a friend into the bargain. And he was too attractive, he had unleashed a feeling in me that I hadn't had for years, which meant that I couldn't eat a thing and had a constant urge to smile. This was impossible, this was taboo: this was beyond all my limits. I loved Michel. And even if I did not love him as passionately as I used to, he was the father of my children, and I had pledged eternal loyalty to him. If he were to find out, I was afraid our marriage would not survive the crisis. The truth would wreck my relationship, and it wasn't worth that. For the time being I must keep out of Simon's way as far as possible.

"Hello, anybody home?" Babette tapped me on the head and looked at me quizzically.

"Sorry. I've got the mother of all hangovers . . ."

"I bet you have. Not that you look shitty, but I saw all those bottles outside this morning. Vodka. How can you drink that rubbish? I expect it was Simon's idea?" The sound of his name made me blush, and I turned away, hoping she would not notice.

"I want to see Hanneke today. Are you coming too?" Babette poured water into the espresso machine, scooped coffee into the container and pressed the button, unleashing an ear-splitting roar. She had already whipped the milk into a thick foam, pressed juice for the children and cleared up the dirty glasses, empty bottles and full ashtrays from the night before. The children ran round the table in their thick winter coats like funny Michelin men, till Babette put a stop to it by raising her voice.

"I'll take them to school," she said, putting on her black sheepskin coat. She looked terrific and proud.

"Are you sure?" I asked, taking a bite of my cheese biscuit.

"I have to get through it sooner or later. I want to get on with my life. For the boys' sake too . . ."

"I understand that, but you've got to give yourself time. People will be all over you at school. Can you cope with that?"

"No way, those women wouldn't dare. They'll gawp at me from a distance and whisper to each other about how pathetic I look. I'm infected, Karen, infected with grief. People can't handle that at all. But I'm used to it, it's been like that since Evert was admitted to hospital. Are you coming with me to see Hanneke later?"

I nodded and was ashamed that Hanneke was not the first thing I thought about this morning. I cleared the table, threw my biscuit away and was just about to go upstairs to fix my face when I heard my mobile bleep twice. A message. My palms were sweaty: I guessed who it was from. I would have to erase it without even looking at it. Hands shaking, I fished the mobile out of my bag and opened the message.

Morning gorgeous, last night was 1derful + worth repeating sober! XXX all over

My heart started fluttering as I hurriedly erased the message. Simon had woken up this morning, and the first thing he thought of was me. He obviously didn't regret what had happened between us. I felt very flattered. What difference does it make? I thought. Why should I deny myself this? We're not hurting anyone.

Still, Patricia deserved my solidarity. Out of respect for her I should keep well out of Simon's way, although their marriage was ultimately his responsibility. There was obviously something not right between them, and that didn't surprise me in the least. Patricia was a control freak, forever busy keeping the house spookily clean. That must get dull in the long run, certainly for a man like Simon. And was I supposed to act as the patron saint of their marriage? My trembling fingers flashed over the small keys.

When?XXX

I pressed "Send", and my message was gone. It was as simple as that. My heart was racing so wildly that I had to sit down on the stairs to regain a little control over myself. It was as if I were ill. I should be torn by feelings of guilt and regret, not sitting on the stairs pining with desire and lust, waiting for the bleep of my phone. Anyway, it wasn't easy to give a quick answer to my question. Probably he was frightened to death by my message, which left so little to the imagination.

"You're really in a bad way, aren't you?" said Babette, laughing when she saw me sitting on the stairs red in the face with my mobile in my hand.

"Who were you calling?" She hung her coat on the coat hook and stood opposite me. I couldn't look her in the eyes.

"I was going to call Ivo, but then I remembered that he's not even allowed to have his mobile on in the hospital." I was a terribly bad liar.

"I talked to Patricia at school. She told me Hanneke's condition is unchanged. Ivo had called Simon. They're going to see her too. If you can't make it, I can drive with them . . ."

"No, I'm OK." My head was almost exploding.

Outside it was milder, and the sky was filled with a thick layer of dark rain clouds. I looked at the shed and realized that, whatever happened, it would always remind me of Simon. I smiled to myself while again going weak at the knees at the thought of him. We got into my car and drove out onto the road. Babette took a George Michael CD out of her bag and asked if she could put it on: it was Evert's favourite and it comforted her to listen to it. She selected the track "Jesus to a Child" and started singing gently along with George's soothing, melancholy voice.

When you find a love
When you know that it exists
Then the lover that you miss
Will come to you on these cold, cold nights

I looked at her immaculately made-up face, which gave nothing away, no pain, no grief, no lack of sleep. I watched her singing along with the music under her breath, clutching her bag tightly to her, as if it were her only support, and I wondered how she found the strength to get up each morning, shower, dry her hair, put on foundation, apply mascara, lipstick, all in the knowledge that her husband was dead and had also tried to kill her and the children.

"How do you keep going, Babette?" I asked.

"I wonder myself sometimes. The best thing is to keep active, not to think. If I give in to it now, I'll never get out of bed again. So I fight it and try as far as possible to focus on the future, organizing a house for myself and the boys and winding up and transferring the business. I can only afford to collapse when that's sewn up."

"Transferring the business?"

"Yes. Everything is being put in Simon's name. He was Evert's partner . . ."

"Hold on a moment. I don't get it . . . Now that Evert is dead, you're automatically co-owner of the business, aren't you?"

"Unfortunately not . . . It's very complicated. But anyway, I wouldn't be able to run the company and certainly not now. But I won't be penniless: I have confidence in Ivo and Simon."

"Ivo has other things on his mind right now."

"Yes . . ."

There was a silence. It started raining softly. Babette gazed outside. I thought of Hanneke, hooked up to machines in a hospital bed.

"Do you know the police asked me if it's possible that someone pushed Hanneke?" We joined the tailback. I braked and changed down.

"No! How did they get that into their heads?"

"Pure guesswork. They think it's one hell of a coincidence that just after Evert's suicide one of his friends should fall off a balcony."

"Did you tell them that Evert and Hanneke had an affair?"

"No."

"I would have understood, you know, if you'd told them. I mean, after Hanneke's act of desperation, we can scarcely go on saying nothing."

"I didn't tell them because I want to spare Ivo suffering, and Hanneke, and you. You asked me not to talk to anyone about it, didn't you? Well, I won't."

She looked at me fearfully.

"They'll ask me too. What shall I say?"

"Whatever you like."

"I don't want to say anything. I want it all to be over. And I'm afraid that if the police get wind of this, they'll be after Ivo like a pack of bloodhounds."

18

Ivo stood huddled in his brown leather coat near the entrance smoking a cigar. He clearly hadn't slept a wink. I kissed his unshaven cheeks, he hugged me and sniffed. "What a load of shit, isn't it? What a mess . . ."

He hugged me even more tightly, and I stroked his bristly head. He let go of me and threw himself into the arms of Babette.

"It's great you've come. I don't know how you managed it. I'm no good at this . . ."

His big body heaved with despair. Babette wriggled free and was able to steer him in the direction of a bench and calm him down a bit. She helped him relight his cigar.

"It's too much for anyone. And how are you supposed to be good at this? You've just got to look after yourself, Ivo, for Hanneke, for your children. Shall I get some coffee?"

He nodded sadly. Babette went inside. I sat next to him and took his hand.

"You're trembling," he remarked, and I pleaded cold and lack of sleep.

"That police cow is back. What a bitch. She's already asked me six times where I was around four. I was stuck in traffic on my way home. Hanneke had phoned to say she would be home by evening. She didn't sound depressed, quite the opposite, she spoke very clearly, as if she knew exactly what she had to do. She said she was going to talk to you, that she was sorry about her behaviour after the funeral, that lots of things had become clear to her that day. She was going to explain it all to me that evening."

"And that's what you told the policewoman?"

"Up to a point: our marriage is none of that cow's business, so I didn't tell her Hanneke said that 'lots of things had become clear to her'. That's something between us. For me the important thing was that she was coming home, that she and I . . ." He swallowed and took a puff on his cigar. "Well, that we could stay together. I'm certain she didn't jump. I mean, why should she? Give me a reason?" He looked at me inquiringly.

"Of course there's a reason . . ." I stammered, and when I looked in his eyes, which were filling with tears, I was immediately sorry I had broached the subject.

"Sorry, Ivo, but I know about Evert and Hanneke. Of course that's not the real reason, I mean, Hanneke would never throw herself off a balcony for something like that, but . . ."

"An accident! That's what it is. She wasn't pushed, and she didn't jump! Who in the world would want to push Hanneke off a balcony?"

"Take it easy. The police have to follow up every lead, that's just their job."

"They revel in it. I can see the jealousy and hatred in their eyes. At last we can screw a rich bastard, I can hear them thinking. Where were you at four o'clock . . . as if I . . . my own wife . . ."

Babette arrived clutching three steaming cups of coffee. Ivo put his hand on my knee and squeezed it gently as a sign of understanding.

"If we start accusing each other to the police, we'll all be in the shit, not just us, but everyone – that's what they want. So watch what you say, Karen, please. My relationship problems are none of their business."

An icy wind blew. I took my cup from Babette and drank a mouthful, shivering in the cold. I looked at Ivo and Babette sitting next to me, leaning against each other, exchanging whispered words of comfort. Their partners had had an affair, and that must and would stay secret. Why? Just because it would be too humiliating for them if it came out? I massaged my temples to suppress my confused thoughts, the suspicions that were proliferating in my head. This concerned my friends, who had always been good to me, Michel and my children. I loved them, and if they hadn't come into my life, I might have gone mad with loneliness. How could I think that any of them had anything to do with the deaths of Evert and Hanneke?

Dorien Jager and a colleague were talking to a gesticulating Simon outside the room where Hanneke lay. For a second it was as if my body would explode there and then when I saw Simon in the distance, but by digging my nails into the heel of my hand and breathing deeply, I was able to keep on my feet and walk beside Babette in a reasonably relaxed way, towards the man whose seed had clung stickily between my legs that very morning. His eyes were a little swollen and his cheeks unshaven. He looked tired and hung-over and as a result more attractive than ever. His eyes narrowed a little when our eyes met, but apart from that he ignored us completely. The conversation with Dorien was obviously not very animated and stopped abruptly as we passed.

Patricia sat glumly at Hanneke's bedside and leaped to her feet when we came in. I forced myself to look her in the eyes and kiss her and managed amazingly well, although a buzzing voice in my head said that I was a loathsome traitor.

"It's not good," she whispered, stroking Hanneke's battered arm. I leaned over Hanneke and planted a cautious kiss on the bandage around her head. I could feel the pressure of tears behind my eyes, but I did not want to cry, because I was frightened I wouldn't be able to stop and would fling myself screaming into Patricia's arms to tell her how sorry I was for what I had done. Babette stood at the foot of the bed, looking at our injured friend with a terrified expression and her hands over her mouth.

"Do you know what I keep thinking?" she muttered in a stifled voice. "That they'll be together soon, somewhere up there, and I'll be down here, alone."

"You mustn't think like that, Babette."

"I should have been dead, and so should my boys. Evert wanted to survive the fire, so he could live with her. That was the plan: we were just ballast."

Patricia caught my eyes and shook her head almost imperceptibly. She put an arm round Babette's shoulder.

"You know that's not how it is. You mustn't torment yourself with those kinds of thoughts. Evert was confused; don't forget that. There was nothing behind it, it was just that he was ill and saw and felt things that weren't there. The old Evert, the one you know, loved you. He didn't want to kill you all."

"She simply followed him. Do you never think that she may have . . . with her lighter? She's crazy, as crazy as Evert!"

"Babette, please!" Patricia motioned towards the door. "Come on. Let's go for a bit of a walk, to see Angela. She's downstairs with Hanneke's mother.

107

We'll go and say hello." Patricia forced her gently out of the room.

I sat on the folding chair beside the bed, laid my head next to Hanneke's and closed my eyes. The bed smelled of blood and iodine. I had once read somewhere that patients in a coma could hear what you said to them. So I whispered softly: "Do you see what a mess we're in, Han? You've got to come back. I need you so much. Everything's going wrong now you're in a coma . . ."

I missed her caustic comments, her hard-edged laugh, her wet jokes, I missed the woman I was in her company.

"I've completely lost the plot . . . all of us have. You've got to tell me what to do. Should I tell the police the truth, or keep mum? I don't know, Han. I don't want to betray anyone . . ."

Well, keep quiet then. I could *hear* her say it. But her thick, swollen lips didn't move. I took hold of her limp hand and stroked her fingers. The nails were broken, and her wedding ring had gone. Only a light strip of skin showed where it had been.

"Why did you never confide in me?" I whispered, swallowing a lump in my throat.

Because you're always on your goddamn moral high horse. She often accused me of that, and it was true, until last night. Whether the discussions in the dinner club were about having affairs, politics, plastic surgery or the division of roles within the family, I was always the one who knew best what was right or wrong, and Hanneke sensed that I would have immediately condemned her affair with Evert and that it would have been a severe test of our friendship.

"It's all your fault! If you hadn't fallen out of that

stupid window, Simon wouldn't have come over to our place, we wouldn't have got drunk, I wouldn't have been so confused right now and would still have been on my high horse . . ."

Ivo came in and went to the other side of the bed. He kissed his fingertips, pressed them to Hanneke's mouth and gave her a loving smile.

"Your father's going to fetch the children, love," he said in a high-pitched, faltering voice, and his chin began trembling.

"Mees and Anna are coming. So you've got to wake up now, sweetie, for your little ones . . ."

There was a roaring and whistling in my ears, and for a moment I felt I couldn't breathe. I hurried out of the room and raced down the corridor to the toilet, where I ran ice-cold water over my wrists. In the mirror I looked puffy and old, with too much make-up on. I splashed the cold water over my face and washed it clean with my hands. "Hanneke mustn't die, Hanneke mustn't die," I murmured to myself. I interlocked my fingers and pressed my knuckles against my forehead.

"Let Hanneke stay alive, please."

19

I needed to eat something greasy and salty to prevent a terrible headache, and holding a plastic tray I joined the queue for the buffet in the hospital restaurant, looking around to see if I could spot any of my friends. It was busy: everywhere there were groups of worried-looking relatives and patients in wheelchairs staring straight ahead, some with tubes coming out of their noses or a drip attached. I hate hospitals, because they are such a reminder of my vulnerability. It is a world I don't want to see, that I'm afraid of: a world of pain, suffering and death.

I put a bottle of diet cola and a tub of fruit salad on my tray, moved further along and ordered two rissoles on bread. Again I looked into the restaurant, searching for Babette, Patricia and Simon, and started to wonder why they were not sitting in the place we had agreed on. Perhaps they had already gone back home. It had become obvious that Babette couldn't handle all this yet. But surely in that case they would have let me know? Why was I always the last to hear about things?

I paid the bill, got cutlery and three sachets of mustard and made for an empty table near the door. Once I was sitting down I turned on my mobile. No new messages. I put my telephone next to me and started on the rissoles.

"Can I join you?"

Dorien Jager did not wait for a reply and sat opposite

me, after setting her tray, on which there were a mug of tomato soup and a sparkling mineral water, on the table. My appetite immediately vanished.

"Right. Wonderful, a bite to eat, but if I order that," Dorien pointed at my plate with a spoon, "I'll put another stone back on in no time."

I smiled, muttered something about my fast metabolism and realized I was dying for a drink, something to clear my head and make me feel less tearful.

"We've got your friend's blood test results back. I've just discussed them with the husband and the parents of the victim."

Dorien blew on her soup and looked at me expectantly. I felt sick.

"And?"

"The victim had traces of both alcohol and benzodiazepines, or sleeping pills, in her blood."

"That could have been from the night before, couldn't it?"

Dorien ate a spoonful of soup and shook her head. "No, the levels were too high for that. She must have taken the substances a few hours before her jump."

"Or her fall."

"It's starting to look more and more as if it was a jump. Why else would she take sleeping pills in broad daylight?"

"Hanneke smokes. Perhaps she wanted to have a cigarette on the balcony and lost her balance because she was under the influence of drugs. That's possible, isn't it, especially in combination with drink? Perhaps she took those pills to calm herself down a bit, to soothe her nerves."

"Benzodiazepines don't calm you down, they put you in a coma."

"Listen, I had a date with her. She had promised her

111

husband she was coming home. Hanneke's a mother! She has so much to live for! There's no way she tried to commit suicide!"

Dorien gave my hand a friendly pat and looked searchingly at me.

"These are the facts. I can't help it. I don't know the woman, I don't know everything that's happened. It's common enough for someone to decide on impulse to end it all, certainly after something as dramatic as you and your friends have been through. Besides, we also know that your friend had been to the hotel twice before, with a man, in the same room."

I tried to return her gaze as neutrally as possible, took a tiny bite of my rissole sandwich, which had meanwhile gone cold. It was like eating cement, and I was frightened I would start retching uncontrollably if I tried to swallow.

"And I can guess who the man was, but I can't start an investigation on the strength of a hunch."

"I've never heard Hanneke talk about any man except her husband."

"I can understand why the others are protecting each other, but not why you are. Judging by the messages on her telephone and the dates in her diary, she's your best friend."

"Why do you think my friends are protecting each other?"

"Because they're all in the clutches of Mr Simon Vogel. We know how deeply Evert Struyk was in . . ."

"How do you mean?"

"Debt. Evert owed him hundreds of thousands. It's not that surprising he should have wanted to end it all. Dying was the only way he could settle his debts, since he was well insured. All arranged by the husband of your badly injured friend, by the way."

112

"What are you getting at? That my friends are some-how implicated in her accident?"

"Why don't you call me Dorien?" asked Dorien Jager.

I shrugged my shoulders. She was beginning to get on my nerves. She spooned up the last of her soup. "I'm not saying anything, that's your conclusion. Perhaps you're trying get to grips with the idea . . ."

I thought of Hanneke, how she was lying there, the pain she must have felt as her body hit the ground . . . I could almost hear the breaking of her bones, the cracking of her skull. Hanneke was vain: she would hate anyone to find her bleeding and mutilated. If she had wanted to put an end to her life, it wouldn't have been like this.

"If your friend is the victim of foul play, don't you think that it should be investigated, that the truth should be brought to light? Or should her children grow up believing their mother no longer felt life with them was worth living?"

I leaped angrily to my feet, knocking my chair over so that everyone looked in my direction. I had to control myself not to run away.

"If you don't mind, Dorien, I'm going back to see my friend," I muttered in a strangled tone, putting the chair upright and grabbing my coat. Dorien grabbed my wrist, pulled me to her and said fiercely in my ear: "Think hard about who it is you're really hurting with that blind loyalty of yours."

Going outside did me good. I filled my lungs with cold air and stared at the people coming and going. There was a mother in a wheelchair with her newborn baby in her arms, an elderly, grey-haired man pushing a walk-ing frame on wheels with a bunch of tulips in the front basket, a boy hiding under a thick black hat with a tribal tattoo on the back of his neck. Taxi-drivers with swollen, red faces were horsing around. I remembered the day when, beaming with pride, I left hospital with my little Annabelle. Michel, overjoyed, coming to collect me with an extravagant bunch of red roses, and the nurses whispering that I should be glad to have such a sweet husband – not all of them were like that by any means. And I was happy, convinced that the birth of our daughter had so deepened our love that nothing could ever come between us. What had happened to us since all those beautiful promises? What had happened to that intense feeling of togetherness? I suddenly felt a powerful longing for Michel as he used to be, when we could really talk to each other without immediately becoming aggressive or defensive. The old Michel would have been able to help me. He would have been able to convince me that above all I must be honest, regardless of the consequences, and if as a result our friends turned their backs on us, they weren't worthy of our friendship. On the other hand, I had promised to keep quiet. It was not up to me to pass on this kind of information to the police, to betray my friends, if they chose to keep the affair between Evert and Hanneke secret. And if they believed that this was unconnected with what had happened, who was I to doubt it?

There was lots of activity round Hanneke's bed. Her parents were on either side with blotchy red faces, looking in horror at their daughter and the machines surrounding her, while on the floor the children were furiously drawing pictures for their mother. I had thought the others would also be here, but there was no sign of Babette, Simon or Patricia. I made my excuses, tiptoed over to Ivo, who was sitting next to his mother-in-law looking desperate, and asked him in a whisper if he knew where everyone was.

There was a strange, tense silence, which frightened me. I put my hand on Ivo's shoulder, but he recoiled and left my hand hanging in midair. He avoided my eyes, and his jaw muscles tensed.

"I think it's better if you go, Karen. Leave us alone," he whispered with pent-up anger.

"I'm sorry?" I asked.

"Yes. Go. You decided to let the cat out of the bag, to betray us, so there's no place for you here anymore."

"Christ, Ivo, that's not true. I swear to you I didn't do it . . ."

I looked at Hanneke's parents, who lowered their eyes, at Mees and Anna, who went on drawing unperturbed. Ivo made a gesture in my direction as if brushing away a troublesome fly. The ground seemed to give way under my feet.

I bent over Hanneke and gave her a tentative kiss.

"I'm thinking of you, dear Han. Please come back to us very soon."

Then I shuffled awkwardly past the children, out of the room.

20

Evert was angry with everyone, but especially with Simon, his best friend, who had had him admitted to hospital against his will, and with Babette: the day after her return, on the advice of Evert's psychiatrist and of all of us, she had applied for him to be sectioned, meaning that he would be forcibly detained for at least three weeks. After the court ruling, the security guards led Evert away cursing and spitting.

At the beginning we took turns to visit him and sat rigid with fear opposite him in the visiting area where he chain-smoked in surly silence and when we left begged us to take him with us, home to his wife and children and howled that everything had got completely out of hand. He was frightened of dying, convinced that they were trying to poison him in there, that it was one big conspiracy. It was awful to see him in that state. Every time we drove away from Amsterdam General Hospital and left him behind in despair, we were in a state of shock but at the same time convinced that this was the best thing for him.

Angela cared for Babette like a Mother Teresa while Evert was in hospital. She ferried the children to and fro, drove Babette to the hospital and back, put her onto a good psychologist to help her get things straightened out for herself, cooked for two families evening after evening and dragged Babette along to birthdays, parties, dinner parties, the gym, the tennis club and yoga. Hanneke and I were amazed at the way Angela immersed herself in Babette's victimhood. "It's as if they were in love!" Hanneke insinuated regularly when we had seen them having coffee in Verdi or making an entrance together at a party. Angela was also beginning to look increasingly like Babette. She had blond highlights put in her hair, lost pounds and suddenly started wearing the same low-cut sweaters, the same tight black trousers, skirts and high boots. They became isolated from the rest of us, to the great annoyance of Patricia, who until Evert was admitted to hospital had been Angela's best friend. "She's got a kind of antenna for lame ducks," she grumbled at the Easter Fair at school, where Babette and Angela again appeared together in the same coordinated clothes. "She appropriates other people's grief for want of anything better to fill her own life with. Now she has something to do, and her new goal is: save Babette!"

I wondered if we were not secretly jealous of the fact that Babette had chosen Angela as her support and comforter. Didn't we all want to provide Babette with good advice, help her and hence feel better people ourselves?

While Evert was getting fewer and fewer visitors, Babette was surrounded by sympathy at all kinds of social occasions. Everyone wanted to know how Evert was doing, but no one dared go and ask Evert himself, using the excuse that they could no longer stand his rage and fear. Nor could we, and we dreamed up impeccable reasons. For example, we felt that he "should do it for himself from now on", that "our visits just upset him" and that "it was as if he didn't want to get better".

Hanneke thought that was all bullshit, and finally

she was the only one, apart from Babette, who continued to visit Evert as regular as clockwork, to take him through the designs she had produced for his latest shop. He was the boss, after all, and she refused to write to him. Those conversations had brought him back to reality and given him a new zest for life, as Evert said on being discharged from the psychiatric department six weeks later: he would remain eternally grateful to Hanneke. He thanked us all for our unconditional support and praised our friendship, which had helped him through this difficult period, but we knew damn well that we had actually abandoned him because we couldn't cope with his illness.

Evert was home again, but he was never completely the enthusiastic, cheerful chatterbox he had once been. The medication that he had had to take for quite a while made him flat and silent. It was no fun sitting next to him in company, because he either said nothing or asked strange questions, which made us uneasy. His presence in the group became oppressive, made conversations laboured and stiff, but none of us dared stand up to him: for fear of hurting him, but even more of being hurt.

"You mustn't take him so seriously," said Babette. "I don't."

"Of course it hurts me to see him like that. He's my best friend, for Christ's sake!" Simon banged on the bar and knocked back the last of his beer. As we did every Saturday, a group of us were sitting at the bar at Verdi's. The children were riding their bikes on the square, and we were having a drink together after doing the shopping. Evert and Babette were not present on this occasion.

118

"You know we can't help him," said Kees, drawing a circle in the air with his finger, indicating to the barman that another round was required. "He's got to do that for himself. Simon and I have tried everything to involve him again. We've played golf with him, tennis, been to see Ajax, we've mountain-biked, propped up the bar for an evening for a chat. But it doesn't make a blind bit of difference. He comes out with weird things and just stares straight ahead. He's got a really negative attitude, and it reaches a point where you've had enough. Life goes on and that's the way it is. You win some, you lose some."

"What are you getting at?"

Michel looked at him in irritation. Simon got the beers from the bar and passed them round. We watched Kees's flushed face expectantly.

"I mean . . . well, that I've kind of given up on him. We haven't got much more to say to each other. Maybe that will change when he's more like his old self."

"How can that happen if we dump him as a friend?"

"Hold on, who's talking about dumping?" Simon put his arm round Michel's shoulders and clinked glasses.

"We're not dropping Evert. It's more like the other way round. He wants more distance from us. He just can't keep up with everything, and that's hardly surprising after what he's been through."

"And if something like that were to happen to *you*, would you want us to treat you like some mental defective?" asked Hanneke in a shrill voice, waving her glass of white wine in Simon's direction.

"The point is: something like that wouldn't happen to me."

"Nonsense. It can happen to anyone."

"No, my sweet, that's not true. You need a predisposition."

Hanneke frowned at him.

"You lot are avoiding Evert as if he has some infectious disease and is still confused. He's been given a clean bill of health, he's back at work, he's doing everything he used to. But he looks at life differently now, and you can't take that."

"How differently do you mean?" asked Kees with a sarcastic smile.

"He knows now that when it comes down to it, money and status don't mean a thing."

Kees and Simon burst out laughing.

"Christ, Han, where did you find that saying embroidered? Come off it!"

"Don't take any notice of those pricks," said Patricia, who up till then had sat talking to Angela with her back towards us. With a show of indignation Hanneke and I turned away from the men and went to join Patricia and Angela.

"Evert will pull through, he's getting a little better every day. Men just find it hard to handle these kinds of things. Let them sound off," said Angela, taking a sip of her wine. Then she rolled up the sleeve of her cuddly white sweater and, beaming with pride, showed us her new watch. Patricia and Hanneke gave little squeaks of delight, and I too homed in admiringly on Angela's wrist. I was just glad that the complicated conversation about Evert was over.

"For our anniversary: I found it on my pillow! It's a Breitling Callistino. The stones are real Swarovski crystals, and the strap is lizard skin . . ."

"Don't let the children hear that last bit, whatever you do!" I laughed.

"Have you seen this, gentlemen? What Angela gets from Kees for her anniversary! That's the way to do it!" cried Hanneke, shoving Angela's arm under their

120

noses. Even the barman came and had a look and felt it should be celebrated with a round on the house.

"Well, you've messed things up for all of us, pal!" said Ivo, punching Kees, who was glowing from all the beer and all the attention, on the arm.

"Must have been to make up for something!"

We went on outdoing each other with wisecracks, our laughter becoming ever louder and shriller, in an attempt to drown out the strange kind of uneasiness that had taken hold since Evert became ill. It was desperate laughter, full of longing for the intimacy and trust we had once had, and I wondered where it had gone, that intense feeling of closeness. The shine had come off, and I found myself wondering more and more often what our friendship was really based on, whether it really existed and whether it had the same value for all of us. Perhaps in my head I had made more of it than was really there, because I had yearned for it so much.

21

Michel knew about Simon and me: that's why he was already home at this time. His car was parked carelessly, not neatly under the carport as always, but in the verge, by the hedge. It obviously didn't matter to him if it got scratched: he must be furious. I went into the house leaden-footed, wondering in panic what to do, what to say, how I could ever work this out. There were two options: to confess everything honestly and swear that it would never happen again or to deny it and pretend to be deeply offended that he could think such a thing of me. For a moment all I wanted was to blurt out the whole story and relieve myself of the burden, hoping it might eventually benefit our relationship. But when I saw Michel sitting so sadly at the table, pulling nervously on a cigarette, I opted for the lie. I couldn't hurt him; it wasn't worth it.

I went up to him as cheerfully as possible and kissed him on the mouth.

"You're very early . . ." I said as casually as possible, and then put a kettle of water on the gas.

"I've got such a dreadful hangover, this headache is driving me crazy. It's a miracle I got home in one piece . . ."

"Yes, you were in a bad way last night." I took the teapot and gave it a thorough rinse. If I looked at Michel now I would turn to dust and beg him on my knees for forgiveness. So I got a clean cloth, put a few drops of steel polish on it and started cleaning all the deposits off the chrome.

"How was Hanneke?"

"Same as yesterday. It's terrible. Ivo's a broken man . . . The children were there this afternoon. They still have no idea . . ."

Michel got up and stood next to me, leaning on the draining board. He looked deep into my eyes. I forced myself to go on breathing calmly and to smile at him. "Tea?" I asked, and Michel shook his head.

"Listen," he began. "Simon phoned me in the car and he was pretty upset. It seems you said something to that policewoman, about Hanneke and Evert having had an affair?"

I gasped for breath. So he already knew, as did Simon, and everyone.

"I didn't tell that cow Dorien Jager a thing! She was the one who started on about Simon, saying that Evert owed him money, that we were protecting each other . . . She tried to get me to admit that Evert and Hanneke had an affair . . ."

"Oh, you needn't tell me about police interrogation techniques! I know how they operate. They confuse you, put pressure on you, and before you know it you've fallen for it."

"Michel, I didn't say a thing. I walked off in a huff. Yes, she confused me. And I have my doubts about Hanneke's so-called attempted suicide, but I didn't give away any of that."

"Darling, you obviously gave her all she needed."

"Perhaps she's found other incriminating evidence."

"Such as?"

"How should I know? I don't know a thing! I never do! I'm always excluded from things! Even Hanneke, to whom I always told everything and trusted absolutely, now turns out to have had all kinds of secrets from me!"

"Obviously she was also frightened that you wouldn't be able to keep her secrets safe."

"What the hell is that supposed to mean?" I was now trembling with suppressed rage.

"Come on, Ka, you blurt everything out. I love you because you're so open and honest, but sometimes . . . sometimes honesty destroys everything. Like now."

"So what do you think is being destroyed?"

"On the basis of what you told that policewoman, they're going to search Ivo's place, and they've impounded Simon's accounts. Clearly suspicions have arisen about Evert's death. It's ridiculous, of course, but anyway, the upshot is that they'll dig up everything and undoubtedly find some shit. Everything will be made public now, and that may have repercussions for my company too."

He retrieved a crumpled packet of cigarettes from the pocket of his jeans, took out a cigarette, bent forward and stuck his cigarette in the flame under the kettle. I turned the extractor hood fan demonstratively to full and poured the boiling water into the gleaming teapot. I was suddenly seized by an intense urge to leave Michel. His friend had committed suicide, my friend was in a coma, and he was thinking about his company.

"What has your company got to do with it?"

"Christ, Ka, don't act so dumb. Simon has a share of my business, and Ivo is my accountant. Do I have to spell it out to you?"

"Yes, please."

"It's the first time you've ever taken an interest. I'll tell you exactly to whom we owe the cash that you just love throwing around. To Simon: he owns fifty-one per cent of the shares in Shootmedia. Because he became my partner we were able to expand, we now have our own studio, and we can make programmes with a unique profile and hold our own with the big producers."

"To hear you talk, it's not your company, but Simon's."

"He's only a shareholder. He doesn't concern himself with the management."

"But he gets something in return, I take it?"

"A share of the profits, which without his input we would never have been able to achieve."

"And why will the company crash now they've started investigating Simon's business practices?"

"If he pulls the plug, for whatever reason, we're finished. Then we'll no longer be able to do what you all find so important: ski, eat out or spend four weeks in some hovel in Tuscany!"

"Christ, Michel, he's your friend and your partner! Why would he do that?"

"He can make me or break me. You only know Simon as a jovial, sociable, fun guy, but in business he can be hard as nails. You need to be, to survive in that world."

"But you entered into a contract with him, I take it? Surely he can't just pull his money out from one day to the next?"

"If he wants to play rough he can squeeze me out, sell the premises, raise the rent and take over if we don't reach the agreed targets. He can also make sure we don't reach those targets. Plus, now the police have started digging into his finances, who knows what may emerge? If they find anything, they can also seize Shootmedia. And that won't be very good for the company image."

I poured the tea into two mugs, although at this moment I felt more like alcohol to calm my pounding heart. Michel made a dismissive gesture indicating that he didn't feel like tea either.

"I'll go and collect the children," he muttered, more to himself than to me.

"There's no need. I'll go. Have a bath or something, clean yourself up. You look as though you've been sleeping under a bridge for a couple of weeks."

"I *want* to collect them."

"OK, go ahead. I'm curious to know if they'll recognize you."

I knew that this comment was really kicking him when he was down, but it just slipped out and it was too late to take it back. With a furious gesture Michel swept the teapot, the ashtray and the mugs off the draining board.

"Christ Almighty! What a poisonous bloody cow you can be sometimes! How dare you . . . I'm working my socks off, for God's sake! For you, for the children! To meet your needs, to keep everybody . . ." he prodded aggressively at my face with his forefinger, "happy! And then you come out with a shitty remark like that! What do you want, you pampered woman? Do you want to drive me crazy, like Evert? Do you want me to stop working? I'd do it tomorrow, you know! I can have a great time playing tennis, doing a bit of freelancing and chatting with the girls! You can bring home the bacon! You wouldn't last a day at what I do!"

He strode out of the kitchen, slamming the door so hard behind him that the glass broke and the slivers crashed to the ground.

"You can count yourself lucky if I last another day with you!" I screamed after him, so loudly that my throat hurt. I charged upstairs and locked myself in the bathroom. Sobbing with anger, I turned on the bath tap. In the course of one day I had managed to turn everyone I loved against me.

126

22

I had two messages, said my mobile. A voicemail message and a text from Simon. I opened the latter first.

We must talk. Tomorrow 9.00 McDonald's car park by roundabout? XXX

A wave of relief went through me and without a moment's hesitation I replied that I would be there. He was still thinking of me. He would reassure me.

On my voicemail there was a message from Angela.
"I've tried to reach you everywhere, but obviously you don't feel like phoning. I know you're home, Michel said so at school. Babette's here, and so is Patricia . . . You've probably heard by now what a mess it all is . . . Well, we'd like you to come over for a moment."
I erased the message and threw my mobile on the bed. From downstairs came the sweet, piping voices of Annabelle and Sophie, who were cooing with pleasure as they romped with their father. I took a clean pair of jeans from the wardrobe and my thick blue sweater, which I always wore when I felt down, put on warm socks and dried my hair. Then I went downstairs and cuddled my daughters, who felt hot and sweaty. Michel avoided my gaze, and I avoided his. The tension between us was like a magnetic field. We preserved a stubborn silence while the girls ran to the kitchen to get their artwork from school and perked up with

relief when they came back. Sophie, beaming, was holding a folded paper tulip, and Annabelle was waving a large sheet of paper on which she had painted a snowman. I said I was proud of them and gave them another big hug, after which they both shot off to their rooms to do some more art.

"I'm off to Angela's," I said deliberately and left without saying goodbye to Michel. I knew it was up to me to put an end to this ridiculous row, since I had started it, but I couldn't yet bring myself to. Everything about him irritated me: his chest-beating about how hard he worked, his reproachful claims that he did everything just to keep me happy, the transparently feeble excuses he used to cover himself and put an end to any discussion about his absence from the home. Our marriage had turned into something nauseatingly clichéd. We were perfect material for an article in a women's magazine on how not to do it.

"Hello, all!" I cried with feigned enthusiasm as I entered Angela's house, where Babette and Patricia were sitting with grim faces at the large, oblong, oak dining table sipping white wine with ice.

"How nice and warm it is in here," I rattled on, kissing all three of them, "it's bitterly cold outside. I'll be glad when it's April again, and we don't have to hunt for mittens, scarves and caps every morning!"

My excited chatter made no impression on the icy atmosphere. Only Babette smiled hesitantly at me, while Patricia and Angela glared like two sulking children. Without a word Angela poured me a glass of wine and pushed it towards me.

"Ice?" she asked sharply, avoiding eye contact, and I shook my head, grinning awkwardly. This was going to be unpleasant.

"Let's get straight to the point," Patricia began, her head trembling with suppressed tension. "We've been talking about it all afternoon, and we're completely in shock. The police have seized Simon's accounts. They've been at his office, and at our home. Right now they're turning my house upside down. The same thing is happening at Ivo's. It's too idiotic for words! As if he hasn't been through enough – it's really appalling. That hideous Dorien Jager, that fat dyke, made disgusting accusations against Simon . . . What in heaven's name did you tell her?"

I took a sip and drew a deep breath.

"Nothing, I swear I told her nothing. She insinuated that we were protecting each other, and I left in a temper. I think she's toying with us, trying to play us off against each other in the hope that we'll start pointing fingers. She's developed some theory, and she's determined to find confirmation, I think."

"She told us literally that you'd expressed doubts about Hanneke's fall and told her outright that Hanneke had an affair with Evert . . ."

I shook my head vehemently.

"What a bitch. That's not true. Really, Babette, I promised you I'd keep it a secret and I did . . ."

Babette avoided my gaze and played vacantly with her glass. Angela interrupted me.

"We all know you're not very good at keeping secrets, Ka."

"What do you mean?"

"You know perfectly well."

"No I don't. Give me an example."

"You once started the story that Kees had been seen in Amsterdam with some blond number . . ."

My jaw dropped. I vaguely remembered this story. I had been told by a mother at school, in the café, after the entry of Saint Nicholas, that a friend of hers had seen Kees out walking in South Amsterdam, hand-in-hand with a young woman. Later I had confided in Hanneke when I'd had a little too much to drink, on the understanding of course that it must stay strictly between ourselves. But that's what it's like among friends: over a glass of wine we confessed everything, to strengthen the feeling of intimacy, although I had never thought that she of all people would trumpet this piece of gossip around.

"That was just a stupid bit of tittle-tattle I heard from a friend of a friend. I didn't even take it seriously . . . You're right, I should have kept my mouth shut. But does that fall under the heading of 'secret'? Do you three never chat about those sorts of things?"

I looked at all of them, searching for some sign of assent or recognition, but they were all staring angrily at their glasses, in which the ice cubes were clinking.

"Let's be honest about it, you've always thought you were too good for us," said Patricia cattily. My face began to burn as if I had a fever.

"What on earth is all this? Come on, we're friends! This is like the third degree!" I choked on my own words, as I realized the unbelievable hypocrisy of what I was about to say. They were right: I was unreliable, a liar, a deceiver. How could I sing the praises of friendship when only last night I had been screwing her husband?

"You're different, you always think you're in the right. You're proud of working, of having a degree, of being so creative. Sometimes you make it very clear that you find us pretty shallow. You and Hanneke, you just laugh at us. And now, when it really matters, you betray us."

"I'm afraid I don't get it. How has Hanneke betrayed you?"

From upstairs came the sudden sound of feet stumbling noisily about and children's shouting. Angela got up, went into the hall and yelled that they mustn't jump off the bunk bed. We smiled awkwardly, glad that the tension had been dispelled for a moment. She came back and put her hands forcefully on my shoulders.

"You mean apart from the fact that she fucked Evert and sullied his funeral with her boozing and hysterical behaviour? We spoke to her about it afterwards, Patricia and I . . ."

"You two? When?' asked Babette in surprise, as if she were only now waking up.

"The morning before she . . ." She made a cutting motion along her neck with the edge of her hand, which turned my stomach.

"She phoned Patricia early in the morning, and, to put it mildly, she wasn't very apologetic. She called us every name under the sun . . ."

Patricia cleared her throat and finished Angela's story.

"I was able to calm her down and arranged to meet her in a coffee bar in P.C. Hooftstraat to talk things out. But I was pretty scared of her, and that's why I asked Angela to come along. Over coffee . . ."

"With which she had a Sambucca, at ten-thirty in the morning," Angela added with a look of fury.

"She said appalling things that I won't repeat here: there's no point. At any rate we were able to convince her that when you're in an emotional state it's dangerous to go around making all kinds of accusations. We left on reasonable terms; she was going to get help and was coming home that evening."

"I think Karen and I have a right to know exactly what she said," said Babette, putting her hand on my shoulder in a gesture of solidarity.

131

"No," replied Patricia resolutely. "I've thought about it, but I'm not going to burden you with it. They're the imaginings of a stressed-out woman, but they could have huge repercussions if the police get wind of them. They've been trying to topple Simon for years: it's simply the price you have to pay for success in this country. Stand out from the crowd, and they'll do everything they can to destroy you. That's why discretion is so important, Karen! If you care at all about Hanneke and Ivo, Simon and me, you won't talk to the police again. Here, between ourselves, we can say anything we like, but outside you must keep mum."

"It's too late," muttered Angela melodramatically.

"If I understand you correctly, Hanneke said something about Simon," I said.

"Perhaps the two of you have already gossiped at length about it, and if so you'll know that Evert and Simon had a business dispute. They were resolving it, but the police suddenly see it as a motive," said Patricia.

Babette banged the table with her hand.

"I just can't take any more of this right now. Please let's stop! Karen is my friend, you're all my friends . . ." She looked at us tearfully in turn. "I believe Karen."

"Well, just as long as you know I've had it up to here, up to here! And I'm not the only one!" said Angela. She looked at Patricia, who rubbed her narrow nose with her brown painted nails. She looked sad and distraught.

"Do the police know you went to see her?" I asked.

"No. It's none of their business! We said goodbye to Hanneke in a perfectly civilized way, and she went back to the hotel to pack her things. She refused a lift. We didn't throw her off the balcony."

"But this is very important for the investigation!" My voice cracked.

"If we tell the police, they'll also want to know what

we were talking about. What good is that to anyone? It won't bring Evert or Hanneke back. This isn't a case of murder, Karen, it's an unfortunate combination of circumstances. Two people from our circle of friends take their own lives in quick succession. Why should we do penance for that?" said Patricia. "I think we both need some space, Karen. I want to concentrate on restoring Simon's good name. I'm going to fight for that, and this kind of squabbling with you I can do without."

The tears were burning my eyes, but I refused to cry.

Patricia rolled her eyes, pursed her lips and suddenly looked very hard.

"I think, Karen, that you doubt us, just as we doubt you. And in my view that removes the basis of our friendship. Simon has been badly discredited. You say you have nothing to do with it . . . I don't know. Meanwhile Simon's reputation has been permanently tarnished. People will say there's no smoke without fire. While all he's done is help you all. That's what he's like. Tell me honestly, Karen: things have been better for you two, haven't they, since he got involved in Michel's business?"

I stared straight ahead while I thought things over and felt myself going cold. Patricia was right: I doubted them, and this sickening conversation only confirmed it. The fog in my head cleared, and with a jolt everything was suddenly crystal clear. I had lost myself in this group. The warmth, the intimacy, our love for each other, they were all in my head. We had admired each other in exchange for admiration. Now the spell was broken, and the naked truth was on the table: one person was dead and another badly injured, and all questions were forbidden.

"Unless I'm mistaken, Patricia, you're terminating our friendship . . ."

"I can't stand betrayal. So if you want to put it like that . . . Yes, I don't think there's any alternative."

"The same goes for me," added Angela. I got up, forcing myself to smile.

"Hey, what kind of idiotic behaviour is this? I don't want this! Patricia, Angela! Surely you're not going to do this, after all that's happened! I need you! Karen, wait, stay here . . ." Babette leaped to her feet and stopped me at the door.

"We can sort this out between us. Don't take this lying down! Perhaps if you say sorry . . ."

"They're accusing me of something I didn't do, and I'm now seriously starting to wonder why I didn't. Your husband is dead, my friend is almost dead . . . It's all wrong, Babette, it's all fucking wrong! Actually they're right: the trust has gone. I clung on desperately, I wanted to believe that what happened to Hanneke was an accident, but I can no longer ignore the facts."

"Wait, I'll go with you . . ." Babette went back into the room and stuttered her goodbyes. I heard her say that she did not want to come between us and Angela answer ingratiatingly that there was no need, that everyone must make their own choice.

23

"I need a cigarette," I said. "Let's go to Verdi's, and I'll buy a packet and finish it over a glass of whisky."

It was bitterly cold in the car; I put the blower on full and directed it at the steamed-up windows. Babette sat beside me shivering.

"I'll join you," she replied, and I looked at her in surprise. If anyone was anti-smoking it was her: I remembered the many arguments between Evert and her when he lit up yet another cigar.

"Yes, I used to smoke, as a teenager. I broke every commandment in my young days."

I drove off and realized that in fact we knew nothing about each other's pasts. What had we talked about for the past two years? About safe things: food, clothes, holidays, the children, each other, lots of tennis and the state of policing. However sad, Evert's death had made us all reveal a different side of ourselves, so that it seemed this tragedy might really deepen our friendship. But the opposite now proved to be the case: his suicide and the attempted murder of his family had been the death knell of the dinner club.

We drove past the dark pines that seemed to lean over the road against a backdrop of freakish moonlight, and I felt remarkably perky and light, as if I had been relieved of a leaden weight.

"Are you all right?" asked Babette with concern and patted my leg.

"Yes. It's strange. I actually feel very happy. I've been

shut out, and I don't care two hoots! I'm wondering what I was afraid of all along . . ."

"Perhaps of what lies ahead?"

"And what does lie ahead?" I said.

"I don't know. But I imagine there'll be some uncomfortable situations. We bump into each other everywhere: at the hospital with Hanneke, at the supermarket, at Verdi's, at school. The children play together, and the men: don't forget them."

"Oh, I thought you meant something else: that they'll come after me, that soon I'll be hanging from a beam somewhere."

"You don't really think . . ."

"I don't know what to think. All I know is that there are secrets, secrets connected with Evert's death and Hanneke's accident, and that people are doing their utmost to cover them up for the sake of something that obviously ranks higher than friendship."

"Money."

Babette said it bluntly and with resignation, as if the word explained everything.

It was quiet at Verdi's. There were a few men in suits at the bar, and couples were eating here and there at the tables. It was January, and the village was hibernating. My stomach was rumbling, but I couldn't eat a thing. Babette went through to the toilet, while I made for a table as far as possible from the other customers and ordered a Jack Daniel's without ice. I left out the cigarettes, since my craving for the soothing effect of nicotine had already subsided. I really ought to phone Michel, but I couldn't face it.

Babette came back looking as elegant as a model. She had put on dark-brown lipstick and let her hair down. She ignored the men who turned round to give her a raunchy appraisal and laughed appreciatively, and throwing her hair back with a nonchalant gesture, she sat down across the table from me.

"I was just thinking," she began, "I'm really so angry! What's happened is so horrendous, but that's what they're like; and if I'm honest, I've known that for a while. They dropped Evert and me like a hot potato, particularly Angela, who suddenly no longer wanted me in her house. Do you know what it is? Patricia and she simply can't handle problems. It's fine as long as it's one big happy party, but woe betide if things get difficult."

"I don't know, Babette," I replied. "They've done a lot for you." I was surprised that she knew about Angela's sudden refusal to have her in the house and wondered who had told her. Not me at any rate.

She raised her glass and I raised mine and she gave me a sweet look.

"Here's to you, Karen. I think you're an amazing woman. You're my only real friend."

The whisky made us warm and rosy. Babette ordered a plate of croquettes, we switched to beer, and I no longer cared that this was the umpteenth evening in succession that I was getting smashed. I loved the way my body finally relaxed, the nagging headache went, and with it my restlessness. What remained were the questions spinning around in my head and crying out to be answered.

"Isn't it odd," I asked Babette, "that Angela and Patricia didn't tell the police they went to see Hanneke?"

"Yes, very," she replied, while trying to fish a remnant of croquette out of the mustard dish. "It shocked me too. I think it's ridiculous that they're refusing to tell us what Hanneke said to them, but I think I know."

I leaned inquisitively over the table towards Babette, and she bent forward. I rubbed my ear, which was red hot.

"Sports Unlimited had big financial problems, and Evert had a dispute about it with Simon, who thought Evert wasn't managing the business properly. Ivo was acting as a go-between in the affair, and it was going pretty well until Evert became psychotic and thought the two of them were plotting against him, while they were just trying to save everything from meltdown."

Babette saw my sceptical, ironic look and shook her head.

"No, really, I'm sure of it. During the time Evert was in Amsterdam General Hospital Simon worked his socks off to save Sports Unlimited from bankruptcy, but the result was that Simon wanted to keep control of the company when he got better. Evert was furious about it – unjustly, since he'd screwed things up himself. But Hanneke doesn't know that, because she's only heard *his* side of the story. I think she accused Simon of something and maybe threatened to go to the police."

"What did Evert 'screw up'?"

"He lost hundreds of thousands on the stock market: dealing in shares and that kind of thing on the Internet. He was addicted, glued to his laptop day and night. At the end he used his company assets. If Simon and Ivo hadn't helped us, I'd be in much worse trouble now."

She gave a pained smile.

"You mean financially."

"Yes. For a while it was really awful: bailiffs on the doorstep every day, standing at the supermarket checkout with a blocked credit card. God, it was humiliating." She took another sip of her beer, and her eyes blurred.

"We never knew. I thought your business was going well. Why did you never tell me? Perhaps we could have helped too."

"It's not something you shout from the rooftops. I was so embarrassed going into the discount supermarket. I always took upmarket bags with me to put the shopping in. Suddenly I found myself in a queue of mothers on income support. The smell of poverty . . ."

A dour expression appeared round her mouth.

"But everyone goes to the discount supermarket sometimes, don't they? It's nothing to be ashamed of, surely?"

She gave me a strange look.

"Of course not. It was just a difficult time, that's all." She shook her head and smiled.

"I find it strange how everything seems to revolve around Simon," I said.

"Do you know what I find strange? Patricia's dogged determination when she said she was going to fight to clear his name: as if he were her child! What on earth can she do about it? It sounds fairly obsessive," replied Babette.

I ran my finger over the plate and collected the crumbs of the deep-fried croquettes.

"I think I really need a cigarette now," I mumbled. Babette waved at the waiter and ordered two beers and a packet of Marlboro Lights. I licked my finger. "Someone threw Hanneke off the balcony to keep her quiet: it's starting to look more and more as if that's what happened. It stands to reason that what she wanted to reveal was connected with Simon: Patricia was the last one to see her alive."

"With Angela, that is."

"Do you think they're capable of killing someone, a friend?"

"Christ, Karen! No. I don't know. Perhaps, on impulse?"

The waiter put down two beers for us and handed us the packet of cigarettes, which he had opened. We both took a cigarette out of the packet, and he very gallantly gave us both a light. I inhaled deeply and immediately had to cough.

Babette reached out to me with one hand and looked at me unhappily.

"Don't let's do this, Karen, accuse each other. It frightens me."

"What do you take me for?"

24

See the moon shine through the branches, friends in your wild
    rumpus pause,
the evening full of splendour's here, the evening of dear Santa
    Claus.
Hearts pounding, we await our treat: who'll have cake and
    who'll be beat . . .

The children sang with straining, high-pitched voices
and were drowned out by the cheerful basses of the
men. We were sitting round Hanneke and Ivo's hearth,
waiting for good Saint Nicholas, who was due any minute. The large table was covered in deep-red velvet
with a golden ribbon tied in a cross over it, with a great
bow in the middle. On the ceiling and along the curtains there were streamers with gold lettering on them
saying 'Welcome Saint Nicholas and Black Peter' and
across the flagstone floor a red carpet actually ran in the
direction of the chair for Santa Claus with its elaborate
baroque decorations.

    Hanneke herself had baked a traditional cake,
Angela had brought a huge pan of spiced wine and
Patricia her renowned bouillabaisse. My contribution
consisted of salmon mousse and two apple tarts, which
were now on the table alongside the dishes of crusty
baguettes, chunks of Roquefort and country Brie,
freshwater crayfish salad, a basket full of hotdogs for
the children and a whole array of bumper-sized squeezable bottles of curry, mayonnaise, mustard, ketchup

and American sauce for fries. We'd be perfect for *Ideal Home*, commented Angela proudly. Except for those squeezable bottles, said Patricia, slightly turning up her nose. Patricia, as Hanneke sometimes said jokingly, was a "style fascist". With her, everything had to be perfect. Squeeze-on sauces were not allowed in her house, and nor were plastic toys. Secretly Hanneke I and sometimes expressed the hope that her boys would later get heavily into piercing and tattooing. For the time being Thom, Thies and Thieu had to wear itchy brown sweaters, corduroy trousers and heavy hiking boots, as if they were the descendants of some Scots laird.

Santa Claus arrived, with four assistants, each carrying a sack full of presents; and the smallest children climbed anxiously onto their parents' laps, while the oldest ones, who no longer believed in the whole thing, eagerly surveyed the presents.

"Where have Evert and Babette got to?" Hanneke whispered in my ear before running into the hall, keying in a telephone number. Angela came and sat next to me and asked in a whispered tone what on earth the matter was. I shrugged my shoulders and tried to concentrate on the youngest children, who, shyly and softly, were chanting "Santa Claus's Capon" for Santa Claus, completely unaware of the disquiet spreading among their mothers.

"Do you understand those two? I don't. This is really not on."

Angela furiously downed the last of her red wine and then enthusiastically applauded the children, who were all given a handful of spiced biscuits.

"I expect they've got a good reason," I whispered back and saw Hanneke joining us again, looking tense.

"This is about the children," said Angela, "not about us."

I looked at her stern, hard face, her red-coated mouth, which was set in a bitter expression, and wondered what she meant. What was wrong with us? And just as I was about to ask, Evert and Babette crept in, smiling apologetically. Babette was radiant and toothpaste-fresh as always and was immediately pulled onto Santa Claus's lap, causing much hilarity among men and children alike, while Evert looked around gloomily, his arms desperately hugging his belly, as if he were in pain. He positioned himself by the door-post, looked blankly ahead of him and was not in the least amused by Babette's off-key rendering of "Look, There Comes the Steamer". Then he disappeared into the kitchen with Hanneke.

"It's absolutely disgusting," mumbled Angela. I hadn't the faintest idea what she meant, and I didn't want to know. I just felt a dislike of her and her endless insinuations.

We sang a few more songs, all the children were given a parcel in turn and were allowed a chat with Saint Nicholas, and when he got up to go, his assistant found a big box wrapped in red foil in the hall. Two men were needed to carry the box into the room, and accompanied by the loud, surprised shouts of the parents, the children descended like a pack of monkeys on the huge parcel. 'Wait,' said Simon, flushed with the excitement and the wine, "there's a note here! A note from Santa! Thies, you're good at reading aloud. Here."

Hands trembling, Thies stammered:

For each mite
Santa's brought gifts tonight

He had a good year
And he holds you dear
So open your parcels here!

The children cheered, we clapped. The paper tore to reveal five large boxes containing videogame consoles.

"You'll have to share with your brothers and sisters," yelled Simon hoarsely above the enthusiastic screams of the children. We parents fell silent. Michel pulled an astonished face at me: we had a mutual agreement that one of these things would never enter our house.

"Christ, Simon . . . You really shouldn't have done that . . ." Michel put out his hand, and Kees slapped him hard on the shoulder. Simon grinned from ear to ear as he received the expressions of thanks.

"Guys, I just get a kick out of giving them something like that. Those kids' faces! I was able to do a deal with someone . . . So . . ."

The mountain of presents in the middle of the room that we ourselves had bought for our children was instantly forgotten, as were the hotdogs, the coke and the squeezable bottles. First they had to try out the consoles.

We all seemed rather taken aback by Simon's huge present. Michel reacted irritably to my question of what we going to do with the thing at home and said that if it were such a problem, he would take it to the office. Ivo and Hanneke had a fight about whose turn it was to make coffee, so Evert offered to fix it, and the children were so euphoric about their games consoles that they unwrapped the other presents dutifully, looking blasé, and sighed with boredom when they were required to read a poem as well.

"What an idiot," sulked Hanneke. "Why does he do

something like that? What's he trying to prove? He's already bought our men, does he have to buy our children as well?"

I thought she was right but tried to shush her to prevent her getting into a fight with Simon after having had one too many. Probably he had done it with the best of intentions: he wanted to share his success with us. He liked giving, and we shouldn't make such a big thing of it. She clinked her glass of white wine against mine and said she would hold her tongue now, for the sake of the children. "But I'm going to mention it to him eventually: he mustn't pull this kind of stunt again – playing sugar daddy, as if we were a bunch of poor slobs."

At that moment there was the loud sound of glass shattering. We looked round and saw Evert, face flushed, grabbing the lapels of Simon's jacket. Simon laughed nervously, stood with his hands in the air and looked at us one by one in an appeal for help.

"Come on, Evert, this is a children's party . . . Don't let's do this, not now . . ."

Evert gave him a good shaking. His chin was trembling, as were his lips, which were pressed tightly together. Tears were trickling down his cheeks. Babette and Patricia leaped to their feet, ran over to their husbands and started tugging at them. Babette screamed hysterically into Evert's ear that he must act normally and let go of Simon. Evert pulled Simon toward him, roared "arsehole" in his face and then pushed him forcibly away.

"He's got to leave me alone!" yelled Evert and then ran out, beside himself. Hanneke went after him, while Patricia tended to a sobbing Babette.

"Uh oh," said Angela, rubbing her hands. "He's having a relapse. Really, he's not right at all . . ." Simon straightened his jacket, splashed some water on his face and made an innocent, uncomprehending gesture with his hands.

"Sorry, boys. Evert and I have a problem ... Business, that is, not personal, but he doesn't seem to be able to keep the two things apart. Phew! I think I'm ready for a beer. And put some nice music on, Ivo. We're not going to let the evening be spoilt by this kind of neurotic fuss."

The following day Hanneke refused to say a word about the incident. She had promised Evert and Babette, she said. "But it won't blow over, Karen. You might as well prepare yourself for the end of the dinner club."

25

A strong wind whistled across the shabby, deserted car
park of McDonald's. Empty coke cups and hamburger
cartons, propelled across the asphalt, were swirling in
the air, and the tall Ronald McDonald bouncy castle
flapped and tugged at the rope securing it to the
ground. It was three minutes to nine: I'd had another
sleepless night and for the umpteenth time I checked
my face in the rear-view mirror. My swollen eyes had
been made even smaller by the application of too
much light eye shadow in an attempt to make them
look fresher and larger; and my skin, which was growing paler and greyer day by day, had been given a
spongy texture by the foundation. This wasn't me. It
couldn't possibly be me, this painted clown, waiting
for her lover on a tacky patch of tarmac. I should leave,
go back home and confess everything to my husband,
not wait here for Simon like an insecure adolescent,
weak at the knees and heart aflutter, hoping that he
would kiss me just once more, that he wouldn't say he
regretted our brief episode of lovemaking in the shed,
that we must leave it at that and forget it, although
those were exactly the words I had resolved to say. If he
should turn up, that is. I felt disgusted with myself and
yet couldn't get the longing for him out of my system.
He was in my mind every second of the day, the mem
ory of sex with him shrouded all my other thoughts.
I had no idea what I felt: was I in love with him or just
a bored mother longing for risk and adventure? At

the same time I was consumed by a fear as violent and stormy as the wind outside. I was as much afraid of Simon as I wanted him, but I was even more afraid of myself, of the feeling that drove me towards him and over which I seemed to have no control. Self-destruction: that was the game I was playing. I had everything others strove for in vain for years, and now I was going to smash it all to pieces. Why? Was it a naïve, romantic idea that we might after all be able to love each other forever and unconditionally? Did we belong together? I shook my head to banish these ridiculous fantasies. We had only made love once and had been drunk and confused at the time. It meant nothing, and I really must stop blowing it up out of all proportion and attributing a purpose and motive to it. I was sitting here pining for a man who wasn't my type at all: too smooth, too self-assured, too superficial. His first pass had been unbelievably crude, and the way he had slid his hand into my jeans greedily and com-placently, and on top of that with Michel sitting oppos-ite, was disgustingly banal – it had nothing to do with romance or love. And the weirdest thing was that I had just let it happen like a purring cat and had revelled in this display of power to the tips of my toes instead of slapping his leering face. To make matters worse, I was now waiting for him, ready to surrender myself again, hot for more, cheating on everything and everyone. The only good thing that could come out of this was that I would find the truth. And so I fooled myself that I was sitting here shivering with cold and fear because I wanted to put a few searching questions to Simon.

Just when I had despaired of his showing up and, feel-ing a hopeless failure, had started the engine to drive back home, a Bordeaux-red Golf pulled into the car park at speed and swung in a wide arc, stopping with the engine running right behind my car and blocking me in. I waited for a moment, annoyed at such impudence, and sounded the horn, but the driver refused to give way. I got out, close to hysteria, intending to scream blue murder at the man to get him to move aside so I could leave, and headed for the Golf, in which sat a grinning Simon, clad in a crisply starched white shirt and a cobalt blue tie in shiny satin. He threw open the door, and I got in smiling timidly, meek as a lamb. Simon leaned across me and kissed me on the mouth, not too forwardly but intimately, sweetly, as if we had been a long-standing couple and he was kissing me to show me how much he still loved me. I melted, all my muscles went limp and heavy, and even if I'd wanted to, I was no longer physically capable of leaving the car. My body had a will of its own that was stronger than me, was drawn to him as if by a magnet. I realized yet again why I had avoided him as far as possible for as long as I'd known him: because I couldn't resist him. When he was close to me I lost my mind, and nothing and no one else interested me. I had been afraid for the past few years that we'd start kissing spontaneously in public.

"Hi, baby." He gave my thigh a quick squeeze, started off, changed gear at lightning speed and joined the motorway like a madman, staring fixedly at the road, while I hunted for words that I could not find because my brain just wasn't working. I could only wonder at myself, for just getting in without asking questions: I, the control freak, the moralist, the chicken. This man was regarded by Dorien Jager as the brains behind Evert's death and Hanneke's near-death. He could just as well be taking me to some remote spot where he would drive me into the drink, car and all.

"This is my town runabout. I never take the BMW into the centre, it's impossible these days, and, besides," he finally looked at me and gave a horny, teasing chuckle, "it's nice having a jalopy no one recognizes you in."

He turned up the volume on the CD player, and from the speakers came the sound of Herman Brood's "Saturday Night".

"I haven't heard that for years," I said.

"I play it every day when I drive to Amsterdam. This music is as great as ever, and Christ, I don't know about you, but it reminds me of good times. Didn't have two pennies to rub together, complete freedom, no responsibilities: it really was a sexy time, and this is sexy music. I use it to psych myself up for the fight . . ."

He clenched his fist and stuck it in the air.

"What fight?"

"My work: bullshitting, bluffing, pulling a fast one: every day new war games. Great, I'm telling you."

"But what exactly do you do? I still don't understand . . ."

"It's easier to ask what I don't do. What it comes down to more or less is juggling with money. Buying premises and selling or renting them to the hotel and catering industries: Kees has set up lots of pubs in my properties. Also investing in businesses like your Michel's. But takeovers too: turning ailing companies around – I enjoy that most: that involves creativity."

I looked at his slim wrist, the sexy way it came out of his shirtsleeve, and at the platinum watch he was wearing, his long, slender fingers that held nonchalantly onto the steering wheel. I swallowed, and my mouth was bone dry. Simon drove fast and in fact proved to be the kind of driver I hated, forcing others to pull over by driving right on their back bumper and if they still wouldn't give way, flashing his lights. A drop of sweat slid down past my armpit, and my hands became moist. Trying to appear as relaxed as possible, I wiped them dry on my skirt, but it was no good.

"To think I'm doing this without a second thought," I mumbled, more to myself than to him. He smiled at me and put his hand reassuringly on the back of my neck, which made me convulse as if I'd had an electric shock.

"We've got to talk, and we're going to. No more, no less. But we can hardly go and sit in Verdi's: it would be all round the village in no time."

He indicated right and left the motorway in the direction of Akersloot. We drove past the Van der Valk motel towards the village, and Simon said with a smirk that it might be nice to call in at the motel. I felt my desire for him flaring up again simply because of the proximity of a bed and had a momentary impulse to suggest we book a room and release the idiotic tension between us once and for all. Just one day with him, that was all I wanted, a memory to cherish for the rest of my life.

"This is an amazing spot," said Simon, stopping at a neglected-looking pub by the water's edge. "No one comes here."

He looked around him like a happy child. I followed him unsteadily over the pebbles on my high heels and eagerly grabbed his proffered warm hand, looking around timidly, as if I were naked or had just stolen something.

We were the only people in the dark, stuffy pub, and the barmaid looked put out to be dragged away from polishing the dilapidated bar. The cheesy sound of a pop song blared from the speakers, and Simon had to shout to order two coffees. The barmaid nodded coolly and simply went on polishing. We made our way to a table in a corner behind a wide pillar and sat down on the rickety chairs.

"This is Holland all over," laughed Simon. "Grey outside and brown inside, traditional and drab."

From inside his jacket came an irritating jingle, and he apologized as he rummaged for the mobile in his pocket. He looked at the screen, and I saw the tension cross his face.

"Right. We'll just turn this off for a bit."

With an exaggerated gesture he pressed the off button, snapped the phone shut and laid it on the table in front of him. The call seemed to have rattled him, however relaxed he tried to seem as he leaned back. His eyes were more restless, almost anxious, as if someone were hard on his heels.

"Simon," I began, finally able to get out a whole sentence without breaking into a sweat, "first of all I want to tell you that I didn't say anything about you or Ivo to Dorien Jager. I don't know what kind of tactics she uses, or why she lied to all of you, but please believe me: I think what has happened is terrible."

"Patricia and Angela are making a terrible fuss. It'll all blow over. The police won't find a thing at my place, because I have no fucking part in any of this. I want to warn you about Dorien Jager. She's a dangerous woman, a real witch who's made it her vocation to poison the lives of everyone who's better off than she is. She's got it in for me – as far as she's concerned, I'm the devil incarnate."

"Why?"

I was dying for a cigarette and, as a substitute, picked at the beads on the shabby table lamp.

"In Holland the prevailing wisdom is that if you've

got money you're probably bent, or at least that you ride roughshod over people. She sees me as some kind of mafia boss. My attempts to save Evert's business from collapse she regards as a hostile takeover, when I only wanted to help him."

"Evert himself wasn't so happy about it."

"Because I sent the administrators in. He did the oddest things: he saw turnover as profit, I think, till it had all gone and it became clear that his company was on the edge of the abyss. What he had conveniently forgotten was that a portion of my assets was also tied up in his business. Not only that: he had only been able to grow like he had because I had invested in the business. Two years ago he was ready to kiss my feet to persuade me to get involved in his business. But if I take a stake, it means that I protect my investment, and so when things don't go to plan, I intervene. That isn't criminal, it's just business. That's how things work in my world, and if I didn't operate like that, I'd never have got where I am today, and nor would Evert for that matter."

"Or Michel, Kees or Ivo either."

"*They* understand very well how things work."

"And how's that?"

"You've got to keep friendship and business separate, that's the first thing. Apart from that, they don't see me as a big player with money to burn but as a partner motivated by profit. I don't take a stake as a friend but as a businessman, and I only do it if I believe that the stake will make money. That's why we always include a target in the contracts we draw up: if the target isn't met, I have the right to step in."

"But doesn't that make them all dependent on you?"

"Only if things go badly, and even then they're better off owing me money than the bank."

"My question is more: can you still be friends and

equals, if you're so involved with each other at the business level?"

"I used to think so."

His gaze slid over my shoulder towards the grey, murky water. The surly waitress brought our coffee. Simon took a brown case from his inside pocket, opened it and carefully extracted a cigar.

"So what has changed?"

"Evert committed suicide. That has to be the ultimate indictment. Imagine if he'd taken Babette and the children with him. I can do business and keep my emotions out of it. When I take a tough line, it's not meant personally: those are the rules. For Evert, it obviously didn't work like that. And yet, when I lie in bed at night and reconsider the whole affair, I know I did nothing wrong, except perhaps that I believed too much in him. I should never have done business with him. If I'd known he was so unstable and jealous . . ."

He lit his cigar with his silver lighter, and I couldn't help noticing that his hand was trembling.

"But what was Evert jealous of, then? After all, he had money, a marvellous house and a nice family."

"Evert wanted to be like me. Everyone wants to be like me, but not everyone blames me because they can't be. Evert did."

I was taken aback by the vehemence and arrogance with which he spoke and at the same time realized that he was right, although it wasn't endearing of him to put it like that. Even Michel wanted to be like Simon: I had seen him change from the moment they became friends. And if I was honest, I wanted a man like Simon too: not so much for his money, as for his sexy, self-assured vibe, his aura of success and the way he obviously enjoyed it. He was as irritating as he was irresistible.

154

I wanted to freeze time. Sit here all day long, have him all to myself, talk as only loving couples can talk. Yes, I was in love with him. The tingling intoxication I found myself in now I was sitting here with him was unmistakably the intoxication of love. And that wasn't good. I must snap out of this before the feeling became so powerful that I really started believing in a relationship with him and was ready to give up everything for him. I knew from experience that I could lose myself completely when I was in love.

Simon put his warm hand on mine, which lay clammy and cold on the table, and looked into my eyes.

"You really are a beautiful, scintillating woman, Karen. I love talking to you."

"I don't think we should do this again."

I could scarcely get the words out.

"It's not sensible, but it is wonderful," said Simon.

"What happened the day before yesterday was fantastic, and I will always cherish the memory, but we must leave it at that, and it must stay secret."

He snorted with laughter.

"My God, yes, I was assuming that. You must never, ever confess these kinds of things. You must promise me: keep denying it. It's just something between us which concerns no one else."

"What was it, Simon? What got into us?"

"It had been coming for quite a while. We did our best to stay away from each other, but the day before yesterday . . . there was no escaping it."

"I feel the same. But I had never thought I was capable of something like that. Do you feel guilty?"

"Baby, you mustn't do that. You have to allow yourself certain things. As long as no one knows and you don't get any weird ideas into your head . . . You only live once and eternal faithfulness sounds nice, but it doesn't work in this day and age."

"What do you mean by weird ideas?"

"That you're in love with me or want to leave Michel. I'm very clear in my mind that I'll never leave Patricia, whatever happens. My kids are growing up with a father and a mother and even if it's one big charade, it's still better than a broken home. That never made anyone any happier."

What he said hit me right in the belly. Not because I had ever thought that he would leave his family for me, or that I would do so for him, or that he was in love with me. His bluntness, which made it clear that he was not in love, was so routine, so cold that I shivered and blushed, as if I had been caught lying. Suddenly I had nothing more to say and just nodded, smiling desperately.

"I'm glad you feel the same," he said, meanwhile glancing at his watch. "I'll take you back. I've got to go to work."

He put money on the table and turned on his telephone, which immediately started beeping.

We walked down the gravel path to the car. Above us lowered dark grey clouds that could bring rain any moment. The wind had dropped, and it was damp and clammy. Simon held the door open for me. I hurried towards him. I did not know what to do with myself and felt rejected.

As I was about to get in and brushed past him, Simon grabbed me by the waist and stopped me.

"Did you mean that: that we've got to leave it at that one time?"

He stroked my sides with his thumbs.

"Yes. I think enough has been wrecked already in the dinner club. And besides, I'm not the sort . . ."

"The sort?"

He took my hand cautiously and played with my fingers. I wanted to find him loathsome, to hit him. I wanted to cry on his shoulder.

"The sort of woman who starts an affair for the hell of it."

"So what we did was a mistake? Are you sorry?"

He looked at me piercingly, and I tried to act as hard-bitten and indifferent as I could.

"Not sorry: it was wonderful, but it's not worth the stress and the lies. At any rate I can't live with them."

Gently I squirmed free of his grasp.

"The dinner club is no more, darling. It's bust, *finito*, down the tubes. That seems obvious to me, so you don't have to stop for their sake . . ."

He ran his finger tenderly across my face. "I'd judged you differently."

He bent over me and licked my ear lobe. His warm breath gave me goose pimples all over.

"How?"

"I thought you were a free woman, not afraid . . ."

And so I am, I thought, that's how I want to be. But getting into something with you would be self-destructive. I want my intelligence back, calm in my head, I want to be happy with myself again, please let me go. But I didn't say that. Instead of pushing him away, I kissed him back and let him put his hands under my sweater. I had never been kissed as wonderfully as by Simon. Never had my breasts so longed for someone's touch as they did for Simon's.

"We can drive round for a bit," he breathed, while his mobile started beeping and tinkling incessantly, bringing me to my senses just in time.

157

"I don't think that's a good idea," I replied hoarsely and tore myself away from him.

Simon answered his phone, and I went and sat in his car with my heart pounding. I could still hear a strange tinkling, that seemed to be coming from a long way off. I checked my mobile, looked under the seats, on the backseat, in the glove compartment and finally in Simon's briefcase, which was behind my seat. That was where the strange ring tone was coming from: obviously he had two telephones. I knocked on the window, pointed to his case and signalled that his other phone was ringing, and he, still talking, gestured for me to give it to him. I pulled the black leather case from behind the seat, clicked it open, took out the tiny red mobile that was vibrating insistently, wound down my window and gave it to Simon.

As I snapped the case shut my eye was caught by a pile of papers on which I could just make out Hanneke's e-mail address. I leafed hurriedly through the papers, keeping one eye on Simon, who had his back to me.

On an impulse, I snatched one of the sheets from the pile and stuffed it into my jacket pocket. Then I shut his case and replaced it neatly behind my seat.

"That was Ivo," mumbled Simon as he came and sat beside me. He seemed to have aged ten years in the space of a few minutes. His face was pale, and the sharp lines at the side of his mouth seemed deeper.

"Christ, Karen, what's wrong with us? Is this a punishment or something? Were things going too well? I sometimes think that this is the price of success and happiness: that's why we get landed with this. We're supposed to learn something from it, but what? What damned use is it?"

He yelled and banged his head on the steering wheel till tears came into his eyes.

"I can't stand it! Not being able to do anything! Anything at all! The man's at rock bottom ... The children ..."

I broke out in a cold sweat. Something had happened to Hanneke.

He looked at me with tears in his eyes.

"They're taking her off life-support." His chin trembled. I wound down the window and breathed in the cold, damp air to stop myself from throwing up.

26

Dearest, Dearest Han,

It's terrible to see the pain you're in and to know that I'm the cause of it. But still there's nothing else I can do except distance myself from you. I've got to. However grateful I am for your support, your trust and belief in me (if I hadn't had you, who knows how deep the hole would have been) and for your understanding, from now on I'm going to do my level best to salvage what I can. I don't want to lose Babette. I don't want to lose my children. So I've decided to accept the situation and to stop fighting her, and to try to understand her.

Yes, I love her, despite everything. What you and I had was beautiful, special and unforgettable, and may have saved my life, but it was also based on fear. We were lonely and lost and were able to take shelter with each other for a while. That's how I see it. But the storm has subsided, the sun has broken through again, and we have to go on. It was never my intention to ruin your marriage and as far as I'm aware nor was it yours. So please, Han, look to the future and try to see what we had as something beautiful that belongs in the past. You will always keep a place in my heart, but however strange it may sound the rest of my heart belongs to Babette. I hope that one day you will find it in yourself to open your heart to Ivo again.

As far as Simon is concerned, you're right, but I can't do anything else, I'm tied to him hand and foot. Apart from which, I don't want to be angry anymore, it's eating

me up inside. The coming year will be dedicated to clear-
ing up the mess that I've caused, both with Simon and
with Babette. Mark my words: I'm going to make sure my
wife starts to love me again and that I get my business
back! Yes, I can already see you retching, but I have to set
myself this goal. And to achieve this I have decided to sell
our house. I want to get away from this f***ing village
and from the dinner club, and away from Simon's sphere
of influence. Start with a clean slate.

    Dearest Han, it will better if we have no further con-
tact and stay away from each other. This is my last mes-
sage to you. We'll bump into each other, in the street, at
friends' places, on the tennis court, hear each other's
names mentioned in other people's stories and that will
certainly hurt, but it will wear off, believe me. I hope that
one day we'll be able to be ordinary friends again and
that Ivo will be able to forgive me.

    Love, Evert

The e-mail had been written a week before the fire. I
kept smoothing the paper gently, as if in this way I
could comfort Hanneke, while the tears dripped from
my eyes onto the table. I read Evert's words again and
again and kept coming to the same conclusion: he
didn't want to die.

I laid my head on the letter and saw it in front
of me. Her body being disconnected from the life-
support system, her strong, young body, which wasn't
meant for death. Was her grief at Evert's death so
great that she had leaped to join him? I shook my
head. Evert had not opted for death, and neither had
she. It was patently obvious: Hanneke knew Evert
had been murdered and had been on the point of
proving it with these e-mails, which were in Simon's
briefcase.

161

I groaned. I felt sick with grief, sick of myself, sick of my friends.

A car drove up our garden path, and I went to the kitchen window to see who was coming. It was Michel. I quickly folded the sheet of paper and stuffed it in my pocket, wiped away my tears and opened the newspaper. Officially I knew nothing about Hanneke's death yet.

"Oh, Karen," murmured Michel when he saw me. He bent over me awkwardly as he put his arms round me.

"What's wrong?" I asked as breezily as possible. "Would you like some coffee?"

"Sit down for a moment. And hold me. Please."

He burrowed through my hair with his nose and sniffed.

"Karen. Something's happened . . . I wanted to tell you myself . . . I drove home at once."

I took his hand and pushed him onto the chair next to me.

"What? What's the matter?"

He sighed and hesitated for a moment. Then he grabbed my shoulders and pulled me to him.

"They're going to take Hanneke off the oxygen this afternoon. There's no point . . . Her brain is so badly damaged . . . In fact, she's already dead."

He held me tight and groaned. His rib cage was heaving.

"Who . . . who says so?"

"Simon. He rang me about half an hour ago. Everyone's gone . . ."

"Everyone?" That word made me feel sick.

Trembling, Michel extricated his cigarettes from his trouser pocket and lit one. I stood up and took one too. He gave me a light. My hands were trembling so badly that I couldn't keep my cigarette over the flame.

And . . ." he said in a hoarse, choked voice, looking away from me, "we're not welcome. Or at least you're not. I know, it's ridiculous. I got very angry. Simon can't help it; he thinks it's awful too. But Ivo is her husband . . . and we must respect his decision."

I suddenly felt cold.

"It doesn't matter. Anyway, I don't want to say good-bye to her surrounded by the very people who may have been responsible for her death."

"Karen . . ."

"It doesn't matter who actually pushed her. Even if she jumped herself, she was driven to it. She had to die, because she knew too much about Evert's death."

"Darling, this is pointless. I understand that you're angry and sad, but please use your head."

"That's exactly what I am doing at last."

Michel rubbed his thumb and forefinger wearily between his eyes. Then he stared pityingly at me.

"Please, Karen, think about what you're coming out with. Stop all this black-and-white talk. Ivo has lost his wife, Babette her husband . . . that's bad enough. Leave them in peace."

"I won't be able to forgive myself if I let this rest. I know that Hanneke would never commit suicide, however drunk and confused she was. I owe it to her children to question that."

He said nothing and put a new cigarette in his mouth. The tears flowed slowly down his stubbly cheeks. For a moment he resembled the vulnerable, sweet man I once fell in love with. I tried to comfort him, but he turned his head away.

"I'm not going to give up everything I've worked so hard for because you've developed some weird conspiracy theory. You can't force me to give up my company, my life. I'm not going to do it. I'm not going to support you. You're alone, completely alone in this."

Evert's letter was burning a hole in my pocket. But I couldn't give it to Michel to read without explaining how I'd come by it.

"I know, Michel, and I hope it won't be too late when I'm eventually able to convince you. For us, I mean."

27

Ivo did not want to see or speak to me. At first he had not even wanted me to come to Hanneke's funeral. Probably out of sheer despair and helplessness, he had directed all his barbs at me. I was a traitor, and he was strengthened in that conviction by Angela and Patricia, who seemed to get angrier with me day by day. At first they said hello in the supermarket, but a week later even that was too much. According to Babette, Angela and Patricia egged each other on to unprecedented heights and had only one topic of conversation: me. They were able to recall more and more negative things about me: the reason they had disliked me from the very first evening in the dinner club, what I had said, worn, done and omitted to do, the way I had been a hanger-on all that time, tolerated because I was so thick with Hanneke and Simon did business with my husband. They had thought all along that I would betray them one day because I secretly looked down on them and thought I was so wonderful. But they had never, ever expected me to be so stupid as to pillory my best friend and her husband by informing on them to the police.

I knew the course such conversations took, as I had sat in on them for two years. The character, the appearance, the marriage and family of the absent person were fully analysed and frequently totally demolished. I had always had the idea that I was the one who had tried to put things in perspective in these conversations, but now I was locked out, I realized that I had played the game just as hard, quite simply because it was fun and a safe way of conversing. We never had to talk about ourselves, our fears, our uncertainties or our relationships. It gave us a feeling of togetherness and of being on the right side. We brought our children up well; they spoiled theirs. We drank in moderation; she was an alcoholic. We had nice husbands; hers was a bastard. We did up our houses tastefully; she let things go. We were good at tennis; she couldn't hit a ball. We chose our clothes carefully; she copied us. We had money and a good life; and she so wanted to be part of it. We were in good shape; she really ought to do something about herself. Our husbands respected their wives; hers was always pawing us.

Strangely enough, being an outcast gave me great strength, and I felt oddly relieved. I didn't collapse, although I was someone who had always wanted to be liked, even by people I didn't like, but I grew stronger every day, as if I were rediscovering myself a little at a time. What remained a terrible problem was the intense and painful longing for Simon that refused to subside. On the contrary, it seemed to be more and more of an obsession, despite my serious doubts about his part in the deaths of Evert and Hanneke. I thought of him the moment I opened my eyes in the morning, while making sandwiches for the children's lunch, biking to school, working at my computer, he haunted my thoughts so that I could scarcely concentrate. Every romantic and melancholy song on the radio, however soupy, set my imagination racing. I had whole conversations with him in my head, in which he explained to me time and again that he had nothing to do with

Hanneke or Evert's death, and then took me in his arms and kissed me passionately. One moment I was convinced that he was the mastermind behind the murders, the next I was sure that he couldn't have had anything to do with it. At night in bed I wrote imaginary letters, e-mails, texts in which I tried to describe my confusing feelings for him and denounced him as the biggest, most disgusting bully, manipulator and seducer on earth. It did not exactly help that he sent me occasional text messages, which I immediately erased without answering them, sometimes superficially friendly (*Wondering how you are. X*), sometimes despairing (*Please let me hear from you. XXXXX*), sometimes explicitly horny (*Lie down on my desk. I unbutton your blouse and find your breasts, your hard nipples, which I kiss, stroke, lick. Your turn! X*).

It was drizzling, and fog blanketed the meadows, in which cows grazed. Michel, the children and I stood dressed in white, each of us holding a red rose, at the side of the Bloemendijk, down which Hanneke's funeral cortege was due to pass at any minute. Friends and family had been invited to the house to take their leave of Hanneke and accompany her to church; acquaintances, business associates and the rest were asked to stand along the route holding a red rose.

The whole village seemed to have turned out. Hundreds of adults and children, solemn-faced, lined the road and it was an impressive sight. I was sure that Hanneke would have loved this.

We all seemed to hold our breath as the white hearse came by at a walking pace carrying the lime-washed oak coffin covered in gorgeous flower arrangements. Ivo was accompanied by Babette, Mees, Anna, his parents and Hanneke's. They walked in a daze behind the hearse, their red faces swollen with grief. A wave of lament rose from the spectators. Michel put an arm round me, and I heard him snivelling. Babette cautiously raised a hand to us.

"Mum?" Annabelle looked at me in astonishment. "Are you crying?" I nodded and smiled at her, while I hugged Sophie.

"Daddy's crying too," Sophie whispered in her big sister's ear, and Annabelle turned around, towards her father, who was drying his eyes with a handkerchief, and took his hand.

"Mees says she's dead, but not really, because she'll always be with him, in his heart . . ."

Patricia and Angela, alone among the mourners, were wearing big black sunglasses. Both hung dramatically on their husbands' arm and ignored us completely. Simon winked pityingly in our direction.

"It's so bloody awful," muttered Michel, putting an arm round me as we joined the great stream of people following the procession.

In the church we found a place at the back, next to a large marble pillar, among the sensation-seekers. Every pew was full. The children climbed playfully into the choir stalls behind the coffin, which was covered in red roses. Above it hung a large black-and-white photo of a radiant Hanneke, being kissed on both cheeks by her children. From the speakers came "Everybody Hurts" by R.E.M., her favourite song, which she had said several times she wanted played at her funeral. I pushed my head onto Michel's shoulder and dug my nails into his arm.

At the front our friends were leaning against each other, Patricia and Angela still hidden behind their sunglasses, and Simon had put his arm round Ivo.

168

"A wonderful performance, don't you think?" someone behind me whispered in my ear. I turned round and looked straight into the face of Dorien Jager.

The undertaker took his place behind the lectern, and an oppressive silence fell. He invited Simon to speak. One couldn't tell if he was nervous, or moved, although by his standards he looked grey and care-worn. He ran his hand through his hair a number of times, put his right hand nonchalantly in his pocket, cleared his throat and told us how hard he found it to stand here, in the presence of the friends and family of this splendid, ebullient young woman, this mother and wife, friend and daughter, and in addition very talented and successful interior designer. He was doing so at the request of his best friend Ivo, who did not feel capable of speaking himself.

"He's good. Charm personified."

Dorien's eyes were boring into my back, and she went on hissing her caustic commentary into my ear, like a little devil on my shoulder. I turned around and asked her to shut up, after which she fortunately held her tongue.

"I thought you would be sitting at the front, with the VIPs . . ." She spoke to me as we came out of the church. Michel went on ahead with Annabelle and Sophie. Dorien leaned against the wall and nervously rolled a cigarette, licked the paper and stuck it behind her ear.

"I'd given up. I've just started again, but I try to smoke as little as possible. I have to allow at least ten minutes between rolling and smoking, I've made a pact with myself."

Her authoritarian, contemptuous attitude had gone. She glanced around timidly and looked as if she hadn't slept for weeks.

"You've got a nerve, turning up here and chattering to me during the service! After the way you landed me in it! Why did you lie? Why did you put words in my mouth that I never said?" I asked her fiercely. She looked right through me with her cold, blue eyes and shrugged her shoulders.

"It's sometimes necessary, to help things along; and even if you didn't say it, I knew you had your doubts. What kind of a friend would you be if you didn't? But console yourself. I paid heavily for my methods. They've taken me off the case . . ."

She looked down and kicked the grass with her chunky shoe.

"Simon blew his horn and abracadabra, I was gone. But anyway, you seem to be out of favour too . . ."

"Thanks to you."

"Go ahead and blame it on me; that's what your kind does. When you get behind the wheel legless and are pulled over, we're the villains, but if one of your brats is run over by a drunk, we're still the villains. Meanwhile you go on moaning that it's getting so unsafe, that we need more police on the beat. While you yourselves find all kinds of ways of dodging tax, as if you were above the law."

"My, my, you should join the Socialist Party. You could go a long way . . ."

"Get stuffed."

She pulled the roll-up from behind her ear and lit up.

"You're blaming Simon when you bent the rules too," I said.

It began raining harder. I pulled up the collar of my coat.

"I saw that woman, who in the photo is laughing so happily with her kiddies, your friend," she pointed accusingly at me, "twitching on the pavement. I found her bag in the room and her mobile, full of telephone numbers of friends, her diary with photos of her kids, full of dates. I knew at once: this is a strong, popular, cheerful woman, not the kind who jumps off a balcony because she's unhappy in love. Believe me, I've seen lots of suicides. If you had seen her lying there like that, *you*'d have sworn to find her murderer at all costs."

Michel came back and gestured in irritation for me to come with him.

"I have to go, but I'd like to talk," I whispered, and Dorien feigned surprise. "Now she tells me. Christ, woman, I have no say anymore! It's no longer my case."

She took a passionate drag on her roll-up, and her eyes shone with pleasure.

"Talking can do no harm. Call me, you've got my card."

Hidden beneath a sea of umbrellas, we said farewell to Hanneke's body, which sank slowly into the grave. Even at my mother's funeral I had not bawled as I did now: my nose and eyes were raw. I was crying not only for the loss of Hanneke but of everything. Here I stood, estranged from everyone, even from my own husband. He tried to comfort me by gently rubbing me warm, giving me tissues and squeezing my hand, which made my grief even greater. I couldn't tear myself away from the big black hole into which Hanneke had disappeared forever, not even after most people had left and made their way to the church hall for salmon and champagne. I stood there while the rain seeped into my high heels. Michel tried tentatively to pull me away, but I refused. I stared at the rose petals that the

171

children, orchestrated by Patricia, had scattered on the coffin and ignored the rain, which was falling more and more heavily.

"Han," I whispered. "I'm going see this through. You were so brave . . . That's why you were my best, best friend, I realize that now. Because you were so brave and tough and honest. And I'm going to make sure that you didn't die for nothing: they're not going to get away with this. I promise you."

Someone took me by the shoulder.

"Hey, baby, what are you standing here mumbling for? You'll catch cold . . ."

Simon. The rain was dripping over his hair, over his face, sliding along his nose towards his sensual mouth.

"What are you promising her?"

"That's none of your business."

"Come on, I'll take you home. You're soaked through."

"So are you, for that matter. Don't you have to go in? To drink champagne, 'just as Hanneke would have wanted'?"

"Don't be so cynical. I didn't arrange it."

"I expect it was your wife, the cow who only a week ago called Hanneke 'a dangerous madwoman'? But anyway, I expect you all have good reason to open the bubbly. I think I'll go in with you and give her some nice text messages of yours to read."

"Fine by me. Michel's in there: he'll find them interesting too."

He held me firmly by my waist and pulled me with him.

I resisted, dug my heels in and poked my elbow between his ribs.

"Let me go, Simon, don't show me up in front of everyone."

He looked at me icily and flexed his jaw muscles.

"You're making yourself completely ridiculous, Karen. Come inside with me, be a strong woman or go home and whine. I've had enough of this. I don't want any more dramas. You're going to behave normally, we're all going to behave normally."

He said it with such authority that I became afraid of him.

"OK. I'll go in with you. I'll fetch Michel and the children, and we'll go home, and from now on you must leave me alone. No more texting, no more calls. Please let's agree to behave normally too."

"If that's what you want, I'll respect that. I won't trouble you anymore."

"Fine."

He turned round and walked off. I stood there trembling and wanted to yell his name very loud.

28

Dorien Jager's flat was an indescribable mess. Moving boxes were piled in the narrow hall, a cat tray next to the door gave off a sickly ammonia-like stench and the floor was strewn with wellingtons, slippers, hiking boots and even a pair of pink mules, as if someone had flung them there in a fit of rage. And that was just the hall: in the small kitchen several days' washing-up was piled on the draining board, and the rubbish bin was bulging, the peel of a squeezed orange lying next to it.

"Don't mind the mess," said Dorien, who was still in her dressing gown, stepping over a pile of old newspapers – but it was impossible not to mind it.

"Have you just moved, or are you about to?" I asked, pointing to the crates full of bottles and jars on the dining table.

"My boyfriend's. He's leaving, tomorrow."

"Oh, sorry . . ." I stood awkwardly in the middle of the room, while Dorien shifted a pile of clothes from one chair to another.

"Doesn't matter. It's better like this. I'll just be glad when this," she gestured rather helplessly around her, "is over. Dividing things up . . . the memories clinging to everything. Coffee?"

"I'd love some."

It was Saturday. I had told Michel I was going to Amsterdam on a shopping spree. Babette had wanted to come with me, but I was able to put her off by saying

I needed a day on my own. She understood immediately and offered to do something nice with the children. When I left, Michel had given me an affectionate kiss on the mouth.

"This is the old Karen," he had laughed. "You go and have a good shop, love." He pressed a two hundred-euro note into my hand, so relieved was he that I hadn't said a word about my conspiracy theories since the funeral.

"Life goes on. We have to go on, together. Patricia and Angela will come round. Please don't let's make the situation worse than it is . . ." In those terms he had tried to comfort me after the funeral. I had looked at him and wondered why he, my own husband, was so keen for the lid to be put back on the cesspit. He, the avant-garde television producer, once a crusader against injustice, now reduced to producing stupid game shows and cheesy reality soaps.

I wanted to start loving him again. I searched high and low for a spark of emotion, a lovely memory that would revive my feelings for him, but nothing surfaced except irritation and revulsion, and I wondered desperately how on earth this could ever be put right. Perhaps if I could prove to him that something underhand was really going on, that would bring us closer together.

"Milk and sugar?" I started out of my gloomy thoughts. Dorien had hoisted herself into a pair of jeans and a lumberjack shirt, obviously hurriedly and with her mind elsewhere, as the shirt had been buttoned lopsidedly. She put two large mugs in the shape of pigs on the table and slid an opened packet of sugar and a large bottle of coffee milk towards me.

"Only sugar thanks," I replied, whereupon she tipped

an enormous scoop of sugar in a dessertspoon into both mugs. I folded my hands round the pig's head and drank a mouthful. The coffee was so strong that my heart immediately started racing.

"I think I've gone a bit over . . ." muttered Dorien, scooping another spoonful of sugar into her mug.

A complacent smile appeared on her face.

"What made you change your mind?"

Suddenly I didn't know where to begin: it was difficult to start confiding in her.

"I know for certain that Hanneke didn't commit suicide," I began. "I know her, and she's not the type."

Dorien sighed.

"Surely you've haven't come all the way here to tell me that? You knew that a week ago, though you refused to admit it. Christ, woman, of course she didn't commit suicide, but try proving that. We have nothing that points to a murder. Apart from that, you're in the wrong place, now I've been taken off the case."

"You said that Simon had fixed that . . ."

"Yes, he sent one of his expensive lawyers to my chief with the story that I was conducting a personal vendetta against him and was collecting evidence by unacceptable methods . . ."

"And so you were. On what grounds were you able to seize Simon and Ivo's accounts just like that and search their houses?"

"Hey, it wasn't me who started that, it was the tax people. It had nothing to do with my investigation. I just took a look, and that was a no-no."

My mouth fell open.

"The Inland Revenue people have been after Simon Vogel for years for tax fraud related to the millions and millions he earned from sex chat lines. I don't know exactly how it works, but I do know that for years he's used shady dealings to avoid tax. He's always got away with it, but now they seem to have got him by the balls . . ."

'Sex chat lines?'

"Yes, that's how he began and that's how he earned his fortune. After he drove my father to his death."

"Your father?"

Dorien pulled a pinch of tobacco from her packet and put it on a cigarette paper.

"My father had a stall on the Albert Cuyp street market. He sold blankets, quilts, loose covers, pillows, that kind of thing. In those days Simon was just a young chancer with the stall next door full of merchandise imported from Thailand, all fake. What were the brands again? Fiorrucci, Kappa, Nike, LaCoste. Polo shirts, socks, sweatbands, that kind of crap. Sold like hot cakes. My father thought it was wonderful what Simon got up to. At the end of the day they'd often go off to the pub together, where he'd turn my father's head with all his plans. One day Simon announced he was giving up the market. He was getting into something that would make him a millionaire: it was still a secret. Dad saw his chance and asked whether he could take over Simon's business on the market."

Dorien's face tautened. She inhaled aggressively and blew out the smoke impatiently.

"No problem, said Simon, but for that kind of trade you needed a nose for what was hip, and you had to go to Thailand, Turkey and India to buy merchandise, which was impossible for my father, with his health. So off he went to Thailand, with a pile of Dad's cash, all his under-the-counter savings. Simon did come back, but without the goods and without the money. He claimed he'd been cheated, but I could tell from the look on his rat's face that he was lying. That was the last time we saw him, although he promised to do everything he could to pay my father back at least half the money he'd lost. My sucker of a father believed him too. He had lost his stall, and Simon's was now run by someone else, probably a mate of his, selling jeans. My Dad's savings had gone, and still he defended Simon. Six months later he died: heart attack. There wasn't even enough left for a decent funeral, and I heard not a word from Simon: no flowers, no note, nothing. He'd swindled forty thousand guilders out of my father. I was fifteen, and my mother had died four years earlier of breast cancer."

When she finally finished, she gave me an almost triumphant look, clearly enjoying my astonishment.

"Yes, Karen, your Simon, with his beautiful suits and his house full of trendy art, began as a market trader and a telephone pimp – and don't let's forget, a con-man. Wherever he goes, he screws people. He never finished secondary school, but he's really smart. He can turn everything and everyone to his own advantage. He manipulates, blackmails, defrauds . . ."

"Yes, yes, stop it. I know. At any rate he was right when he said you were pursuing a personal vendetta against him . . ."

The overdose of caffeine combined with this devastating news made me shiver. Dorien got up and came back with the coffee jug. I refused politely and asked for a glass of water.

"What do you reckon I thought," she shouted from the kitchen, "when I saw his name in the letter of condolence in the paper? And saw him pop up as one of the first visitors to the hospital where Hanneke was?"

She gave me a glass of water and I took a paraceta-mol from my bag to fight the headache that was coming on.

"I can imagine you found it odd and that you immediately grabbed the opportunity to expose him. But of course it could just as well be a combination of circumstances. None of this proves that Simon is a murderer. However terrible I think it all is for you, you can't blame him for your father's death and in revenge try to pin the death of Evert and Hanneke on him."

"I'm certain he's got something to do with it," she hissed fanatically, waving her raised finger.

"His wife, Patricia, went to see Hanneke. She was the last one to see her, together with Angela."

Now it was Dorien's turn to stare me open-mouthed.

"They went to see her to talk to her about what had happened at Evert's funeral."

"They didn't tell me."

"And I have a letter. From Evert to Hanneke."

I pulled the piece of paper out of my back pocket and laid it on the table.

"May I?"

I nodded. My cheeks were burning. Dorien's eyes rapidly scanned Evert's words.

"This is unbelievable' she muttered and frowned at me. "Unbelievable."

"This isn't exactly a letter written by someone want-ing to die, although that doesn't mean anything in itself. How did you come by it?"

"Does it matter?"

Dorien rolled her eyes in irritation.

"Jesus, woman. What are you after?"

"I found it in Simon's briefcase."

"Ah."

She looked at me searchingly.

"Well, are you going to tell me?"

"What?"

"What you were doing in Simon's briefcase."

The blood crept slowly from my neck to my face.

"Have you got a thing going with that prick or what?"

"That's none of your business," I stammered. "Perhaps this isn't such a good idea . . ."

"Karen, you can tell me. I'm no longer on this case, I can keep my mouth shut, really. Come on."

"Yes, something happened between Simon and me. We were drunk, it was a one-off. Afterwards we talked it over together and that's when I found that letter among various other e-mails in his briefcase. By accident: he asked me to get his telephone out of it."

"Careless of him."

She got up and went over to the window, which looked out over other blocks of flats.

"Right." She sighed. I blushed and waited for her disapproval. "We can nail him with this, Karen," she said.

"I don't believe he's a murderer. I'm more inclined to think he's protecting someone, Patricia, for example . . . After all, she went to see Hanneke. She may have taken these e-mails from her and then pushed her off the balcony."

"I think it's more likely she's protecting *him*, her golden boy. Bah."

Dorien exhaled the smoke and stubbed her cigarette out furiously on a coke can on the windowsill.

"They're whores, those women. They may be worse than their menfolk. They'll put up with anything for a few sparklers. They're shit, really. As long as they can drive a convertible, shop in P.C. Hooftstraat and lie on their backsides beside a swimming pool in the south of France. Whatever else their men get up to,

180

they couldn't care less. And do you know what bugs me most? That these kinds of women crop up as heroines in the magazines. All you see on the covers are blond, pneumatic bimbos, who've done nothing but land a rich guy. In past you had to have some talent to be a celebrity, nowadays you just need dough, irrespective of where it comes from."

"I think we're getting off the subject."

"Sorry, but that kind of thing always makes me so angry."

"My question is: what should I do with this e-mail? Can your people use it?"

"I can't use it, because I'm not allowed to get involved. I know from colleagues that they're about to close the case. There's no proof that Hanneke was pushed, and the only link they can find with Evert's death is their affair. For them it's just a love drama. This e-mail makes no difference to that: all it proves is that they had an affair and that he was in conflict with Simon, but we already knew that."

"And what about Patricia and Angela seeing Hanneke just before her fall?"

"That's certainly interesting, especially the fact that they lied about it. But that still doesn't make them murderesses. Their meeting might have convinced Hanneke that life no longer had any meaning. They'll say they lied about it out of guilt and fear."

I sucked in my lower lip and bit it. Dorien came back and sat on the corner of the table close to me.

"Didn't you say there were more e-mails in his brief-case? You must get your hands on them: you're the only one who can do that."

She put her hand on my shoulder.

"I've broken it off with him . . ."

"Oh, come on. You can wind guys like that round

your little finger. Flatter him a bit and you'll have him where you want him in no time."

"I don't know. Suppose he catches me . . ."

"Then you'll think up an excuse."

"I don't want to end up twitching on the pavement or as a charred corpse."

"I'll protect you. You'll tell me where you've arranged to meet, and I'll stay close to you. If things get heavy, just press one key on your phone and I'll be there."

I shook my head and covered my face with my hands. I had to do this for Hanneke's sake, but the idea of betraying Simon in such a despicable way made me gasp for breath.

"Jesus, you're in love with the prick!"

"I can't help it . . ." I snivelled.

"Come off it. Of course you can help it. You're not an adolescent, are you?"

She handed me a crumpled packet of paper tissues.

"Come on, Karen. You've got to be strong. This is the only way. If I could, I'd do it myself, but I'm afraid Simon wouldn't want to fuck me."

"He's probably long since destroyed those e-mails . . ."

"Possibly. On the other hand, why didn't he do it at once? Perhaps there's a reason why he's keeping them."

"I'm frightened . . ."

"That your affair will come to light . . ."

"That too."

"I promise you that won't happen. I'll think of something."

29

I turned off at the first petrol station, bought a packet of cigarettes and bottle of diet coke and went back and sat in my car. Michel wasn't expecting me home for ages yet. I took my mobile out of my bag, hesitated for moment and put it on the seat next to me. I lit a cigarette and stared at the surly faces of the passers-by, observed their hurried gestures and felt far removed from this perfectly normal world. I was alone, as alone as Hanneke and Evert had felt for months, and I could suddenly vividly imagine how that could drive you mad. I picked up my mobile and keyed in the message without hesitation.

> *"Can't get you out of my mind. Let's see each other 1 x more. x"*

I pressed "Send" before I was overtaken by doubt. Then I twisted the screw-top off the cola bottle and put it to my mouth.

Sorry, Simon, I thought, as the fizzing carbon dioxide in my mouth brought tears to my eyes. I can't think of any other way.

I started the car and shot off towards Amsterdam, in order to spend the two hundred euros I had been given by Michel. I couldn't go home without buying anything.

Slightly dazed and hyper, I wandered through my old

neighbourhood in the Jordaan. I walked down the cosy narrow shopping streets, stared into shop windows without seeing a thing, my hand clutching my telephone, unable to abandon myself to the impulsive shopping in which I had been so expertly instructed by my friends. Walking into a shop and choosing the rack with the colour you had decided on for yourself that season. This winter we had gone *en masse* for black, nice and easy. Then feeling the material. Is it comfortable, warm or, on the contrary, cool and lightweight, not too synthetic? Trendy yet timeless? Do you wear anything on top or under it? Do you dare wear it? But especially: is it exclusive enough? The price was of secondary importance; it was never discussed unless it was so exorbitant that it could be bragged about. For example, Patricia had once bought a calfskin jacket from Dolce & Gabbana, her favourite label, under the pretence of love at first sight, which to her horror, so she said, cost five thousand euros. It's steep, but you've got something for your money, she had laughed proudly. Three weeks later Angela was wearing the same jacket, which had caused some consternation. She maintained that it had completely slipped her mind that Patricia already had it and promised that henceforth she would confer first before wearing it to a party. But, for Patricia, it took the shine off, and she never wore the thing again.

I bought wellingtons with ladybird prints for Annabelle and an umbrella in the shape of a frog's head for Sophie, a big red scarf that I already knew I would never wear and high-heeled, pointed black boots in the sale. Walking through our old neighbourhood, past the pub where Michel and I had first met, across the bridge where he had kissed me and asked if he could please come home with me, I thought of him with affection for the first time in months.

As I was ordering a cappuccino in the Paleis café, my mobile vibrated in my pocket, and I jumped as if someone had jabbed me with a pin. The waitress looked me in surprise.

"Sorry. Message. That thing frightens the life out of me every time," I smiled apologetically, and she smiled back in sympathy.

Hi Mum, we've been to a film and now we're going for a Happy Meal! Kisses, Anna and Sophie

It was now over two hours since I had texted Simon. Surely he should have reacted by now. Perhaps this was his way of punishing me: it was too vain of me to think that he would want to see me one last time after all that had happened. Probably it had been nothing to him but an easy lay. After I'd started playing up, he had written me off. The plan that Dorien and I had dreamed up suddenly seemed utterly pointless and absurd. I had just let myself be swept along in her hate campaign.

The waitress brought my cappuccino, and I paid her immediately. I hurriedly gulped down the weak, milky slop, put on my coat and collected my bags. I was suddenly dying to go home, to make it all cosy again. I decided to stop off in the village on the way back and buy all kinds of wonderful things. And once home I would turn off my phone in order to devote myself completely to Michel and the children. We would have a communal bath and then curl up in front of the television in our pyjamas, or even better, play a game together, accompanied by tea and apple tart. In bed I would not lie beside Michel like a board, hoping he would keep away from me, but would snuggle up to him and tell him I loved him, that we didn't need anyone else. And if his hands wandered over my body, I would give into it and be aware that they were his hands, the hands of my own husband, whom I loved, with whom I wanted and with whom I had to spend the rest of my life, with whom I could be happy if only I did my best. And from now on I would.

I parked my car behind Food Fair, a themed shopping mall containing an upmarket greengrocer's, a Fish Palace, a Cheese Corner, a free-range butcher and La Boulangerie. I gulped down an oyster in the fishmonger's and bought five slabs of smoked salmon, sampled some olives at Cheese Corner and left with a large piece of unpasteurized Brie, some Roquefort and a mild, overripe goat's cheese. At the baker's I was allowed to try some warm pesto ciabatta, which was so delectable that I immediately bought five, along with their famous apple tart.

Outside it had gone dark, and it was again raining unrelentingly, so clutching all my bags – cursing the weather, the winter and this country – I ran through the puddles to my car, where I threw my shopping on the backseat and eased breathlessly into the driving seat.

"Don't be alarmed," said Simon.

I *was* alarmed. So badly that I could only breathe in a high-pitched squeak. I put both hands on my chest in an attempt to calm my wildly pounding heart.

"God, Simon! Bloody hell! You've just about given me a heart attack!"

He put his hand on my back, making me recoil and bang my head on the windscreen.

186

"Damn you!" I hid my head in my hands to stop him seeing my tears. He was soaked to the skin and smelled of drink.

"Sorry," he said. "I didn't mean to give you a fright, but I saw you in the car and when you got out I called to you but you didn't hear me . . . I didn't want to talk to you in the shop, you understand, so I waited for you, but it was raining so hard and your car wasn't locked, which is very silly of you, by the way."

"What do you want?"

"Hold on a minute! You texted me! First you ask me to leave you alone, and three days later you suddenly want to see me again! And now you look at me as if I'm a serial killer . . . It might be better if I asked you that question."

I couldn't control the trembling.

"I'm just a bit confused, I think."

"You wanted to see me one more time, so here I am!"

He spread his arms and grinned. "Or have you changed your mind again?"

"By 'seeing' I had something else in mind than being ambushed by you."

I tried to think of him as a vulgar market trader, as a rotten telephone pimp, as a cold, calculating murderer, but it was no good; the longing for him took hold of me, and he smelled it as a dog smelled blood. He stretched out his arm and ran his finger cautiously along the back of my neck.

"So what did you mean?"

I swallowed the saliva that was filling my mouth.

"Meeting somewhere, far away from here . . ."

His eyes began to shine, and he grinned from ear to ear.

"Oh! You mean somewhere where there's a bed?"

His other hand stroked my thigh, moving higher

and higher. His thumb found my crotch. "Something like that," I stammered, pushing his hand away from my thighs. "Simon, we mustn't do this here. We just can't."

"No one can see us. We'll just make sure the windows steam up quickly."

"My car may be recognized."

"So let's drive off . . ."

He lifted my chin and forced me to look at him. I became frightened of myself, of my willingness to surrender to him again. It no longer mattered to me that we were in the middle of the village in a car park where everyone could see us, that Dorien had told me this morning what a shady character he actually was, or that I had just made all those good resolutions about Michel and the children.

He pressed a kiss on my lips, so sweet and soft that it was as if he really cared for me, felt what I felt, so that I wasn't alone. I put my hands against his cold cheeks, actually to stop him, but instead I kissed him back as tenderly as possible. His breathing became heavier and his kisses more insistent. He took my hand and pressed it against his erection.

"Well," he groaned in my ear, "tell me then . . ."

"What?" I pulled my hand back: things were going too fast for me.

"Tell me. What you want to do with me, somewhere far away . . ."

He fiddled with the buttons of my blouse and put his face between my breasts, which he cupped in both hands and pressed together. I couldn't get the words out. His head came up again, and he against kissed me greedily, pushing his hand down my trousers.

"Then I'll tell you," he breathed. "I want to fuck you, Karen, and I'm going to fuck you. Somewhere far away from here, in a bed, very long and very hard."

His finger slid slowly and purposefully inside my wetness. I shuddered.

"Unless you don't want to. Just say . . ."

"No," I stammered. This had to stop. People were walking past. There was a child's car seat in the back, and people who knew me would recognize my vehicle. A warm tingling sensation spread through my lower belly and up my inner thighs, in the direction of my crotch and just as it was threatening to engulf me, he withdrew his hand and said: "You're right. This isn't a good place."

I gasped for breath like a fish out of water.

"Sorry, Karen, I got carried away. I was so glad to hear from you . . . and then I saw you passing. I felt a great urge to talk to you."

"So I noticed."

He ran his hands through his curly hair, and for an instant I saw real confusion on his face.

"When I'm close to you I just can't keep my hands off you."

There was a moment's silence as we looked into each other's eyes. His eyes darkened as he began talking again.

"My life has turned into a nightmare since Evert's death. Do you know we had stones through our windows last night? And that we keep getting nuisance calls? The moment we answer, they hang up. Patricia's afraid. She wants to leave the village, leave the country even. She keeps talking about Marbella. And if it goes on like this, we'll have to."

"Shouldn't you report it to the police?"

"No, I don't think that's very sensible. That crowd are not exactly my best friends. Besides, I see that

Dorien Jager as quite capable of . . . I had her suspended, because she went far beyond her brief. She's so hysterical, she might be the one behind this."

"But why would she do something like that?"

"Because she's not right in the head." He sighed. "The police are not my pals, and I'm not their pal. People like me have to fend for ourselves, we're outlaws in this country. If you've made a slip in your taxes, oh yes, they know where to find you, but if someone is harassing you, they're suddenly short-staffed."

Simon stared thoughtfully into space for a moment, then turned to me and opened his arms wide.

"Come here. Come to me for a moment."

I laid my head against his broad, muscular chest. He ruffled my hair with his fingers. It was a wonderful, peaceful moment, as still as the eye of the storm.

"I have to go now," he mumbled, "but I want to arrange to meet. Then I'll make sure I have more time. Just leave it to me."

"Monday is my only day."

It had to happen as soon as possible.

"OK. I'll keep Monday free. I'll call you."

He put his hands round my face and gave me a sweet, boyish smile.

"Bye, my Karen," he said and kissed me on the tip of my nose. Then he was gone.

30

My house smelled of scented candles. I hated scented candles: this must have been Babette's idea. Cheerful sounds were coming from the kitchen. The place had never been so tidy: shoes were lined up under the coat hooks, which had coats hanging neatly on them, and on the dresser in the hall there were welcoming orange tea lights among the framed family photos that were usually obscured by scarves, mittens and hats. An oppressive feeling of sadness came over me, as if I no longer belonged here, as if I were an outsider about to disrupt a happy family scene. What on earth had I got myself into? Was my quest for truth worth losing my family little by little? I realized that I hadn't really devoted any time to my children for weeks and probably wouldn't be able to do so now either. My head was too full.

I joined Babette, Michel and the children at table, had a glass of wine pushed in my direction and looked at the children, who were totally absorbed in the game. Every so often Babette tried to catch my eye. I could see from her face that she had been crying a lot. Michel played happily with the children and occasionally smiled at me with the same artificiality.

"I've brought all sorts of goodies," I called out and got up again to unpack the bags I had left on the draining board. I put the cheese on a board, popped the salmon into the oven for a bit and cut the baguettes, after which I started emptying the dishwasher. Restlessness was raging through my body, and to calm it I downed my wine in three gulps.

"My, you're spoiling us," said Michel and put his arm round my waist to pull me onto his lap. His hand slid down my back.

"Did you have a good time? Have you perked up a bit?"

I nodded.

"It was wonderful to walk through Amsterdam again."

"Great. We've had a terrific time here too. I took the children to a film."

Beau, Luuk and Sophie started chattering away enthusiastically all at once. Babette gave me a strange stare.

We played another game of Trivial Pursuits, emptied a second bottle of Chablis, ate the warm salmon with a sauce that Babette threw together, chatted a bit more about the delights of Amsterdam and let the children watch a DVD with warm chocolate milk and apple tart. Over a third glass of wine we shared memories of Evert. Again Babette told us that she would never have smelled the fire if she hadn't fallen out of bed. She told us how, woozy from the sleeping pills Evert had put in her wine, she had gone to the boys' room and found Beau in bed but no sign of Luuk. With Beau in her arms, she had run downstairs, while the fire in the kitchen was spreading and she could scarcely see anything because of the smoke, got him outside, laid him in the shed and ran back inside to look for Luuk, whom she found in his parents' bed. He did that often when he was frightened, crept into bed with them. But that night Babette had gone to bed in the guest room – they had had a fight. The questions were churning round in her head: would Evert have done it even if they hadn't had a row? Would they all be dead now if she had simply slept in her own bed? Why hadn't she spotted that Evert was having another psychotic episode? Could she have saved Evert if she had tried harder? If she hadn't been so terribly angry with him? We listened, were touched and moved and occasionally cried. We comforted her by saying that she had done what she could. If she had tried to save Evert, she probably wouldn't have been alive today. She had done the right thing and she must resign herself to the fact that certain questions would never be answered. I didn't dare ask whether she had ever doubted that Evert had started the fire himself, or whether he was the one who had drugged them. But the thought that someone else was responsible, that someone in our circle of friends might be capable of killing even two children in such a dreadful way, was so abhorrent that I was deeply ashamed. I was suddenly certain that Simon had nothing to do with this, whatever Dorien Jager said. He wasn't a child murderer. It was impossible, inconceivable that I should put the life I was used to, my marriage and my family at risk for a child murderer.

"I'm going to put the children in the bath," muttered Michel, somewhat the worse for wear and upset by Babette's story. He left the kitchen.

"You've got a nice husband," said Babette when he had gone, and she divided the last of the wine between our glasses.

"Yes," I replied, feeling my cheeks going red. At any rate he did his best to be nice.

"I mean it, Karen. Don't destroy it." She looked at me sternly.

"How do you mean?"

"I'm not stupid. Why did you simply have to go to Amsterdam by yourself?"

I didn't know what to answer. The wine was clouding my thoughts. I wanted to tell her the truth, but at the same time was frightened that that would ruin everything.

There was an awkward silence.

"Karen, I live in your house, I tell you everything. You can trust me . . ."

A strange squeaking sound came from my throat.

She took my hand and began stroking it.

"I'm on your side. That's why you must tell me what's going on, so I can help you. After all you've done for me." Her eyes softened.

"I'm afraid," I said hoarsely, "that I'm in deep, deep trouble. I've completely lost the plot. I no longer know what's true and what isn't, whether I'm doing the right thing or not. One moment I feel strong and I'm convinced I've got to do it, that it's the only way to get my life back, that I owe it to Hanneke, and the next I feel a wreck, a traitor, a thoroughly evil woman . . ."

My head hung in my hands and my tears were dripping onto the table. Babette stroked my hair, patted me on the shoulder and when none of that helped she fetched me a glass of water.

"Here, drink up. You've had too much alcohol. I can't make head or tail of it. What do you have to do?"

I emptied the glass of water, dabbed my eyes dry with a tissue from the box Babette had put on the table, blew my nose and laid my head on the table. I couldn't look at her as I told her this.

"I went to see Dorien Jager. She told me how Simon

194

operates, how ruthless he is when it comes to making money. Did you know that he started out with sex chat lines? That he used to work on the market?"

"Yes, I've heard that . . . But that's not a crime, is it? And what has that got to do with you? Or with Hanneke?"

"You knew?"

"Yes. But what's so terrible about that? Sex chat lines are just another form of trade . . . They're not drugs or anything."

"Did you also know that the house searches at his and Ivo's places were ordered not by Dorien but by the tax people?"

"No, I didn't know that . . ."

"He has e-mails, from Evert to Hanneke."

"What?"

"In his briefcase. I saw them and grabbed one and gave it to Dorien."

"My God . . ." She got up and fetched a glass of water, which she held to her cheek.

"Why didn't you show it to me? An e-mail from *my* husband!" She gasped for breath. "What did it say?"

"That the affair between him and Hanneke must end. He was going to fight to save your marriage. It wasn't exactly a letter from someone who wanted to end his own life and his family's. Nor did he come across as psychotic."

Her head slumped between her shoulders, and she grabbed onto the chair. For a moment I thought she was going to fall. I was able to get up, ready to catch her, but she shooed me away.

"Leave it. I'm OK." She pulled the chair toward her and sat down on it. "I think I'm going to smoke one of Michel's cigarettes."

I fetched Michel's Marlboros from the extractor

hood, took out two cigarettes, lit them and gave one to Babette.

"I assume," she began softly, "that you've thought about what you're insinuating . . ."

"I think of nothing else. But after what you told us again this evening . . . Who would be capable of something as disgusting as that? Only a lunatic, someone without any feeling."

"Evert was very ill, Karen. I don't think any of you realized how bad he was, not even Hanneke. The evening before the fire I found him naked in the wardrobe, scrubbing himself clean with a nailbrush and bleach. He thought he was contaminated, that we had all been contaminated by extraterrestrial beings. He had seen them, he said. Then I knew he had stopped taking his medication. I put him under the shower and gave him his pills mixed with tea, as he refused to take them normally. Then I was going to ring the doctor, but he begged me in tears not to have him taken away again. He said he would die in there, that he would kill himself. What do you do in a case like that?"

Her lips were trembling. She took a drag on her cigarette.

"He was my husband, I loved him. I couldn't take him there again. I thought: this time we'll solve it together. So I'm also partly responsible for what happened."

"No, Babette, you can't say that . . ." I said, searching for words to relieve her of this dreadful burden of guilt. Michel came in and shrank back when he saw us sitting there so distraught.

"Are we OK, ladies?" We both nodded and smiled through our tears. I gestured to him that it would be better if he left us alone.

"You must never tell anyone about this," said Babette,

grasping my wrist with both hands. I shook my head and kissed her on the forehead.

"Of course not."

We were silent, apart from the occasional sniff. I put a kettle of water on the gas, got two cups and two plates, upon which I put two big slices of apple tart, and gave one to Babette. "Delicious," she sighed and tried to look at me gratefully.

"What I don't understand is how Simon got hold of those e-mails. And why should he lie about that investigation by the taxman? Something's not right . . ."

I poured tea into the cups and looked anxiously at Babette, frightened that I would confuse her again. "Sorry to keep going on. But now we've started."

"It doesn't matter. I have another question. What were you doing in Simon's briefcase?"

"Well. That's another story . . ."

She leaned across the table towards me.

"I don't think so. Why are you so obsessed with him?"

"I'm not obsessed with him."

"Yes you are. You keep coming back to him."

I lowered my eyes and tried to think of some way of getting out of this fix.

"You don't have to lie to me, Karen. I saw you."

My heart missed a beat.

"What are you talking about?"

"That night when you all got so pissed. You and Simon were kissing by the shed. I was woken up by the noise you were making. I looked out of the window and there you were . . ."

Babette stared at me impassively.

"I don't know what got into me that night. We were so out of it, so drunk. It only happened once.

Afterwards we talked and decided to leave it at that and not to tell anyone. After that talk I found those e-mails in his briefcase. Will you please promise me that this won't go any further?"

"You've no need to ask. Of course."

A worried expression crossed her face.

"Simon is just about the last person on the planet you should fall for . . ."

"I know." I cringed with shame.

" 'He's fucked more women than I've had hot dinners,' Evert always said." Babette seemed to say this deliberately as crudely as possible, so that it would hit home – and it did. It felt like a kick in my stomach.

"Does Patricia know?" I asked softly.

"Patricia doesn't want to know. What good would it do her? If she plays up, she can kiss her Range Rover goodbye."

"Simon told me he'll never leave her," I said.

Babette grinned cynically.

"OK, so you go to bed with the man you suspect of having thrown Hanneke out of the window."

"He's got something to hide at any rate, and I want to find out what."

"That's why you're going to bed with him."

"It only happened once."

"It beats me. I'd just advise you to stop. I know what a mess it can create. Believe me, when you've been through it . . . No fuck is that good."

"You mean with Evert and Hanneke?"

She nodded.

"And you? Did you ever cheat on Evert?"

"I can't imagine touching some strange body. I can't understand how you can. I could only do that if I loved someone very much, and I can only do it with one man at a time."

Michel was already asleep when I crawled into bed next to him after putting on my flannel pyjamas in the dark. With a groan he snuggled up to me, jammed his leg over mine and slid his hand onto my belly. In the last few days he had done his best to make something of our marriage again. The one who refused to play ball on all fronts was me, I wanted someone else, I neglected him and the children, did not confide in him and, instead of admitting that honestly, hurled one accusation after another at him, blamed him for everything that was wrong between us, secretly even the fact that I wanted Simon. Michel must never know that. It would destroy him. I had set this in motion and now I had to bear the crushing feeling of guilt alone.

"What was all that just now?" He mumbled hoarsely, while his hand slid up and came to rest on my breast.

"Nothing. We were talking about Evert. She misses him."

"Hmm. It's hard for her to see us so happy . . ."

He began stroking my nipple hesitantly, very cautiously, frightened of being rejected, as if he were begging for love, while Simon again loomed up in my head. We made love in the dark, for the first time in weeks, without kissing, and when Michel came in me I said I loved him. He stayed on top of me for minutes, sighing and snuffling. For a moment I thought he was crying. I broke out in a sweat. Consolingly I stroked his wet back and asked him if he was OK.

"You bet!" he laughed. He looked at me so sweetly I thought the earth would swallow me up.

"You're terrific, do you know that? Made for love. It's just as well other people don't know how wonderful you are in bed . . ." He slumped beside me and sighed with pleasure. I laid my head on his chest and clung to him.

"Only with you . . ." I mumbled. Michel pulled the duvet tightly round us and then rocked me gently to and fro. "Now let's get a good night's sleep, close to each other. You've got to stay close to me tonight."

"OK," I whispered hoarsely, although everything in me was screaming for distance. I felt his body relax and listened to his heavy breathing, which changed to gentle snoring. I knew that once again I wouldn't sleep a wink.

The glowing red figures on our alarm showed it was three-thirty in the morning. My thoughts were still racing at full speed. All my dinner club friends had been in the frame as suspects, even my own husband, although in his case I couldn't think of a single motive and knew for certain that he would never be able to hurt anyone. One question kept nagging at me: why had Angela refused so suddenly to take Babette into her house, when she had previously agreed to? I was increasingly convinced that the answer to that question was connected with everything that had happened. There was a secret, another secret that Angela had not wanted to share with me, or Babette, however hard she tried to give the impression of sincerity and honesty. There was only one way of finding out what it was. And for that I would have to eat very humble pie.

31

Angela opened the door in her ice-blue tennis outfit and was startled when she saw it was me.

"Karen," she said, pressing her lips together as she stood in the doorway. "What brings you here?"

She surveyed me from head to toe as if I were a filthy, mangy stray dog. I wanted to melt into thin air. When I asked if I could come in, her small grey eyes opened wide as if I had made an indecent proposal.

"I'm not sure I'm so keen on that idea . . ."

She stood feet astride and crossed her arms. I burst out laughing; it was a nervous, hiccupping giggle.

"God, Angela, please let's stop this idiotic behaviour. I want to talk to you, and I think you ought to give me a chance."

She sighed and took a step back.

"OK. But I haven't got long: I'm playing tennis with Patricia at ten-thirty."

From the living room came the sound of a vacuum cleaner. Angela went ahead of me and asked her cleaner to vacuum upstairs. The shy woman squeezed past me apologetically and made for the stairs.

"Right, I might as well make a cappuccino . . ."

"Lovely," I said.

She came back with two perfect cappuccinos and sat down opposite me in the black leather armchair.

I rubbed my hands together; they were frozen.

"Angela, I've come to say that I think it's a terrible

shame the way things have turned out. I feel really bad about it. I'm not sleeping, and I'm brooding the whole time. I miss you all . . . Unfortunately I can't turn the clock back, but I hope it will help if I say I'm sorry."

A triumphant look came into her eyes.

"So you admit you were in the wrong?"

"Yes."

"Well . . ."

"I can't remember exactly what I said to the police, but obviously it was incriminating enough. It was never my intention to betray anyone. I'm sorry. I'd really like to patch things up with all of you."

I raised my hand in the air in apology.

"I should have kept my mouth shut, but I was terribly confused by Hanneke's accident, so soon after Evert – who wasn't? As a result I said things I didn't mean."

Angela shot a suspicious glance at me.

"Don't you think it would be better to say this to Patricia and Simon?"

I replied softly that she was right, but that I was still too embarrassed and that I'd always been able to talk to her. That was why I'd come to her first. She slowly thawed.

"Do you know, Angela, you're different? I don't know how to put it into words. I've always felt safe with you: there's more depth to you than the others. At any rate you're not so quick to pass judgement. That's why I think you're the only one who can help me."

A cautious smile appeared on her severe face.

"I simply try to be open with everyone. I believe everyone deserves a second chance, and that includes you. For that matter, I think what you are doing now is very good. I really think you've grown as a person, to be able to do this."

That's how easy it was with narcissistic friendships.

At last I knew how it worked: it was bartering compliments. I put out my hand and made eye contact with her. My eyes even grew moist. She took my hand and looked at me forgivingly.

"It's OK. Let's forgive and forget, and let's look to the future from now on. And please don't start crying."

I shook my head and blinked my tears away dramatically.

"You're right. We've got to get on with our lives. That's what I want too. It's just . . ." I fell silent and lowered my head. Angela slid forward and put her cappuccino on the table.

"What? Come on. Tell me."

"There's something that keeps bugging me. I can't get it out of my head. It's probably my fault. It's Babette: I think I'm beginning to understand why you didn't want her in your house."

"Oh God," she murmured. "I thought she'd behave at your place and not try it on with you."

I tried to suppress my astonishment and act as if I knew exactly what she was talking about.

"Perhaps you should have warned me."

"Damn," she said, and her face darkened again. She wound her finger nervously through her hair, looking gravely at me.

"I thought about it, but it didn't seem right. She'd just been widowed . . . and she'd barely survived a fire. That's why at first I felt we should look after her, but the closer the moment got, the more afraid I became. After all I'd been through it with her once before, it caused me a lot of pain. Kees swore to me that it would never happen again, that he had learned his lesson, but I didn't dare take the risk. And then I thought: she'll be better off with Karen. Michel is as loyal as the day is long. My Kees likes the ladies, he likes talking to them and likes flirting with them. I know that, and it's fine by me, but there are limits. For me at least, for Babette obviously not."

"How do you mean?"

"Surely you remember she was in and out of here the whole time just after Evert had been admitted? And I went into hospital for a few days for that knee operation? Babette cooked for Kees and the children. Well, that's when it happened. I found out because I discovered a message from her on his telephone, saying she had liked it so much and was wondering why he was suddenly ignoring her. I confronted him with it, and he admitted it at once. So did she for that matter. It didn't mean anything, he said. He had taken her home, and she had felt so unhappy and so lonely at the thought of having to go in alone, she was completely beside herself. Kees went in with her and put on some tea, comforted her, and well, one thing led to another."

Her rage seemed to flare up again.

"I was so angry with her. And I still am, sometimes!" she fumed.

I thought of Babette saying that she could not bear to think of touching some other, strange body, and I felt the anger taking hold of me too.

"Why did you never tell me this before?"

"I think you sort these things out in private. Once it's out in the open, your marriage really goes down the drain. Everyone sticks their nose in."

"That's why you stayed friends with her," I said.

"Take a word of advice from me, Karen. Hysterical scenes don't get you anywhere. Maintaining your friendship, at least for the outside world, is the best way of keeping someone like that away from your man. When the cat's away, the mice will play. If you dump them both, you're giving them carte blanche to continue with their sleazy goings-on. Stay in there is my motto."

I covered my face with my hands and shook my head.

"What am I to do now, Angela? What kind of woman is she, who lives in my house, sits at my kitchen table and perhaps . . .?"

"Is fucking your husband? You know, men like pathetic women: it gives them a feeling of power. She's very good at exploiting that. But do you think she'd have done it if your Michel had been a bus driver? No way."

I was glad when she looked at her watch and said we had to bring our conversation to an end. I had an urgent need for some fresh air. We went to the hall together and put on our coats. This woman, whom for two years I had regarded as a good friend, was now a stranger to me. I was certain that if Michel had been a bus driver, she wouldn't have wanted to know me either.

Angela looked in the mirror and hastily retouched her make-up. Then she took me by the shoulders and gave them a squeeze of encouragement.

"Right, my girl, all the best. And don't you worry, I won't breathe a word."

"Nor will I," I croaked.

"And don't risk your family, it's not worth it. Forgive them, that's the best thing in the long run."

I smiled wanly and got my bike.

There was already a tentative feeling of spring in the air, but the hesitant birdsong, the sound that normally heralded better, warmer and happier times, meant nothing to me now. The talk with Angela had shocked me deeply: Babette had lied to me, and I wondered why.

I pedalled hard. Could Michel really have succumbed to her charms? A few months ago I would have refused to believe this, but now I wasn't certain of anything. It was quite possible, certainly if she had used the "poor little me" line. Michel was a man, and like all men he liked to play the knight in shining armour. She had probably first showered him with compliments. What a good man he was, so sweet, such a perfect father, I should be glad of a man like him. I saw clearly how she must have gone about it, how her wonderful brown eyes filled with tears, how she slowly opened her arms wide and nestled her head against my husband, how her narrow shoulders jerked, how his nose disappeared into her thick, glossy and fragrant hair, how he was overcome by so much grief and beauty, how she raised her head and looked at him helplessly and anxiously, how he wiped her tears away with his thumbs and kissed her comfortingly, how she cautiously opened her mouth, how she left it up to him whether he took advantage of her vulnerability.

I looked at the sky, at the clouds slowly drifting by beyond the bare trees, and I wobbled. Perhaps I was crazy, at the end of my tether, stressed out. Fantasy and reality were dangerously confused in my mind. I had got so worked up that I was now on the verge of a psychosis myself and was seeing everyone as the potential murderer. Like Evert.

In the village I bought a packet of cigarettes and three magazines and then went into the perfume shop. I wasn't looking for anything in particular, I was just wandering around, stopping at the shelves of perfume without seeing anything, putting lipstick on my hand, picking up bottles containing the latest anti-wrinkle serums: I smelled them, put them back, let myself be sprayed by the Shiseido girl with their newest fragrance and was startled when a heavily made-up woman asked if she could help me. "I don't think so," I stammered hazily and fled the shop.

I didn't want to go home, to find Babette at my kitchen table, drinking from my coffee cup, reading my paper or perhaps in my bed with my husband.

I turned into the alley by the church and went to Verdi's.

I saw no one I knew through the window, so I went inside, sat at a table in a corner at the back and ordered a latte and a glass of water. Then I picked up my mobile. There was a voicemail message from Babette. She would be out the whole day today: first in Amsterdam to see her therapist, and then she was going to look at houses with her estate agent.

"Yes, yes," I muttered. Then I opened the text, which turned out to be from Simon.

Tomorrow, 2 p.m., swimming pool suite 342 VdValk Hotel, Akersloot. Be there!!!

I sighed. What a shambles my life was. I rang Dorien. She answered immediately.

"Hey, Karen. You OK?"

"Yes. Uh, not really . . ."

"Any new developments?"

I told her about the talk I'd had with Angela and my date with Simon, puffing away on my cigarette. When I'd finished, there was a moment's silence at the other end.

When she spoke, she sounded severe.

"You're too emotional. Put those emotions aside for a moment, otherwise it'll go pear-shaped."

"We're talking about my husband and a woman who's living in my house."

"Look at what we've got in concrete terms. Those two, Patricia and Angela, went to see Hanneke just before her death. Perhaps Angela was using Babette as a red herring."

"She lied to me, about not being able to bear the thought of touching anyone else."

"That doesn't make her a murderess. Christ, woman, everyone lies about those kinds of things – you too."

"I'll still e-mail you a photo of her. Perhaps you can show it to the owner of the hotel."

"OK, if you want . . ."

"I'm going to Hanneke's house this afternoon: I've still got a key. Perhaps she made other copies of those e-mails, or they're still on her computer. If I can find her password, I can easily get them, and then I can call off the date with Simon."

"Simon and Ivo could just as easily have found those e-mails and deleted them."

"It's worth trying. There must be something."

I looked up and saw Babette heading towards me with a radiant smile. My blood froze.

"I've got to hang up. I'll be in touch."

She kissed me three times. Her cheeks were cold. She took off her coat and had a red sleeveless dress on, ridiculously flimsy for the time of year. Her arms were full of goose pimples. She twirled and asked me what I thought of it. I said it looked divine on her. After that I didn't know what else to say. She stammered that she had arranged to meet the estate agent here. It was time for her to stand on her own feet. She hugged me again and whispered emotionally: "If I hadn't had you. I'm going to pay you back, really. As soon as everything is fixed, and I've got my own house . . ."

I was able to conjure up a smile.

"I was just going," I said. I saw her look at my half-full cup of coffee and the smouldering cigarette in the ashtray.

"Oh. OK . . ." She looked at me quizzically. Then she took my hand.

"Was that him?"

"Who?"

"Simon. On the phone."

"No."

"Hey, Karen, could I have a copy of that letter perhaps? Would you ask Dorien?"

"Certainly."

I had an overwhelming urge to run out of the place but managed to control myself and left calmly, looked around again with a smile and slid my bike key extremely calmly into the lock, turned it, got on my bike and gave a friendly wave as I cycled off. Once I was out of sight, I looked at my watch. It was one-thirty. The children would be out of school in three-quarters of an hour. I must be finished by then.

32

"Hello?" I called. "Hello, Ivo?" I had opened the back door with the key I still had in my possession and was now in the kitchen. The chairs were on the table, and the place smelled of household soap, which had been used to clean the floor. My eyes were drawn to the mantelpiece with the large portrait of Hanneke on it surrounded by candles. I went over to it, kissed my fingers and pressed then against the cold glass.

"Yes?" I turned around, and there stood a woman in a headscarf looking at me expectantly.

"Good afternoon." I put out my hand. "I'm Karen van de Made, a friend of Hanneke's. I've come to collect some things. Mr Smit knows about it."

She picked up her bucket and went on mopping.

"Fine," she muttered, mopping the floor with slow strokes.

Hanneke's room was in chaos. It was as big a mess up there as the ground floor of their house was clean and neat. Books, colour samples and drawings were scattered over her desk, among them a full ashtray and mouldy, congealed half-full cups of coffee. The walls were covered in drawings and photos of Mees and Anna, radiant in a boat, on the beach, in the swimming pool, on Saint Nicholas's lap, surveying a huge pancake, as babies asleep in their cradles, being peacefully breast-fed, their faces covered in ice cream and chocolate, sitting on Ivo's shoulders . . . It broke my heart. I picked out a photo, of the dinner club in Portugal. All in bathing suits, tanned, arms round each other, smiling blissfully. How pleased we had been with each other and with ourselves. I swallowed a few times and popped the photo in my bag. Everything lying here, a rusty pair of secateurs, a stick of lip protector, piles of magazine pieces on home decoration, a couple of lighters, a dish full of shells, a pair of silver high heels, everything reminded me painfully that Hanneke had gone.

I turned on her computer, which made a faint hum, and went through the whole pile of papers next to her printer. Bills, a list of telephone numbers of all the children in Mees's class, tax demands, a travel brochure, an invitation to a home design fair, a birth announcement. I stuffed an unopened envelope from the telephone company into my bag and turned my attention to the computer. I clicked on the mail icon and opened her mailbox. She had 145 new messages, mainly e-mails offering penis enlargements, Viagra, Xanax, loans and blind dates, reactions to quotations, confirmations from contractors, kitchen and bathroom companies and in addition four fairly desperate-sounding messages from someone called Mo.

You're not responding to the forum anymore and you're always offline . . . I'm worried about you. Just let me know how you are. I'm thinking of you and I know what you're going through.
XMO

Han, please let me hear from you! I saw the announcement of the death in the paper. Was that your love? How awful. I'm there for you. I can also come to you. XXX

211

Tried to call your mobile. Where are you? How are you?
Please, if you don't want to have any more to do with us,
just say. We've been through so much together . . . Let me
at least know why you're not responding.

This is my last message. I'll go on thinking about you
and whatever it is you can always call/e-mail me.
Perhaps you've lost my mobile number. Here it is:
06–43332231. I hope to hear from you at some point,
but I take it that you've changed tack and opted for your
family. We're no use to you with that. I want you to know
I respect your decision. Love and all the best, MO

I hurriedly wrote this Mo's mobile number on an empty envelope and erased all her messages.

"Are you OK?" asked the cleaner. I hadn't heard her come in. She was wearing a bright-red winter coat and was standing with the key in her hand.

"I'm off now. I'll lock up. You have to go."

33

The cleaner cycled off in the opposite direction. I watched her go till she was a red dot and then cycled off over the crunching gravel, down the long, lonely road through the polder. Relieved that I had at least found something, I breathed in the smell of silage, the rural smell that would always be associated in my memory with Hanneke, clutched my bag under my arm and pedalled on hard.

At first the deep growling sound did not impinge upon me, I was in such a hurry. I was determined to stop Babette collecting my children from school. But suddenly I realized I was being followed by something that sounded more like a truck than a car. I looked round. A large, brand-new Range Rover loomed up behind me swerving dangerously, and flashing its headlights. I couldn't see who was at the wheel.

"Fuck," I panted. "Fuck!" I pedalled on, so fast that my thighs and lungs were on fire. My mobile rang and for some strange reason that sound made me even more anxious. Someone was trying to reach me while I was about to be murdered. And I couldn't do a thing. I could pedal as hard as I liked, but I could never outrun that car. I could grab my mobile, but I would be dead before I could call for help. The roar of the engine was right behind me. There was a furious beeping of the horn and the screech of brakes: "Please . . . please . . ." Then I jerked my handlebars round and bumped along across the wet grass. Reed stalks cut my face, scraped my arms and legs, the smell of tar and rotting leaves rose up, and slowly the stinking water crept into my boots, my trousers and my sleeves. There was a thud and then a gurgling sound. I clawed at the reed stalks with my hands and opened my mouth, which filled with the sweet, sandy water, as did my nose. I kicked and thrashed around, my head rose above the water, and I squealed like a stuck pig. Someone swore, called me a stupid cow and pulled me roughly out of the water by my armpits.

"If you don't stop this hysterical nonsense right away, I'm going to hit you."

I looked up, straight into the face of a flushed, cursing Ivo.

Dripping and sobbing, I sat at the edge of the ditch with Ivo's leather jacket wrapped round me, while he pulled my bike out of the water, swearing all the while.

"Look what you've done to me! My shoes are ruined . . . Have you gone crazy or what?"

My teeth wouldn't stop chattering. I was shivering all over, and my jaws were so stiff with cold that I couldn't get a word out. Ivo's dog licked my face and sat next to me quietly wheezing and wagging his tail.

"Come on," said Ivo, standing severely in front of me. "You'll just have to pick the bike up yourself, later."

He put out his hand and hoisted me to my feet. He went to his car, placed a piece of plastic over the seat and patted it to indicate I could sit down. Ivo grabbed my legs and began tugging at my boots. When they eventually came off with a squelch, ditchwater gushed out. Then he pulled my socks off, squeezed them and stuffed them into a plastic bag, together with my boots. His thoughtfulness touched me. He slammed the door shut, walked round the car opened the back flap for the dog, sat next to me and started the engine, avoiding looking at me. He put the car into reverse, backed out, turned the wheel impatiently and drove onto the road, back towards his house.

"You've got a nerve, forcing your way into my house after all that's happened," he said angrily, his eyes fixed to the road, "and then taking off like a thief in the night. What's wrong with you, Karen?"

He looked at me for the first time. His eyes were tired and sad.

"I could ask you the same thing," I replied, my teeth still chattering; Ivo turned the blower to full.

"Driving up behind me like an idiot. I thought you were going to kill me. I didn't know it was you, did I?"

"I'd ordered this car for Hanneke . . ." He seemed to cringe as he spoke her name and started to whisper.

"I'd forgotten all about it, can you believe it? Who remembers a new car when his wife dies?"

He stroked the dashboard lovingly.

"Then yesterday they rang. Your car's ready. At first I didn't want to go and collect it. We picked it together, Hanneke and I. She loved this white upholstery so much, with walnut trim. So South of France."

I showered till my skin glowed red, and all the fine ditch sand – which was everywhere, in my hair, nose and ears, between my toes and under my nails, and even grinding between my teeth – had disappeared down the drain. Then I dried myself off in front of the tall, unforgiving mirror and surveyed my battered body and face. A deep gash ran along my cheek towards my eye, and a number of more superficial wheals. Along my left side too and across my belly there were red stripes. My heart was still beating as if a murderer was on my trail and there was also fear in my eyes. I carefully smeared calendula cream on my wounds and then held the pile of clothes that Ivo had put out for me to my nose in the hope of catching some trace of Hanneke, but all I could smell was water softener. I donned her smooth, black Björn Borg panties, which were a little tight, as were her jeans, put on her close-fitting white T-shirt and then her red cashmere sweater, which tickled the back of my neck, and looked at myself in the mirror again. Again the thought that I would never see her again hit me like a blow. Whatever happened, whatever I did, whatever truth came to light, it wouldn't bring her back, although occasionally I felt subconsciously that it might. She was drifting further and further away from me. Her smell had already gone from her clothes. In a little while the clothes themselves would have been disposed of. Her children would forget what she looked like, the sound of her voice, how she smelled, what she sang, what she liked. At a certain moment the manner of her death would no longer even matter. I hugged myself and closed my eyes. I hoped and prayed that there was some beautiful afterlife and that she was there, with Evert.

"Keep them," muttered Ivo, pointing to Hanneke's clothes. I stroked the sweater and said I was very pleased with it. He took a bottle of beer out of the fridge, opened it and put it to his mouth. Then he sat on the draining board and gave me a piercing look.

"What are you up to, Karen? What were you doing here?"

"Actually I came for your cleaner," I began, "and then I realized that there were still a lot of things of mine lying around here. Some books and CDs, my

Discman. I thought, why don't I take them while I'm here . . .?"

Ivo cleared his throat, took another big swig of beer, jumped off the draining board and went to the pantry, from where he returned with my sodden bag.

"I didn't find any books, CDs or a Discman in here, but I did find a telephone bill of my wife's!"

In a fury he threw the bag on the table. I flinched, as all my things flew over the floor.

"Why?" he shouted, pointing at me, his nostrils flared. "A bloodsucker, that's what you are! You need to see a shrink!"

"Ivo, please," I said softly. "I can understand that you're angry . . ."

"Angry? Furious, you mean! Looking behind my back for . . . for what actually? What are you so desperate to prove? Why are you so determined to drag our marriage through the dirt?"

He paced restlessly to and fro, stroking his short-cropped hair.

"Hanneke screwed Evert: everyone knows that by now, thanks to you. But what good does it do you to raise doubts about their deaths, spread insinuations? Does even more have to be destroyed?"

He hit the kitchen unit next to me with the flat of his hand. I turned my head away and heard him breathing heavily through his nose. I tried to swallow my fear.

"Don't you have any doubts?" I asked cautiously, cowering, bracing myself for another outburst.

"No," he said gruffly, more to himself than to me. He picked at the label of his beer bottle and stared at the ground. "She hadn't been herself for months, and after the fire it was as if she were slowly drowning in her grief. If I blame anyone, it's myself. I couldn't bear to see her mourning someone else so deeply, scarcely noticing the children, tucked away in her study smoking all day long. I was just angry at her, whereas, if I'd been open about it . . . I'd have tried harder to talk to her . . ."

His eyes filled with tears, which he brushed away with an angry gesture. I put my hand on his arm, but he shook it off.

"There's no point. You've got to stop this, Karen. Look to the future, please. It's in everyone's best interest. Focus on your husband and children: they need you. Don't worry about the past: what matters is your family and the future. If anyone has learned that lesson the hard way, it's me."

"How do you mean?"

"I mean I should have forgiven her instead of constantly punishing her. If I had, she might still be here. But I wouldn't listen to her."

It hurt me to see him blaming himself for Hanneke's death. I would have liked to take him in my arms and whisper in his ear that it wasn't his fault, that he had been a good, loving husband to her and that his reaction to her affair with Evert was only natural, but I knew he did not want to share his pain with me. Without a word I picked up my keys, my dripping wet purse and my mobile off the draining board and put them in my bag. "I know you hate me now," I said in a hoarse voice, "but I want to tell you I feel for you. And whatever happens, or has happened, you can always count on me for help. Go ahead and direct your anger at me, if that helps, but believe me, everything I do, I do for love of Hanneke, the same as you."

He did not look up when I put my hand on his shoulder.

"Just leave us alone. That's all the help I want from you," he said.

"OK," I replied, and taking hold of the big plastic bag containing my clothes, I swung my wet handbag over my shoulder, said goodbye and went through the door. Only when I got outside did I realize I was swaying with giddiness.

34

I saw them all sitting round the table drinking hot chocolate, while my girls talked animatedly to Babette, who was plaiting Annabelle's hair. A wave of nauseous disgust swept through me. I could no longer bear to watch how she tended my children with her poisonous tentacles.

Babette gave me a strange look when I came in looking dishevelled in Hanneke's clothes and carried my daughters off upstairs. I just managed to squeeze out a smile and announce that they had promised to clear up their rooms and that I was going to work upstairs.

Of course she came after me. She put her arm round me and asked if I was OK. What I was doing in Hanneke's clothes? How had I got that scratch on my face? I shrugged my shoulders and said the clothes had been hanging in my wardrobe, and I had suddenly had a great urge to put them on, and had walked into a branch in the garden. She didn't press me any further. She hung around me like a lapdog until I asked her to go away. I said I wanted to do some things on the computer, and she left slowly.

I rummaged in my bag and fished out my mobile. Water was dripping out of it and the screen was grey. Everything had gone. Dorien's number, Simon's, his message, everything. I couldn't reply to Simon, and Dorien couldn't help me if I got into difficulties. Wearily I laid my head next to the keyboard and tried to control my feeling of panic a little by breathing deeply.

The envelope on which I had written Mo's number was still in my bag. Although the writing was soaked and blurred, I could still decipher it. With trembling fingers I keyed in the numbers on my work telephone. Mo answered almost at once. There was a background hiss, from which I concluded she was in the car. I gave my name and said I was a friend of Hanneke Lemstra. She had to think for a moment. Her voice sounded nice, if rather high-pitched and rasping.

"You e-mail her," I said, which was followed by silence. When she spoke again, she seemed to be on her guard.

"OK. Now I get it: you mean Han64. That's what she called herself in the forum. We were in intensive contact for a while, but not for the past few weeks."

I realized that she did not know Hanneke was dead and that the news would hit her hard.

"Are you driving?" I asked.

"Yes, but that doesn't matter, I'm phoning hands-free. Tell me, what's the matter with her?"

"I think you should just pull the car over to the side of the road . . ."

"Oh, all right. I can see a petrol station up ahead, I'm turning off . . ."

I listened to the roar of cars and tried to imagine what this Mo looked like. Judging by her voice, she was my age. I heard her brake, turn off the car radio and light up a cigarette.

"I've stopped now," she said. She took a deep drag on her cigarette. "You're frightening me, though."

I spoke falteringly. At the other end of the line there was the occasional cry of horror.

"How awful! How terrible! And I simply thought she didn't want any more to do with us . . . Suicide, you say? That can't be true? I just don't believe it!"

"Sorry to spring the news on you like this," I went on,

"but I have to ask you a few things. You see, I don't believe she committed suicide either."

Another silence. I could hear her sniffing.

"She was so upbeat. She was really an example to us all."

"Who are 'us'?"

"The forum. We know each other through the Internet. Via the relationship forum. We wrote to each other about our problems."

"And what problems were they?"

"Well, I'm not sure if I can tell you just like that . . ."

"I was Hanneke's best friend. Whatever you tell me will remain between us."

"You may say that, but you could be from the police. At any rate, I'm not going to testify, not under any circumstances."

"I promise I'll never trouble you again after this."

"I'm not sure . . ."

Deep rage welled up in me.

"Listen, I think Hanneke was murdered. You're the only person who can help me, who can tell me what she was involved with before she died."

She sighed and blew her nose audibly.

"Hanneke had an affair," she began.

"I'd got that far myself."

"We met when she responded to my appeal in the forum. She wanted to contact women like me who loved two men. We supported each other. You know, it's so difficult leading a secret life alongside your day-to-day one, not being able to share your feelings with anyone without being condemned or betrayed. On the Internet we could talk to each other, cry, and give each other advice day and night."

"How long ago is it since she responded to your appeal?"

"About six months. Her affair didn't last all that long. He ended it after a month. I assume you know her lover is dead too?"

"Yes," I said. "I knew him well. Why did he end the affair?"

"They were found out. Someone had seen them together and told his wife. He immediately opted for his marriage, although his wife, if I'm to believe Han, is a dreadful person."

"What did Hanneke say about her?"

I looked over my shoulder at the door. It was shut.

"The weirdest thing she told us was that he had to pay his own wife for sex. She belittled him and took him to the cleaners financially. Those are her words, not mine. To tell the truth, I thought all the things she said went a bit far. I mean, a woman abusing her husband seems a bit farfetched."

"Abusing?"

An anxious feeling came over me. I was suddenly no longer sure if I wanted to hear all this, if I wanted to know. If you dig deep enough, you'll find shit everywhere, Michel had said, and there was already quite a stench.

"She talked about it, yes. The wife apparently sometimes hit him, and he did nothing to stop her, for fear of never seeing the children again, but also because he had a reputation to keep up. But I'm not so sure: a man is so much stronger . . . What kind of wimp lets himself be beaten up by his own wife?"

"That's probably exactly the reaction he was afraid of."

"I must say I had a funny feeling when I heard he was dead. Hanneke just wrote: 'There's been a disaster. My love is dead.' We were all shocked, partly because she was so often worried about him."

"That forum of yours, can I still find it on the Internet?"

"Sure. At www.relationships-online.nl, under the heading 'Two loves'."

I typed in the URL.

"Thanks, Mo, for your frankness. I'll take a look."

"I want to remain anonymous. I'm married with three children. If you need to know anything else, ask me via Hotmail. You'll find my address at the forum."

"I understand. Thanks, and all the best."

"You too."

I surfed through the messages, amazed that there were so many women with two loves who still found time to chat endlessly about it. I found Hanneke, or Han64, in the message archive. I scrolled through to her very first message.

Dear Mo,

I have 2 loves in my life too at this moment. I've been married to 1 for 8 years, the other I've known for 2 years. He's a friend of my husband's and his wife is a friend of mine. Complicated, you see. I'll call him no2 for convenience. Our relationship became more serious when he was admitted to hospital because of a severe burnout. I was once admitted myself, as a student, so I knew better than anyone what he was going through, how lonely and misunderstood you feel, how terrible it is when friends start avoiding you and stare at you as if you've turned into a monkey. I wanted to support him and be there for him, because back then there had been no one there for me.

To cut a long story short, something grew between us, our conversations became more and more intense and familiar and it soon emerged that we were both stuck in difficult marriages that we could not talk to anyone about. Our other friends all have perfect relationships, from the outside at least, and they all like to put on a perfect front. When there are problems, no one wants to know, I've noticed.

Since no2 has been back home, our relationship has become sexual. The desire was great, we both longed for true, passionate love, and my feelings for him are so huge and powerful . . .

I feel terribly guilty about this relationship, and yet I cannot bring myself to end it. I've never been so happy and at the same time unhappy. I live for the stolen moments we have together and between times I want him so badly that it hurts.

Perhaps we were both looking for excitement or consolation, I don't know. The problem remains that we have fallen deeply in love, which is forbidden. It's not allowed. I don't want to hurt my no1 and more importantly I want to spare my children this misery. And no2 made it plain long ago that he will never leave his wife, because he can't live without his children.

I could go on typing for hours, but that will do no one any good. Remember I feel for you and you're not the only one.

The tears ran down my cheeks over my hand, which was clapped to my mouth. It was as if Hanneke were talking to me, as if she were still there, not physically, but her words were floating in cyberspace, she had left me something after all. True, not intentionally, and well hidden, but I had found her words, and they had touched me deeply. I was one of those friends with apparently perfect relationships, who had been deaf to her problems. I ran my clammy hands through my hair and hunted through my memories, but I knew for sure that she had never tried to talk to me about her problems with Ivo. Nor did I know that she had been admitted to hospital herself.

Well, so it's happened. We've been caught. Someone who calls themselves a friend saw us together and told his wife. All hell let loose, especially at his place. We've spoken to each other for just 10 minutes on the phone and he was completely freaked out. She scratched him, hit him, kicked him, swore at him and threatened he'll never see his sons again. Go ahead and hit me back, she shouted, then I'll have even more reason to divorce you. How can he love someone like that, choose a hysterical bitch like that over me? I said he should go to the police, but according to him there's no point. He thinks he's in the wrong and for the time being he doesn't want to see me or speak to me. He's now determined to do all he can to save his marriage, he said, and then I got angry, stupid cow that I am. He cried and said there was no other way, that he could never be happy in the knowledge that he had destroyed two families. And that's true of course, damn it. But my God, how it hurts. I'll stop now, as it seems she's on her way. I keep going to the loo the whole time, I'm so nervous.

Bye for now.

. . .

God what a crisis. Talked all night with no1, yelled, cried. No2 was here with his wife and we had a decent conversation. When other people are around she behaves like the most empathetic, sweetest wife there is . . .

No1 has now shut himself away in his study. He feels so deceived. It is dreadful to see how much it's hurting him. It breaks my heart. For the first time in months I have some sort of feeling for him, but now he rejects me. I don't know if this will ever come right. I'm frightened I shall soon find myself alone. My no1 is mainly worried that the whole village will get to know. I've promised him not to talk to anyone about it.

. . .

We haven't been in touch for a month now and I still check every hour to see if there's a message on my mobile. When will this restlessness be over? It's driving me mad. We only see each other these days when other people are present, and I have the feeling that everyone is watching us. He's not in good shape, I can see that. He's so withdrawn, he drinks a lot and makes trouble. I think his wife is taking her revenge. She's trying to seduce all our men. It just makes you sick that no one can see what she's really like. I don't dare say anything: I'm frightened she'll hurt him even more if I do. I can't understand it anymore. Now they're suddenly going to move . . . She's got something up her sleeve, I just feel it. I'm scared and alone. Fortunately I have all of you.

. . .

There's been a disaster. My love is dead.

That was her last message. I exited and clicked on the MSN icon with my mouse. There I entered hannekelemstra@hotmail.com and tried various passwords. At the fifth attempt I got through; her password turned out to be just her home address.

There are no messages in this folder

it said on screen. All her incoming and outgoing messages had been deleted. Someone had beaten me to it.

227

35

I don't remember how I got through that evening, how I sat there at the table with Babette, Michel and the children, while my head felt as if a swarm of bees were raging through it. I managed to smile now and again, to chew on a piece of steak, to swallow it despite fierce resistance from my tightening throat and to act as if I were listening to the children's enthusiastic school stories. When Michel touched me, I jumped as if I'd had an electric shock, and whenever I looked at Babette, I was filled with revulsion. At any rate it was clear that this woman must leave my house: her presence was like an infectious, lethal virus. But it was impossible to arrange things that very evening without awakening suspicion.

I inquired as casually as possible about her appointment with the estate agent, and she sighed and replied that it was so difficult finding a nice house to let that met her requirements. She had had such a wonderful place. She had always thought she would grow old in that house. Again she threw her tears into the fray, as she summed up everything that had been so wonderful about it: sitting together by the fire, waking up and looking out over the woods, her cosy kitchen, where we had had so many parties.

Shut your trap, I thought, spare me this play-acting. But Michel went along with it one hundred per cent and after the third wine was crying too.

I poured water in my wine. I wanted to stay sober. I

used a headache as an excuse, and that was no lie. I cleared the table, put the dirty dishes in the dish-washer, washed the pans, shut out the conversation that Michel and Babette were having and said I was going upstairs with the children. Once there I ran the bath, settled the children in front of the TV and looked for Dorien Jager's visiting card. I had realized I must still have it. I called her on Michel's mobile and told her all about Hanneke's messages on the Internet. She promised to look and said that, sadly, it still didn't prove anything.

"Evert was admitted to hospital, sectioned. We can't prove that he was actually mistreated. It could just as well be a psychotic fantasy. Mail me a photo of her, and I'll take it to the hotel owner this evening. I can tell you now that she has no criminal record, that's all been checked."

She said I must be careful and also be on my guard against Simon.

"Dorien?" I asked to drag out our conversation, to postpone the lonely anxious night that lay ahead of me. "Perhaps I should stop this, accept the situation. Sometimes I don't know anymore who I'm doing this for. For Hanneke, yes, and for you . . ."

"For yourself, Karen. You're doing it for yourself. *You're* not corrupt."

We hung up, and there I sat, on our bed, numb and shivering with nerves, with Michel's mobile in my hand. I pressed "Menu" and then "Messages". For the first time in my life I was checking up on my husband. The inbox was empty.

The knot in my stomach was throbbing painfully against my midriff. I threw the phone away and buried my head in his pillow, breathed in the familiar smell of his hair, his skin, his sleep and cried for us.

After I had more or less pulled myself together, I put the children into the warm, foaming bath. I washed their backs, their flaxen hair, felt their loose teeth and counted the new bruises they'd acquired in the playground. Then I dried their thin little bodies, one by one, tickled them and stuck my nose in their damp necks. They put their pyjamas on, and they were allowed to sleep all four in one room. The boys dragged their mattresses doggedly into the girls' room, while we moved the dolls' house aside, after which they all crawled under a single duvet and I read to them from a children's book. I would have liked to stay here, with these rosy, innocent children, lock the door and wait among the Barbies and baby-dolls until it was all over.

Three o'clock came, and I was still not asleep. I had meanwhile convinced myself that it was a conspiracy: everyone had a hand in the murders of Evert and Hanneke, who had been eliminated because they were dissidents, resisting the power that Simon exerted over us. He had a finger in everyone's pie, our success was his success, but if he pulled the plug, everything would burst like a bubble.

Outside the wind developed into yet another westerly gale. A heavy hailstorm rattled against the windows. I was cold, despite my pyjamas, the thick duvet and a warm, snoring man beside me. The cold came from inside: my blood had turned to ice water. I was so frightened of the thoughts that were bombarding me that I could scarcely breathe. I had to get out of this bed: I couldn't lie next to Michel for another minute. If it was a conspiracy, then he was in it too. Perhaps he had opposed this plan but ultimately could not help agreeing. I looked at his peacefully sleeping, rumpled face, the face of my husband, the father of Annabelle and Sophie, and felt as if it was a stranger lying there. Carefully, I crept out from under the duvet, slid my ice-cold feet into slippers and threw a dressing gown round my shoulders. Michel turned over and went on snoring. I tiptoed to the door, left the bedroom and crept down the stairs, panting the whole time as if something was hard on my heels.

The kitchen smelled stuffy, and it was freezing cold. My teeth were chattering; I put the oven on and opened the oven door. Then I got a small saucepan from the cupboard, into which I poured a splash of milk, all the while brooding, incapable of bringing my thoughts under control or giving them direction. When the milk boiled I poured it into a large beaker, added a dash of cognac and sat down shivering in the wave of warmth emanating from the oven.

I forced myself to think everything through again, step by step, starting with the e-mail that Evert had sent to Hanneke. It had been a completely normal, rational message. Nothing indicated that Evert wanted to die or was psychotic, or that he intended to do his family any harm. What did become clear was that he was in a conflict with Simon and that he couldn't win. I drank a mouthful of the warm milk. The alcohol gave me a pleasant burning sensation in my throat. Babette had been near enough to Evert to switch his pills and drug her children and herself.

I took Michel's cigarettes off the mantelpiece, turned on the extractor hood and lit one. I inhaled deeply and looked at Babette's gold hairclip, which lay in front of me on the draining board. Why should she take such huge risks?

I forget how long I sat there by the oven smoking,

enjoying the warmth slowly flowing back into my bones. Thoughts and memories confirming my theory tumbled over each other in my head, and it was impossible to go back to sleep. I was on my own, but that didn't matter. It was actually a wonderful feeling to think for myself again, not to be directed by Michel or the dinner club. I suddenly understood too why Hanneke had fled to a hotel, because I had the same impulse to go away, to hide till I had thought of a solution or had found proof. The hardest thing would be to go on acting as normally as possible.

I was getting up to put another dash of cognac in my milk, which had gone cold, when I heard faint footsteps on the gravel path. It was a quarter to five, I could see from the clock on the oven. Not exactly the hour for visitors and still far too early for the paper delivery. Babette and Michel were asleep. The footsteps came closer and seemed to be heading straight for the kitchen door. There was no longer any point in running away or hiding. Whoever was walking outside would see me. My heart pounded loudly, and my chest began to hurt. If this was it, if someone had come to get me, I would defend myself, I knew: I felt capable of using force. I shuffled to the knife block and grasped the cold, plastic handle of the kitchen knife. I would stab. Someone put a key in the lock and pushed up the handle. The door slowly swung open, and I could stand it no longer. My yell seemed to come from somewhere else, not from my own tense, panicking body.

"Fuck off!" I screamed. "Fuck off, or I'll call the police!"

With a trembling hand I pulled the knife out of the block. In the doorway stood Babette, wrapped in a beige raincoat over her white satin pyjamas. Wet hair was clinging to her face, which was red and blotchy. She stared at me, fearful and astonished.

Her breath was wheezing, which made her sound like an animal at bay. Michel had charged into the kitchen without pulling on a pair of underpants and stood there between us stark naked with his hair sticking up and groggy with sleep. I was trembling from head to toe and couldn't get a single word out.

"Sorry. Sorry, Sorry," squeaked Babette, also trembling, her eyes flashing from me to Michel.

"Christ almighty. Have you two gone completely mad?" Michel was panting too. From the hall came the patter of children's feet and anxious crying.

"You're delicious!" whispered Michel in my ear, and he ran to the children but realized half way that he was stark naked. He grabbed my fake fur coat, put it round his shoulders and took care of the four children, who were sitting crying their eyes out on the stairs.

"Karen? Sorry. I didn't want to give you a fright. I didn't see you . . ."

Babette put out a trembling hand to me. I was still pressed against the draining board, the knife in my hands. I looked at the gleaming, sharp blade and realized it was probably long enough to have gone right through her if I had thrust – and I would have if necessary. The powerful wave of aggression that surged through me when the door opened had completely blinded me, and for a moment I had lost my grip and wanted to kill her or whoever it was who had come to threaten my family – finish them off. I could no longer claim I would never hurt a fly. I had felt evil, the almost orgiastic thrill of it, and obviously I was an infinitely worse person than I had ever imagined.

I laid the knife on the draining board and looked severely at Babette.

"Where have you been? It's five in the morning, for Christ's sake . . ."

"I couldn't sleep, sorry."

She lowered her eyes and fiddled with the belt of her raincoat.

"But surely you don't go out on a night like this? It's blowing a gale out there!"

"I drove around for a bit. I just had to get out, I was going mad. My head was too full, and . . ." Her voice fell to a whisper. "I keep thinking of what you said about Evert's letter to Hanneke, that he didn't sound like someone who wanted to die . . . That really got through to me, but it also brought something up. Something that was already there, a thought I found so terrifying that I kept pushing it away. It's terrible, it's disgusting, but it's also quite logical. I think you're right."

The children trooped bashfully into the kitchen with their tear-stained faces to give us a kiss and to see if all was well. Sophie and Annabelle both put their arms round my neck.

"We thought someone was coming to murder us, Mum!" I stroked their skinny backs.

"Of course they weren't! Mummy was just frightened by Babette, and Babette was frightened by Mummy. No one's coming to murder us, no one at all. You've got a very strong Daddy and a very strong Mummy, so there's no need to be frightened!"

Beau and Luuk leaned against their mother, as pale as ghosts. Babette kissed them and urged them to go back to bed. All four of them trotted calmly back upstairs with Michel.

"You think I'm right. What about?" I asked hesitantly.

234

Babette whispered in an ominously soft voice.

"If Evert was murdered, if that fire was an attack on our family, then only one person could have done it: Hanneke."

"No," I murmured, "no, I don't believe it."

"Wait, listen." She touched my shoulder cautiously. "Evert had broken off with her. She was at her wit's end. You know that she drank a lot, certainly for the last few months, and that she wasn't in good shape. She had a motive, and she had access to our house . . . A week later she committed suicide. It's so obvious that I find it odd the police didn't investigate the possibility."

I could scarcely bear her touch, her words, her proximity.

"Let's go to bed. We're so tired that we'll start saying very strange things."

"Why did I have to listen to you all yesterday evening and you now refuse to listen to me?" Her nostrils flared, and she looked at me petulantly.

"Tomorrow," I said, "we'll talk some more tomorrow," and I shuffled upstairs. I lay awake until I was certain she had also gone to her room.

36

I drove frantically around the car park of the motel, my hands so moist that I had scarcely any grip on the steering wheel, looking for a parking space where my car would not be immediately recognized. I felt sick with nerves. My stomach was grumbling and rumbling, and I was sweating like a pig.

I reversed into a parking spot, almost hitting the side of the car next to me, opened my compact and looked again at my frightened face, like a battered rabbit in the glare of the headlamps. I pinched my cheeks to conjure up a bit of colour, put some gloss on my lips, sprayed some more perfume into my black silk blouse, which was clammy with sweat and sticking to me, put some chewing gum in my mouth and started chewing on it impatiently. My mobile was broken, and I hadn't been able to reach Dorien again. I could only hope she would be there.

In the old fashioned wood-panelled lobby there was a bustle of chattering business people, shuffling elderly guests, exhausted mothers pushing laden buggies and the occasional timid-looking couple presumably out for some extramarital sex. Families and groups were being welcomed with large signs and directed to the various rooms, but nowhere was there a sign pointing the way to the individual suites. So there was nothing for it but to ask the girl at reception: something I dreaded. I tried to make myself invisible, as far as that was possible in the harshly lit, open lobby, and at the same time not to appear too obviously nervous. The man in front of me checked in, while telephoning someone to say he was forced to stay at least another day in London, winking at me in a gesture of complicity. I blushed.

When the receptionist asked in a friendly voice how she could help me, I blushed even more deeply and had to clear my throat before I could get the question out. She said brightly that Mr Simons had already checked in and gave me directions, without asking for my name or passport. I suppressed the urge to concoct some elaborate excuse why I had arranged to meet him here: she had probably heard all the excuses before. I walked behind the tubs of exotic palms towards the disappointingly grey, shabby corridor and kept repeating in my mind what I had to do and say, although images of us making love became more and more intrusive.

I knocked, gently at first, then louder. I heard music: Herman Brood. I banged on the door. Simon's shirt was hanging open, and he was stroking his flat belly, running his fingers through the wayward black hair on his chest. His dark, longish hair hung over his eyes. He reached out to the cut on my cheek; we said nothing. For the first time he looked lonely and vulnerable. His head lay heavily on the back of my neck, and he murmured my name. I pushed the door shut. We stood there for minutes on end, silent and sighing, stroking each other's tense back, until Simon broke free, took my head in his hands and kissed me on the lips. It moved me, because it felt like a farewell. His hypnotic blue eyes were bloodshot and looked frenzied, and I could smell that he had been drinking.

"I'll have one too," I said, pointing to the bottle of Stolichnaya on the fake walnut table. Simon went over to it and poured me a glass. The room was spacious, with a king-size bed in the middle, covered with a synthetic pink bedspread, but the swimming pool was so small it was scarcely worthy of the name. Two teak deckchairs made the illusion of luxury complete, and I wondered if anyone ever sat in them.

"Don't you think this is great?" Simon asked with a laugh, waving his glass round.

"Fabulous," I said, thinking that it was actually a vulgar, kitschy set-up and, if I had been here with Michel, I could have had a good laugh about it.

Simon sat down on the swaying waterbed and patted the place next to him. "God, Karen, I'm glad you're here," he sighed, all the while looking at the floor. His attitude disturbed me. This wasn't the Simon I knew, full of daring and self-confidence. I sat down next to him, and he laid his hand on my knee, picked at my skirt and sighed again. He was sitting there as if weighed down by some huge burden.

"Are you having second thoughts?" I asked tentatively and swirled the vodka round in my glass before downing it in one.

"No," he replied. "Yes and no, I don't know. There's so much going on . . . I'm not relaxed. Sorry."

"Why's that?"

I looked at him, at the tiny wrinkles round his eyes, his heavy eyebrows, his jaw muscles, his wonderful full lips with their sensual curves, and I felt a burning desire making my body go weak. I resisted the feeling: I must keep my head.

Simon let himself fall back and looked at me expectantly, perhaps hoping that I would take the initiative.

"What were you doing at Ivo's?"

238

"He's probably already told you himself."

"Yes. To tell the truth, I was a bit shocked."

"So was I," I said, getting up and refilling our glasses. This was my last glass, to calm me down. After this I must switch to water. Under no circumstances must I lose control of myself. "At him, I mean, at the way he chased after me."

"What are you after, Karen? You could just as well ask straight out, couldn't you? Him, or me . . ." His hand was burning on my back. I stared at his flat, hairy belly. Would it ever fade, this idiotic desire?

I lay down next to him and looked him in the eyes. He returned my gaze with a look of pity.

"OK," I said, "I'll just ask you: do you think Hanneke committed suicide?"

He screwed up his eyes.

"I believe what the police have concluded after a thorough investigation, which is that under the influence of drink and pills she jumped or fell from the balcony."

"The other day you said you were no friend of the police, that you don't trust them . . ."

"In this case we shall have to . . ."

It was almost unbearable to be so close and not kiss each other.

"Why do all of you refuse to see the truth? Why are Patricia and Angela hushing up their visit to Hanneke? Why are you suppressing the e-mail correspondence between Evert and Hanneke? And more importantly" – my heart beat wildly, while he smiled mockingly – "how did you get hold of the e-mails?"

He laid a cool hand on my glowing cheek.

"My very own Miss Marple."

His hand slid from my neck to my breast, where it stopped, level with my heart.

239

"My," he said, "it's going wild."

"Simon . . ."

He stood up with a jerk, grabbed his glass and emptied it. He stood in front of me and looked down at me, full of concern.

"I can't answer, and believe me, I'm acting in your interests. You've got to stop, really got to stop this. Trust me when I say that I've got everything under control, that it will be resolved."

He leaned over me, smelling of coconut.

"Karen, don't let's waste our precious time . . ."

For a moment I couldn't believe that it was me, lying here looking at this splendid man, that this suite had been reserved for us to make love in, that I was experiencing this, that this man had chosen me. It was too good to be true; he couldn't possibly want this because I was so irresistibly attractive: I wasn't. For him I was probably nothing more than a trophy, one of many. And with this realization came shame and guilt: goose pimples spread over my arms, my legs, my breasts, and I longed to disappear, like a grey mouse into a crack behind the wardrobe, and I suddenly felt uglier and more gullible than ever.

"Just trust me," murmured Simon and kissed me, but the disgust had taken hold, and there was no stopping it. I was disgusted at myself, at how I was lying there, skirt pushed up and blouse half-unbuttoned, at him, his airs and graces, this play-acting, at the way I had let myself be used and manipulated and at us, two adults, a father and a mother, this sleazy deceit.

I rolled away from him off the bed, buttoning up my blouse.

"This is so wrong, so wrong," I stammered and could no longer look at him.

240

"Oh God, now we get a scene . . ." he said softly and in an irritated tone.

"Simon, how can you ask me to trust you under these circumstances? If anyone should know you're not to be trusted, I should . . ."

"Christ, Karen, you're being bloody difficult. There's as much at stake for me as for you, perhaps more."

"Stop it! Stop that vacuous bullshit!"

My fear vanished, together with the knot in my stomach, and was replaced by rage.

"What's at stake? What are you frightened of? You're going to tell me right *now*!" I yelled at him. I took my cigarettes out of my bag and lit one, sucked in the nicotine, trembling with rage, and watched him collapse. His shoulders began to heave, and a strange strangled hiccup came from his throat. He was crying: Simon Vogel, the six-million-dollar man, as Hanneke and I had dubbed him sarcastically, was crying his eyes out.

"Don't yell at me. I can't stand it . . . Christ, Karen . . . please . . ."

He reached out to me. I stood there as if frozen.

"I'm a little man, Karen, I may seem big, but I'm not. I'm scared . . . can you imagine that? Simon Vogel scared . . . This is going to cost me everything I've built up, fought for. Everything . . ."

He spoke quickly and breathlessly, as if talking to himself.

"I didn't want to doubt her just after it happened. I knew things were difficult between them, that she wanted to leave him, that he had refused a divorce. And in a funny way . . . you know, I was scared of him. Scared he would do something to me, after all that had happened, harm me in business too . . . the way he looked at me now and then . . . So in my heart of hearts I was relieved . . ."

His voice broke. I went cold, icy cold.

"What are you talking about? Begin at the beginning . . ."

"Babette, that crazy, sick woman. Last night again, sitting in her car, staring at our house . . . She rings me all day long, e-mails me, texts me, threatens to tell Patricia everything. I don't know how to stop her. Imagine how I felt when that house went up in flames . . . with Evert in it, and Beau and Luuk . . ."

"How *you* felt?"

"I'd broken off with her. I told her she belonged with Evert, that he didn't deserve to lose his wife to me. Evert knew about us: the cow had confessed everything. But anyway, I'd had enough: the fun had gone out of it by then . . . The way she kept chasing me . . . even e-mailed nude photos to the office . . ."

He made a helpless gesture. A tear hung from the tip of his nose, which he brushed away with the sleeve of his shirt.

"She wanted more and more, while I . . . I don't want to leave Patricia. I've got what I want: perhaps not sexually, but what marriage still has good sex? That's part of the deal: you only get really good sex on the sly."

I wanted to punch him, smack on his straight nose, till the blood spurted, jam my knee in his crotch and see him crawl, groaning across the floor.

"In the hospital she said: at least now he's not in our way anymore. I had the fright of my life, no kidding."

"So you had your suspicions all that time, and you said nothing to the police?"

"You don't understand, Karen, it doesn't work like that. Suppose I'd spoken up. What would that have meant for my family, my business? When it's not even certain that she did it?"

242

"And when Hanneke fell? Did you still have your doubts?"

"I don't know . . . No, not really. Babette brought me the e-mails in which Evert wrote about our affair and our problems with the tax people . . . Evert and I had a business in food supplements for athletes. He sold them through his outlets and to sports centres. Supposedly we got the pills from Switzerland, but in fact the stuff came from South America. Well, anyway, long story, but the idea was that we could channel lots of money into our Swiss bank account. It was a wonderful scheme, until we found the tax people on our doorstep. His signature was on all the contracts, and the Swiss account was in his name, so he took the rap, since I was just a sleeping partner . . . Anyway, in the e-mails Hanneke eggs him on against me and Babette, all grist to Dorien Jager's mill . . . Hanneke threatened to take it to the police."

"Patricia knows about it too . . ."

"Patricia didn't believe a word of what Hanneke was saying . . ."

"Oh, fuck off. You all know it doesn't add up! Even Ivo . . . His own wife is murdered! My God, and the lot of you keep mum!" I yelled.

"Ivo fixed all the contracts, the bookkeeping. It earned him a lot of money, but he'll be irreparably damaged if it gets out how he's cooked the books. What can he do? After all, he's got to provide for his kids . . ."

"Are you going to kill me too, Simon, now you've told me all this? Because I won't keep quiet, even if you offer me millions . . ."

"I haven't killed anyone."

"Yes you have. You're just as responsible for their deaths as Babette, but you're such a coward, such a creep, you'll just wait still she beats my brains out."

"I've thought about ending it all . . ."

There was a knock at the door. I started.

"Don't be afraid, I think it's the wine I ordered."

Simon wiped his eyes dry with his sleeve.

"Open up."

I looked through the spy-hole and saw no one. They'd probably left the bottle outside. I opened the door and first heard a hissing sound. In a reflex I pushed the door shut again, but the person on the other side was stronger and the hissing continued, there was no escaping it; my eyes seemed to be burning and bulging out of their sockets, and my throat swelled so violently that I couldn't breathe.

Somewhere far off I could hear Simon yelling. The door slammed shut and suddenly I felt an intense, overwhelming pain in my leg that spilled over into the rest of my body, as if I were being blown up. I jerked, left the ground, my teeth bored into my tongue, and I crashed back and lay twitching on the floor. The metallic taste of blood trickled into my throat, mixed with vomit that seemed to congeal, and took my breath away, and I couldn't see a thing. There was the shattering of glass and hysterical cursing. Simon begged tearfully for forgiveness, for his life, while I crawled across the rough, synthetic carpeting, trembling with pain. My nails broke one by one, my fingers bled and my heart, my poor heart, pounded in panic, as if about to give out at any moment.

37

Someone was tugging at my legs. I tried to resist, but I still had no control over my muscles. Simon was groaning like a wounded dog, and Babette was cursing.

"Spare me that whining, Simon Vogel, and help me."

"I can't see a thing . . . I'm blind. Jesus, Babette! What have you done to me? My face . . ." he squeaked and started groaning again.

She let go of my legs.

"Bloody hell! You wimp! It's all you deserve! If you don't shut your trap, I'll personally scratch your eyes out!"

A little feeling returned to my painfully tingling body, but I kept as limp as possible. I heard her stamping around the room, turning on a tap, returning and then the splashing of water, after which Simon gave a yell.

"If you scream like that once more, I'll give you what that whore over there just had!"

Her angry footsteps came back in my direction, and before I knew it another jolt went through me, and again I shot into the air shuddering with cramp and pain. The surge of current went straight to my heart, the pump faltered, stopped for a moment, and then began fluttering like a butterfly in my chest. A searing pain forced its way from my neck into my head.

Simon sniffed.

"To think you're meeting her here of all places,

Simon! Here, in our room! God, I think that's the worst bit of all!"

Something scorched, Simon groaned under his breath.

"Traitor! You dirty fraud!"

"Babette . . . Please . . ."

All the strength had gone from his voice. I tried to move my swollen tongue, to get my rigid jaws apart. I couldn't. Very gingerly I wiggled my toes, flexed and relaxed the muscles in my buttocks and legs, moved my fingers. I heard her coming towards me. She stopped by my head and bent over me. I could hear her breathing and smell her heavy perfume.

"You mean nothing to him, Karen. You're not worthy of him. Simon belongs to me. That was obvious right from the start. We're a beautiful couple, don't you think?"

She grabbed me by my hair and pulled my head back, while she forced her knee into my back. My body was still paralysed. She slipped what felt like a satin shawl round my neck.

I heard Simon stumbling about. Probably he still couldn't see, like me.

"I saw him, and I knew he belonged to me. We were destined to meet. He needed a woman like me, and I needed a man like him. I found it strange that no one could see that."

She slowly pulled the shawl tighter. I gasped for breath and tried to throw her off me. My muscles refused. My head started buzzing, and I retched.

"Babette, stop it, please! Let her go!" Simon wailed. "You're right, we belong together! But if you kill her, we can never be together again . . ."

She laughed hysterically and loosened the shawl a little. I took wheezing breaths.

"You know I can make you or break you. Not that I want to. I just want you to choose *me*, Simon. Because you know too that we're the perfect couple . . ."

I blinked. The burning feeling was subsiding. I turned my head to the side and saw Simon slumped dejectedly in a chair.

"If you love me, Babette, you'll give me time. Then everything will come right, I promise you . . ."

"I've given you enough time, and no one's standing in the way of our happiness anymore, Simon! So why do you just drop me? Why do you go and fuck her?"

She pushed her knee into my neck, so hard that my neck vertebrae cracked. I thought of Hanneke, twitching on a cold, filthy Amsterdam pavement, of Evert in the flames, of the despairing, tearstained faces of their children. I mustn't be afraid.

"There's still Patricia . . . and my boys, your boys . . ."

"Patricia! Patricia! She doesn't give you what I give you, does she? You said so yourself . . . If you could start all over, you'd do it with me. The two of us would be a wonderful team. You said I knew how to appreciate you . . . So don't start talking about that drab little woman!"

She let go of me and charged furiously towards him. I heard glass breaking. Simon raised his hands in self-defence. I saw hazily that she was turning back towards me and lay as limply as possible, preparing myself for another jolt of electricity. There was just a kick in the belly.

"You're my girl, Babette. She's not: she came on to me . . . I was missing you . . ."

I could hear from his voice that he had regained his composure and knew from the silence that ensued that he had touched a chord in her. I assumed he was lying to play for time.

"But why do you refuse to talk to me? Why do you suddenly avoid me? You mustn't do that, Simon, it drives me crazy!"

She wandered about crying, differently than I had ever heard her cry: this was the sound of a madwoman.

"I was frightened, Babette . . . Surely you understand that? I thought, it's better if we stay away from each other for a bit . . . but I missed you, darling. I really did . . ."

His wheedling made me sick.

"She's got to go," I heard her whisper. He didn't answer. I wondered if he would sacrifice me to his own safety. I slid almost imperceptibly closer to them, biting back my pain.

"In the swimming pool," she whispered. "I'll hit her with this, and you throw her in. Then I know for sure."

"What?" asked Simon anxiously.

"That you love me."

"No, Babette, we can't do that . . ."

She came towards me. I tensed all my muscles, into which the feeling had now returned, and knew that I had one second. My fury gave me strength. I threw myself forward, onto Simon's heavy briefcase, which was under the hat stand, jumped up and swung it. The briefcase hit her head with full force. The sharp edge hit her temple. It cracked. I hit her again, in the face this time. She wobbled. The stun gun flew out of her hand, and she fell groaning and bleeding to the ground. Simon grabbed the pistol and said that that was enough. But I didn't want to stop. My head was ringing, every particle of me was seething with fury. Again I raised the briefcase, I heard Simon cry "Hold on!" and turned towards him, wanting to hit him in his arrogant face, break his nose, rip his beautiful mouth.

"You don't want to do that, Karen. I was lying, it was

all lies, to calm her down . . . Stop, Karen, stop, let's sit down and think of a solution . . ."

I hit him in the stomach with the briefcase, making him double up and fall groaning to the floor.

Then I went to the telephone by the bed and with trembling fingers keyed in Dorien's number. I still had the briefcase in my hand.

Simon coughed and slowly sat up. He swore and hoisted himself onto the bed.

"Wait. Are you calling the police? Karen . . . Let's first think carefully about what we're going to tell them . . ." he stammered.

"We're not thinking up anything at all. We're going to say exactly what happened."

"Karen, this is in your interest too . . ."

"I'm very well aware what my interests are. The truth, at last, even if it hurts."

"And Michel? He'll curse you . . ."

"Perhaps, but I'm not afraid of that anymore."

Dorien banged on the door and called out my name. When I saw her, I began crying.

"There's an ambulance on its way," she said and put her arm round me. A policeman came in behind her and bent over Babette. He shouted something into his walkie-talkie. I asked him if she was dead, and he said no.

Dorien grabbed me by the shoulders and said it was over. She led me to a chair and gave me a glass of water. The policemen took care of Simon.

"She was seen near the hotel, Karen, the hotel owner recognized her. She must have followed you two. I was actually on my way to your place with him to take her in for questioning." She pointed to the policeman.

"I thought you'd been taken off the case . . ."

"I was able to talk my chief round with that e-mail and the hotel owner's statement."

I looked at the crumpled figure of Babette, her wonderful legs, her slim, tanned arms, the gold bracelet round her wrist.

Another, older man came in, with grey curly hair, who introduced himself as Gijs van Diemen and rattled off a string of sentences, about how I wasn't obliged to say anything, and that anything I did say could be used in evidence and that he could ring my lawyer. I looked at Dorien. "I haven't done anything wrong . . . She came . . ."

I pointed to Babette.

"She sprayed tear gas in my eyes and hit me with that thing."

"Best not say anything," whispered Dorien, gently rubbing my back.

Simon was given the same caution as I was. He looked at me, his face contorted with pain and fear, while tears glistened in his eyes. I realized that he wasn't crying about what had happened but about what awaited him.

38

The scale of my deceit hit me like a ton of bricks when I got home and found Michel completely beside himself. Although I was more convinced than ever that I wanted to be with him, I was afraid that there was no way back, that I might have brought the truth to light, but in so doing had destroyed my own life and my own family.

I repeated the story many times, answered all his questions as honestly as possible, although it hurt him terribly: lying would have been even more painful. It was a relief finally to be able to tell the truth. Every word brought me closer to him, I felt, closer to the relationship we had once had and as I told him I realized how much I had underestimated him, what a mistake it had been to think that he could not handle this. We yelled, we cried, he threw a wine glass across the kitchen and threatened in a shrill voice to beat the hell out of Simon, we smoked a packet of cigarettes together and talked all night and the following nights. There were conversations that kept ending in fights, with him going to sleep with the children and me lying awake in our big bed.

He asked me why I had had sex with Simon, why I had decided not to tell him, why I had forced him, Michel, out of my life little by little without ever talking to him about it; and I could only answer that I didn't know. I didn't know where it had gone wrong, when I had started to focus on outsiders instead of on him. I said he was partly to blame for that. Just like me he had abandoned his ideals, had reneged on the agreements between us. We were to live together in this village, run this family together. He had left me in the lurch, here in the country.

I begged for forgiveness. Michel admitted cautiously that he had made mistakes too. It took weeks, months before we slowly began to feel at ease in each other's company again, could touch each other again in a natural way and finally, tentatively, make love. We were not there, not by a long way, and from time to time the reproaches crackled and flared up again, and it was difficult to regain his trust, to be honestly intimate again. Sometimes we wondered if staying together was the right choice and whether we were doing it just for the children, but now we wondered aloud and in so doing gave each other another chance.

We both wanted to move and start afresh elsewhere: not back to town but certainly closer to Michel's office. Away from the whispering outside school, away from the sneaky glances in the supermarket and the ambiguous comments in the café, and especially away from my former friends, who shot across the street like frightened rabbits when they saw me approaching or turned on their heel if they saw me in the queue at the checkout. One day Michel came home furiously waving *Quote* magazine, which featured an interview with Simon. He talked about Ivo, whom he called raving mad and whom he'd apparently fired, said that he'd "made a deal" with the tax people and that as a rich man, he could buy anything he wanted but sometimes the wrong people were brought along. All expecting some of his wealth to come trickling down to them. "I acted too naïvely, I was too easy-going.

People took advantage of that with great regularity, I now realize." After reading the piece, which also featured a photo of Simon and Patricia beaming blissfully in their garden, Michel threw the magazine in the fire. He had accounts to settle with Simon too, and it wasn't a pretty fight.

The morning before the move I cycled through the village one last time, past the church and the blossoming chestnut trees, bought a bunch of white roses on the square and saw them sitting on the terrace at Verdi's: Patricia and Angela. Shopping bags parked next to their seats. They were both laughing loudly but fell silent when they saw me walking past. I smiled, and they turned their heads away. I jumped on my bike and waved. They stared after me, dumbstruck.

Near the cemetery I realized that the birds were singing, that it smelled of summer and that the cow parsley was head-high again. Cow parsley would always remind me of Hanneke, of the long summer days in her garden, of dancing with the children and of her hoarse, guffawing laugh. More than ever I had the feeling I was carrying her with me, that I had taken on some of her toughness. I smiled for no good reason, felt as light as a feather in the wind and hummed a silly old song about summer that just popped into my head.

D.B.

Elwood Reid

"Raunchy, seamy, cocksure, perversely juicy, so surprising in its vivid convolutions of plot and character that you keep turning back a few pages to see how the author is getting away with it." Jim Harrison, author of *Legends of the Fall*

In 1971 a man calling himself D.B. Cooper hijacked a flight, claimed his ransom without harming a soul and vanished. He parachuted out of the plane over the dense woods of the Pacific Northwest with $200,000 strapped to his body. Elwood Reid uses this true story as a starting point, imagining Cooper as Phil Fitch, a Vietnam vet with a failed marriage who decides the time has come to do something that will save him from a life of punching time cards and wondering what could have been. Fitch ends up in Mexico, where he drifts until a turn of bad luck forces him to return home.

Meanwhile, retired FBI agent Frank Marshall, struggling with his new life of leisure – fishing, drinking too much, tempted to embark on an affair with a female witness – decides to help a young agent determined to solve the case of D.B. Cooper. An odyssey, a manhunt, a gripping and frequently hilarious tale.

PRAISE FOR *D.B.*

"Wild and alive, an epic manhunt and brutal social portrait, *D.B.* is the road trip of your dreams – Hunter Thompson does the driving, but John Steinbeck holds the map." Mark Costello, author of *Big If*

"Masterfully told, *D.B.* ranks among the best and most entertaining books of the year." *Pittsburgh Tribune*

"Elwood Reid ascends to the top of his generation with this novel." Mark Richard, author of *Fishboy*

"Smart and direct prose . . . By shifting the reader's attention from the overtly dramatic to the psychological, Reid has written something much more engaging than the mere suspense novel *D.B.* might have been."
The New York Times Book Review

£9.99
Crime paperback original
ISBN 1-904738-19-2/978-1904738-19-0
www.bitterlemonpress.com

FEVER

Friedrich Glauser

"With good reason, the German language prize for detective fiction is named after Glauser. . . He has Simenon's ability to turn a stereotype into a person, and the moral complexity to appeal to justice over the head of police procedure."
Times Literary Supplement

When two women are "accidentally" killed by gas leaks, Sergeant Studer investigates the thinly disguised double murder in Bern and Basel. The trail leads to a geologist dead from a tropical fever in a Moroccan Foreign Legion post and a murky oil deal involving rapacious politicians and their henchmen. With the help of a hashish-induced dream and the common sense of his stay-at-home wife, Studer solves the multiple riddles on offer. But assigning guilt remains an elusive affair.

Fever, a European crime classic, was first published in 1936 and is the third in the Sergeant Studer series published by Bitter Lemon Press.

Praise for Glauser's other Sergeant Studer novels

"*Thumbprint* is a fine example of the craft of detective writing in a period which fans will regard as the golden age of crime fiction." *Sunday Telegraph*

"*Thumbprint* is a genuine curiosity that compares to the dank poetry of Simenon and reveals the enormous debt owed by Dürenmatt, Switzerland's most famous crime writer, for whom this should be seen as a template." *Guardian*

"A despairing plot about the reality of madness and life, leavened at regular intervals with strong doses of bittersweet irony. The idiosyncratic investigation of *In Matto's Realm* and its laconic detective have not aged one iota." *Guardian*

"Glauser was among the best European crime writers of the inter-war years. The detail, place and sinister characters are so intelligently sculpted that the sense of foreboding is palpable." *Glasgow Herald*

£9.99/$14.95
Crime paperback original
ISBN 1–904738–14–1/978–1904738–14–5
www.bitterlemonpress.com

FRAMED

Tonino Benacquista

"One of France's leading crime and mystery authors."
Guardian

Antoine's life is good. During the day he hangs pictures for the most fashionable art galleries in Paris. Evenings he dedicates to the silky moves and subtle tactics of billiards, his true passion. But when Antoine is attacked by an art thief in a gallery his world begins to fall apart. His maverick investigation triggers two murders – he finds himself the prime suspect for one of them – as he uncovers a cesspool of art fraud. A game of billiards decides the outcome of this violently funny tale, laced with brilliant riffs about the world of modern art and the parasites that infest it.

In 2004 Bitter Lemon Press introduced Tonino Benacquista to English-speaking readers with the critically acclaimed novel *Holy Smoke*.

PRAISE FOR *FRAMED*

"Screenwriter for the award-winning French crime movie *The Beat That My Heart Skipped*, Tonino Benacquista is also a wonderful observer of everyday life, petty evil and the ordinariness of crime. The pace never falters as personal grief collides with outrageous humour and a biting running commentary on the crooked world of modern art."
Guardian

"Edgy, offbeat black comedy." *The Times*

"Flip and frantic foray into art galleries and billiards halls of modern Paris." *Evening Standard*

"A black comedy that is set in Paris but reflects its author's boisterous Italian sensibility. The manic tale is told by an apprentice picture-hanger who encounters a thief in a fashionable art gallery and becomes so caught up in a case of art fraud that he himself 'touches up' a Kandinsky."
New York Times

£9.99/$14.95
Crime paperback original
ISBN 1–904738–16–8/978–1904738–16–9
www.bitterlemonpress.com

HAVANA BLACK

Leonardo Padura

A MARIO CONDE MYSTERY

"The mission of that enterprising Bitter Lemon Press is to publish English translations of the best foreign crime fiction. The newest addition to its list is the prize-winning Cuban novelist Leonardo Padura" *The Telegraph*

The brutally mutilated body of Miguel Forcade is discovered washed up on a Havana beach. Head smashed in by a baseball bat, genitals cut off with a blunt knife. Forcade was once responsible for confiscating art works from the bourgeoisie fleeing the revolution. Had he really returned from exile just to visit his ailing father?

Lieutenant Mario Conde immerses himself in Cuba's dark history, expropriations of priceless paintings now vanished without trace, corruption and old families who appear to have lost much, but not everything.

Padura evokes the disillusionment of a generation, yet this novel is a eulogy to Cuba, and to the great friendships of those who chose to stay and fight for survival.

PRAISE FOR *HAVANA BLACK*

"A great plot, perfectly executed with huge atmosphere. You can almost smell the cigar smoke, rum and cheap women." *Daily Mirror*

"This is a strong tasting book. A rich feast of wit and feeling." *The Independent*

"Well-plotted second volume of Padura's seething, steamy Havana Quartet. This densely packed mystery should attract readers outside the genre." *Publishers Weekly*

"Lt. Mario Conde, known on the street as 'the Count,' is prone to metaphysical reflection on the history of his melancholy land but the city of Havana keeps bursting through his meditations, looking very much alive." *New York Times*

£9.99/$14.95
Crime paperback original
ISBN 1–904738–15–X/978–1904738–15–2
www.bitterlemonpress.com

THE MANNEQUIN MAN

Luca Di Fulvio

Shortlisted for the European Crime Writing Prize

"Di Fulvio exposes souls with the skills of a surgeon, It's like turning the pages of something forbidden – seduction, elegant and dangerous." *Alan Rickman*

"Know why she's smiling?" he asked, pointing a small torch at the corpse. "Fish hooks. Two fish hooks at the corners of her mouth, a bit of nylon, pull it round the back of the head and tie a knot. Pretty straightforward, right?" Amaldi noticed the metallic glint at the corners of the taut mouth.

Inspector Amaldi has enough problems. A city choked by a pestilent rubbish strike, a beautiful student harassed by a telephone stalker, a colleague dying of cancer and the mysterious disappearance of arson files concerning the city's orphanage. Then the bodies begin to appear.

This novel of violence and decay, with its vividly portrayed characters, takes place over a few oppressive weeks in an unnamed Italian city that strongly evokes Genoa.

The Italian press refers to Di Fulvio as a grittier, Italian Thomas Harris, and *Eyes of Crystal*, the film of the novel, was launched at the 2004 Venice Film Festival.

" A novel that caresses and kisses in order to violate the reader with greater ease." *Rolling Stone*

"A powerful psycho-thriller of spine-shivering intensity . . . written with immense intelligence and passionate menace. Not to be read alone at night." *The Times*

"A wonderful first novel that will seduce the fans of deranged murderers in the style of Hannibal Lecter. And beautifully written to boot." *RTL*

£9.99/$14.95
Crime paperback original
ISBN 1–904738–13–3/978–1904738–13–8
www.bitterlemonpress.com

NIGHT BUS

Giampiero Rigosi

"An ironic and relentless thriller. A chase that won't let you catch your breath until the last page." – *Carlo Lucarelli*

Leila is young, beautiful and a hustler. She robs hapless men picked up in the night clubs of Bologna. Easy money, until she ends up with a document at the centre of a plot of political blackmail. In an atmosphere of intense paranoia two secret service operatives, a goon hired by the blackmailer and the police all pursue Leila for the document and a suitcase full of dollars meant to be the pay-off. She joins forces with Francesco, a bus driver and gambling addict on the run from the Bear, a terrifying debt collector. Suitcases and blackmail notes change hands at a frenetic pace against a background of torture and murder. A savagely funny crime adventure with an Italian twist

"The caper novel in which the hero is a loveable rogue is very much an American genre, in which Elmore Leonard and Donald Westlake have excelled . . . So this debut Italian novel comes as pure delight. Frenetic, savagely funny, this is first rate and witty entertainment." *Guardian*

"The taut, muscular prose and noirish moods of the novel owe something to Elmore Leonard, though with a more obvious cinematic quality . . . In a character-based black comedy in the style of Quentin Tarantino we are entertained by recipes for Italian meals as devised by beloved mamma but cooked by an assassin, slapstick scenes of blundering criminality, and hilarious descriptions of physical appearance. Without forsaking the thriller's requirements of plot and pace, Rigosi provides a bitter satire on ambition and stupidity, greed and gullibility. A spider's web in which all politicians are corrupt, all families dysfunctional, all friendships based on business or fear, and all our illusions about love and sex no better than a chance encounter with a toothless transsexual." *The Times Literary Supplement*

£9.99/$14.95
Crime paperback original
ISBN 1–904738–11–7/978–1904738–11–4
www.bitterlemonpress.com

SOMEONE ELSE

Tonino Benacquista

"A great read from one of France's best crime writers.
A tale peppered with humour, unpredictable twists and a
healthy dose of suspense. It all makes for a cracking read,
with witty insights into the vagaries of human nature."
Guardian

Who hasn't wanted to become "someone else"? The person
you've always wanted to be . . . the person who won't give up
half way to your dreams and desires?

One evening two men who have just met at a Paris tennis
club make a bet: they give each other exactly three years to
radically alter their lives. Thierry, a picture framer with a
steady clientele, has always wanted to be a private investiga-
tor. Nicolas is a shy, teetotal executive trying not to fall off
the corporate ladder. But becoming someone else is not
without risk; at the very least, the risk of finding yourself.

"Benacquista writes with humor and verve. This novel is less
a mystery than a deftly constructed diptych of existential
escapism: each story offers a unique map to new possibilities
in the midst of suffocating lives." *Rain Taxi*

"This has been a big hit in France, and it is easy to see why –
Thierry's attempts to slip into a story by Simenon and
Nicolas's explosive encounter with vodka make for
unexpected, cynical comedy." *The Times*

"Exuberantly written, Benacquista's book is another triumph
for the genre-bending approach to crime fiction."
Tangled Web

Winner of the RTL-LIRE Prize.

£9.99/$14.95
Crime paperback original
ISBN 1–904738–12–5/978–1904738–12–1
www.bitterlemonpress.com

A WALK IN THE DARK

Gianrico Carofiglio

"Carofiglio writes crisp, ironical novels that are as much love stories and philosophical treatises as they are legal thrillers."
New Yorker

When Martina accuses her ex-boyfriend – the son of a powerful local judge – of assault and battery, no witnesses can be persuaded to testify on her behalf and one lawyer after another refuses to represent her. Guido Guerrieri knows the case could bring his legal career to a premature and messy end but he cannot resist the appeal of a hopeless cause. Nor deny an attraction to Sister Claudia, the young woman in charge of the shelter where Martina is living, who shares his love of martial arts and his virulent hatred of injustice.

Gianrico Carofiglio is an anti-Mafia prosecutor in southern Italy. *A Walk in the Dark,* his second novel featuring defence counsel Guerrieri, follows on from the success of *Involuntary Witness.*

PRAISE FOR *A WALK IN THE DARK*

"This novel raises the standard for crime fiction. Carofiglio's deft touch has given us a story that is both literary and gritty – and one that speeds along like the best legal thrillers. His insights into human nature – good and bad – are breathtaking." *Jeffery Deaver*

"*A Walk in the Dark*, features an engagingly complex, emotional and moody defence lawyer, Guido Guerrieri, who takes on cases shunned by his colleagues. In passing, Carofiglio provides a fascinating insight into the workings of the Italian criminal justice system." *Observer*

"Part legal thriller, part insight into a man fighting his own demons. Every character in Carofiglio's fiction has a story to tell and they are always worth hearing . . . this powerfully affecting novel benefits from veracity as well as tight writing." *Daily Mail*

£9.99/$14.95
Crime paperback original
ISBN 1–904738–17–6/978–1904738–17–6
www.bitterlemonpress.com